CLAYTON'S HONOR

A British Agent Novel

MK McCLINTOCK

Trappers Peak Publishing
Montana

PRAISE FOR
THE BRITISH AGENT NOVELS

"Ms. McClintock weaves a thick tapestry of mystery and romance in her historical setting . . . Multiple twists and unexpected alliances hook the reader into her complex tale . . . Bravo Ms. McClintock!"
—*InD'Tale Magazine* (on *Blackwood Crossing*)

"This is a wonderful book with suspense to keep me on the edge of my seat and surprises to keep me guessing. The main characters—a feisty heroine and a strong, gentle hero—are just the kind I love and the villains are worthy of being hated."
—Verna Mitchell, author of *Somewhere Beyond the Blue*

"Ms. McClintock succeeds in masterfully weaving both genres meticulously together until mystery lovers are sold on romance and romance lovers love the mystery!
—*InD'Tale Magazine* (on *Alaina Claiborne*)

"The balance between romance, mystery, and adventure was perfect. Usually one outweighs the other, so I was pleasantly surprised. In addition, the plot had some unexpected twists, which made the story that much more interesting. With memorable characters and an entertaining plot, *Alaina Claiborne* has it all. —*Readers' Favorite*

"A mystery entwined with an ongoing hopeful romance between Devon and Anne, *Clayton's Honor* is utterly enticing and captivating!" —*InD'tale Magazine*

Published in the United States of America
Trappers Peak Publishing
Bigfork, Montana

McClintock, MK
Clayton's Honor; novel/MK McClintock
ISBN-10: 0991330676
ISBN-13: 978-0991330676

Cover design and formatting by MK McClintock
Cover images from Dreamstime

"Connemara Cradle Song" Copyright © 1951 Delya (Delia) Murphy
Used with permission by Rowan Browne, Ireland

PRINTED IN THE UNITED STATES OF AMERICA

Other Books by this Author

BRITISH AGENT NOVELS

Alaina Claiborne
Blackwood Crossing
Clayton's Honor

MONTANA GALLAGHER SERIES

Gallagher's Pride
Gallagher's Hope
Gallagher's Choice
An Angel Called Gallagher
Journey to Hawk's Peak
Wild Montana Winds
The Healer of Briarwood

For a complete listing of all MK McClintock novels and short stories, visit www.mkmcclintock.com.

AUTHOR'S NOTE

Dearest Reader,

Much like Scotland, Ireland has intrigued me and captured my imagination. I knew when it came time to write a story with a main character like Anne Doyle, she would be a lot like the amazing and strong Irishwomen I've had the pleasure of knowing in my life. Devon Clayton, our hero, deserved someone special, but I also knew the woman would have to be possessed of a kind and gentle spirit, with uncommon compassion and a fierce sense of justice. Anne turned out to be a perfect match for Devon's charismatic and protective personality. I hope you enjoy their story as much as I have.

It should also be known that I write fiction, not history. My stories are meant to entertain and offer the reader an escape into another time and place. While I remain true to the era and customs, there are times when I exercise a certain artistic license in order to find a balance between what we believe, what was, and what we can relate to in our modern day. It is never my intention to offend the historical purists.

Happy Reading,

-MK

For Stephen, Melissa, and Eva.

Go gcasaimid le chéile arís ar pháirceanna glasa na hÉireann.

(May we meet again on Ireland's green fields.)

I would like to give special thanks to . . .

Ronan Browne, grandson of Irish singer Delia Murphy, for the generous use of stanzas from the "Connemara Cradle Song."

Pól Deeds of An Droichead in Belfast (Béal Feirste) for ensuring the accuracy of the beautiful Irish language in this story.

Maria McCool, Irish singer, for graciously allowing the use of her beautiful rendition of "Ar Éirinn Ní Neosfainn Cé Hí" for the *Clayton's Honor* book trailer.

Susan Stuphen for her generous gift to Rozalyn "Roz" Patricia. May your friendship never wane and your kindness be emulated.

Lorraine Fico-White—rock-star editor, teacher, and friend. The solitary nature of writing suits me perfectly, but without you, my stories would languish in a drawer far too long. Thank you for your commitment and hard work.

One

Scáthanna agus Eagla
(Shadows and Fear)

County Wexford, Ireland
February 4, 1892

Could they hear her? If she moved deeper into the shadows, could she sneak away? If she loosened the grip on her lungs and took the deep breath she desperately needed, would they find her? The heady stench of copper filled the air of the great hall, the dank stone walls doing little to block the scent of death. The carpets beneath her slippered feet masked her first step. Back one, and then two. She ducked behind a heavy tapestry, one of the few left in the old castle.

Masked under a cloak of clouds and desperation, she escaped out the servants' entrance, confident that the cook and single housemaid would not see her. Wet slush and rain combined to make her retreat difficult. She could not risk discovery by hailing someone and beseeching them for a ride. Her own two feet must carry her the miles to Brannon Cottage.

The noise of the carriage wheels competed with that of the storm, but she did not mistake the sound of the small rocks as they ground and rolled over one another. She hurried behind a nearby copse of blackthorn and waited. Lights from the carriage lanterns broke through the darkness as the conveyance approached. The man in the driver's seat sang "She Is Far from the Land" faintly heard through the wind. After he passed, Anne set one foot in front of the other and paused. Her fear overpowered her desire for warmth. She could do this. It was only four miles.

One worn slipper almost fell from her foot when she stepped in a small slush of wet snow. Colder now, she pressed forward. One mile. Two miles. Three. She must reach him before they realized she was gone. Anne flailed and her body lurched to the ground. Her arm scraped over a sharp stone that sliced through her cloak. The faint clatter of bottles in her satchel managed to reach her ears over the harsh howl of the winds.

Anne rose to all fours and then stopped and knelt on the sodden road, choking back a trail of tears as they coursed down her already wet skin. She tucked soaked locks of her long hair beneath her wet bonnet. Drawing on pure need, Anne pushed up from the ground and continued down the dirt road. She did not know the Brannons well. They visited Ireland once or twice a year, and yet the only person on this earth she could hope to trust was currently on holiday and using the Brannons' cottage. Ten years had passed since she'd last seen him.

The tidy two-story stone structure appeared as though from the fog. Soft, white flakes fell in time with her heavy breaths but lasted only the time it took for her to reach the front door.

With knuckles cold and weak, Anne managed to knock. The sound of fist against wood was pathetic even to her. She knocked louder and waited. She heard someone remove the door latch and a tall, familiar man opened the portal. "Anne, whatever are you doing here?"

"I'm sorry, Charles. You sent word you'd be here, and I know we were to meet tomorrow."

A beautiful woman with soft red curls stepped into the front room, still clad in her robe. "I heard you open the door. Is everything all right?" The woman looked at Anne.

Charles motioned the woman forward. "This is my cousin, Anne Doyle. Anne, this is my wife, Rhona."

Rhona reached out and welcomed her. "You're shivering and cold. Come and sit by the fire."

Anne wanted to cry all over again. Kindness had been a rare commodity in her life these past few years.

Charles helped her into a chair and covered her with a blanket. "What are you doing out alone on a night like this?"

Anne's eyes welled with tears. "Something terrible has happened. I need your help." Anne lifted her leather bag over her head and set it on the floor, revealing the long and bloody tear in her cloak.

Charles leapt back to her side and lifted her arm. "What's happened?"

Anne held her arm close. "I fell. It doesn't hurt."

"We're still going to tend your wound," Rhona said. "I'll be right back with some hot water and cloths."

When Rhona returned, Charles had helped Anne remove her cloak, and Rhona set to work. "I don't know if I can do much other than slow the bleeding. Charles, perhaps you can—"

"There are supplies in my bag," Anne said.

Charles picked up the leather satchel and rummaged through its contents. "You have your own apothecary in here. What is this about?"

"It's what I do." Anne grimaced, an action not lost on her cousin.

"Never mind." Charles took over and carefully cleaned the wound and applied a liquid per Anne's instructions. "This will need a few stitches. Can you bear it?"

Anne glanced at Charles in surprise. "You know how?"

Charles nodded. "It's not my first time."

Anne closed her eyes while Charles stitched four even lines into her skin and bandaged the wound. For all of her experience administering to others, she'd never had the misfortune to require sutures.

"The wound isn't deep, but I want to know how you came by it."

Anne looked first to Charles and then to Rhona.

"You can trust Rhona." Charles set aside Anne's bag and covered his cousin's hands with his own. "Whatever's happened, I'm here for you. We're here for you."

"I saw something I shouldn't have, and I wish I could erase it from my memory." Anne gripped Charles's hand. "Someone I believed to be a friend to my father has killed a man."

"You witnessed this?"

Anne nodded and watched as Charles's jaw tightened. "I don't believe they saw me, else I would have been found by now."

"They?"

"I heard another man's voice, or thought I did."

After he covered Anne with a second blanket, Charles sat down on the edge of the settee next to his wife. Rhona's hand immediately settled on her husband's arm. Anne had not seen Charles in years, but she had to trust someone.

Charles leaned toward her and set his elbows on his knees. One might think he was in casual conversation with a friend, but Anne saw the alertness of his body, as though he was prepared to move at any second.

"Who is this man, the one your family called friend?"

"He's powerful. He could bring your family great difficulty. I came to you for help to get my family away, but I do not wish to put you in greater danger. I've been away for four days tending to a villager's child, and only just returned home to see . . ." Anne steadied her eyes on Rhona. "I know I ask much of my cousin, but there is no one else."

Rhona's gray eyes revealed a woman of warmth, compassion, and understanding, but how could this woman know anything of what Anne faced?

"You do not ask too much, Anne. However," Rhona smiled at her husband despite the grim circumstances, "to withhold any information would be to put Charles at risk."

"Lord Gaspar, Marquess of Lochnabar."

Charles released her hands and stood. His expression bordered on indifference, but Anne recognized intense concentration when she saw it.

Charles said, "I know Lord Gaspar."

Anne leaned back into the chair, her eyes firmly held by Charles's gaze. "How well do you know him?"

"Not on friendly terms, I assure you." Charles quietly paced the small room.

Anne listened in fascination as he spoke not to her or his wife but to them both. His mind seemed to move from one thought to the next. "He was once a man of great influence. Our paths crossed a few times in London during my earlier days at the agency, but he was never under investigation, at least to my knowledge. Devon knows him better than I do."

"Devon?"

Charles nodded. "A friend. We need to get you back to England."

Anne shook her head and stood. "I can't. My family is here, and I won't leave them."

"Your mother."

"Yes, and sister. They rarely leave the castle. When I returned home, I went to check on them both, but they weren't in their beds. I heard noises down the hall, and you know the rest. They have to still be there."

"I haven't met your sister. Claire is her name, correct? Your father wrote of her only once, but you he spoke of often. She was a sickly child if I recall."

Anne automatically stiffened in an effort to stand in defense for her sister. When she realized how rigid her body had become, she forced her limbs to relax. Charles was not like the few others who had met her sister, ridiculing the child until there was no choice but to hide her from society. It mattered little to Anne what others thought of her or even her parents, but on more than one occasion, she'd discovered how fiercely protective of her younger sister she could be.

"The doctor called it mongolism. I didn't know what the word meant at the time, but he may as well have branded her a leper. There were whispers in the village which claimed Claire should be institutionalized, but my parents wouldn't hear of it. I believe they hid Claire away to shield her from the gossip, but I like to think most people would have accepted her." Anne looked away, squeezed her eyes closed, and held back a few tears but without great success. A warm and smooth hand pressed down on hers. Anne turned back, her smile taking some effort.

"How old is Claire?"

Anne wiped away the tears, and this time her smile was genuine. "Eight years. She is the most beautiful and dearest child." She stood once more and faced Charles.

"Tomorrow, I'll bring them here to Brannon Cottage, and we'll leave for England."

"It's not going to be easy, Charles. Lord Gaspar may still be at Ballinrock Castle, and I told you, I don't know where my mother and Claire are. I need to return and search, but I couldn't do it alone, not without Lord Gaspar finding out what I saw. If I find them and they're hurt . . ."

"Why would Gaspar be at your home?"

"There are things you don't know. My father—"

Charles pulled her into his arms, and she held on. His

embrace reminded her of her father, and she knew Charles would protect her just as her father would have.

"It doesn't matter right now. There will be more time for discussion when you and your family are safe." Charles eased her back. "Tell me what I need to know about your home. I haven't been there since I was a boy."

Anne cringed. "It is not the same. I should go back with you."

"No. I understand that I cannot force you to stay here, but I ask for your safety and for your family's."

Anne finally acquiesced. "I can't imagine Lord Gaspar would still be there, not after what he's done, but if he suspects that I've witnessed . . ."

"I don't need an excuse to descend upon Ballinrock Castle without notice. I am your closest living male relative, and as such, I may visit at my leisure."

Charles smiled, but Anne sensed it was merely for her benefit.

He asked, "Just tell me who else might be there, how many staff, and if anything else significant has changed. I'll leave before the sun has risen."

Charles insisted he be told every detail, and Anne spent the next few minutes carefully answering questions about who occupied which rooms. Most of the rooms in Ballinrock were empty.

"What of the staff?"

One of Anne's greatest regrets was her inability to keep the full staff employed. "Most have gone. You won't have any difficulty once you tell them . . . my God, Charles, I didn't think about them. I saw no one else except for Lord Gaspar and the other man. How could the servants be there and not hear? What if he's done away—"

"Don't think that way. If I remember correctly, the servants' quarters are far removed from the main rooms."

Anne nodded. "Of course, you're right."

Rhona arrived with a bowl of warm soup and tea, both of which Anne gratefully accepted but could not imagine consuming.

Rhona said, "I understand your worry. I would have risked everything for my brother." Pain was unmistakable in Rhona's voice. "Your mother and sister will be safe."

"I pray that is true because if anything should befall . . ."

Anne's absence would not go unnoticed for long, but she doubted her cousin would allow her to accompany him if she asked again. Charles would see for himself soon enough the lies, deception, and secrets which plagued her family.

Two

An Fhírinne agus an Bhréag
(Truth and Deceit)

A footman answered the door. Haverly, the man Charles once knew as the butler, would have been disgraced if he thought a guest was not treated properly or to see the house in such disrepair. No clock perched on the mantel to tell Charles just how long he'd waited. He pulled out his pocket watch. Twenty minutes. Either they'd already forgotten he'd arrived, or the servants were desperately trying to find someone who could greet him.

Anne had warned him that Ballinrock Castle was not the grand edifice he'd memorialized in his mind as one of the finest castles in Ireland. Walls where tapestries once hung were now bare, with nothing to show of the castle's former grandeur. Crystal from the impressive chandelier in the foyer had been stripped. The few tables left lay bare of pictures and trinkets. He walked across the length of the room over carpets which had managed to survive where most of the other possessions had not.

Soft footsteps stopped in the hallway just outside the parlor door. When the door opened, Charles admitted his surprise. He didn't imagine the head housekeeper to be one so young, but the clothing and a ring of keys which hung from her belt confirmed her position.

"Lord Blackwood, I am Mrs. Keegan, the housekeeper. I am sorry, but Lady Anne is in the village." She remained by the door and awaited his response.

"Is she now?" Charles couldn't fathom what game the housekeeper played, or if perhaps she was scared of someone, but he'd be a good sport. "Might you know when she'll return?"

"Her ladyship did not inform me."

Charles studied her. This woman had no reason to fear retribution from him. Why lie? He couldn't say, but he was curious enough to learn the reason.

"I will be staying." Charles walked toward her and watched her take one almost indiscernible step backward. He stopped and asked, "Might Lady Doyle be in residence?"

The housekeeper's eyes opened wide and her lips parted, but she did not immediately speak.

"I'm sorry, my lord, she's not here."

"No matter. I'll stay until Lady Anne returns." Charles glanced out the window, devoid of curtains, to the unkempt grounds. "It has been far too long since I've visited."

Mrs. Keegan wound her hands around a silver watch chain. "Is there anything else?"

"No, my lord. I will see that a room is made up for you immediately. May I bring you a tray and tea to tide you over until dinner?"

"That won't be necessary."

A short time later, Charles followed the housekeeper down the quiet hallway where he stopped the footman who had met him at the front door and asked him to come to his room in ten minutes. The footman shared a glance with the housekeeper and quickly nodded. The upstairs room where Charles was meant to stay the night was one of great familiarity. He'd slept in the room next door during his last visit, many years ago, one of many fond memories with his Irish cousins.

Not once had Mrs. Keegan asked about luggage, nor did she wait around after Charles thanked and dismissed her. He perused the room, now empty of its once finer furnishings, and searched the desk for stationery, locating a few sheets of old paper. Charles quickly penned a message before the footman arrived exactly ten minutes after Charles had pulled him aside.

"What is your name?"

"Alby, my lord."

"Is there a telegraph office nearby, Alby?"

The footman stood with one hand behind his back and nodded once. "Yes, my lord."

Charles handed the young man the folded paper along with a two-pound banknote. "I need this seen to immediately. I'll be out walking the property when you return. Please notify me when the message has been sent."

The footman stared at the banknote, and Charles realized this was likely more than one month's wages. His eyes lit up with eager anticipation. "Yes, my lord. Right away."

Charles counted on that eagerness to expedite the delivery. He needed more information and quickly. If the murder Anne claimed to witness had taken place, the servants were either unaware, exceptional liars, or frightened for their own lives.

STEAM ROSE FROM THE bath, so graciously drawn by Rhona. Rivulets of hot water dripped down Anne's skin, but she bore them no mind. She held her knees against her chest, her cheek resting against her hands. She muffled her cries so Rhona couldn't hear her.

Anne attempted to block the images, but they remained with her. A hand gripped the long blade gleaming with blood. The cries of the young man before his body fell to the stone floor, convulsing for seconds before his eyes went blank. She stood beyond the door, hidden and transfixed by the grisly scene. The coppery stench of death and blood permeated the air all around her.

"Anne?"

Her legs splashed back into the water as her mind rejoined her body in the bath chamber. Rhona's soft voice, filled with concern, called out once more. "Are you all right?"

Anne wiped the tears and bath water from her face. "Yes, thank you." She cleared her throat for her voice sounded weak and unconvincing even to her. "I'll be out shortly."

She patted her body dry with the bath towel and buried her face in the cloth, drawing in deep breaths to help calm the quick thudding of her heart. Rhona had set out scented water, and on impulse, Anne lifted the glass stopper and drew in the fragrant lavender. Such a luxury, and at a time when her family was in danger, and perhaps now even Charles. She replaced the scent and donned the clothes Rhona set out for her to wear. Rhona was close enough to Anne in height and size that the garments fit well. Anne let down her golden-colored hair, secured in a knot for the bath, and drew the brush through a few times before she braided it down her back.

She would flee with her mother and sister to England, but it would not end there.

Afternoon transitioned into evening. Rhona appeared calm—too calm in Anne's opinion—while she prepared a light supper. It was just the two of them in the cozy cottage kitchen for no servants had traveled with the newlyweds. Anne appreciated the quiet as she sat at the kitchen table and enjoyed a cup of tea while her mind wandered.

There had been no word from Charles since he left in the morning. Perhaps it was too soon, but if Charles had found her mother and sister, she'd hoped they would have returned by now.

Anne wasn't one to wait idly by doing nothing, but what choice did she have? Brannon Cottage offered her safety while the fate of her family was uncertain.

"Anne?"

"I'm sorry. I'm restless from the waiting. How do you do it?"

Rhona glanced sideways at Anne and smiled while she pulled a cast-iron dish from the small oven. "I experienced a similar unease when Charles and the others fought to protect me. With my younger brother's life at stake, I almost married a man I didn't love. My father and I had a tenuous relationship, but I didn't imagine the depths of his treachery. The end could have been far worse had they not been there. Don't fret. Charles knows exactly what he's doing."

Anne nodded and looked down at her unfinished tea and scone. She couldn't stomach another morsel until she knew her mother and sister were safe. "My father once told me about Charles's work for the British government. He spoke of Charles as though he bore the weight of the world's problems and yet managed to solve them at the same time. He believed Charles to be a gallant and trustworthy man, though he hadn't seen him in many years."

Rhona smiled softly. "Charles is all those things, and more."

"I was pleased when I heard of your marriage. I am only sorry I could not have been there."

"Few were. Tristan and his wife, Alaina, and their son, Christian. Devon, of course, and Braden."

Anne reached into her memories, but only Tristan sounded familiar. "My father mentioned Tristan—he went to school with Charles. Who are the other two?"

"Devon Clayton also went to school with them, and he worked with Charles. Devon is a bit of a mystery and not easy to know beneath the surface. I would trust him with my life, as I would Charles and Tristan."

Rhona set the dish on the counter and wound her hands into a cloth. Anne saw that the distant look in Rhona's eyes contained pleasant memories. Rhona said, "Braden, Lord Crawford, is an unexpected and recent friend, and much like a father to me."

Anne still ached for her father. In the evening hours when her mother and sister had retired, and not a sound echoed off the stone walls of the castle, Anne longed to hear her father's boisterous laugh. A laugh she remembered from the days before he realized Claire would never be a normal child, and before Anne discovered the debts, lies, and secrets. And yet, her heart could not beat without remembering the good in him, too.

They ate their supper in companionable silence, though neither of them finished more than a few bites. Afterward, Anne helped Rhona clear the table, and then she motioned Anne into the cozy living room where a fire burned low in the hearth. Poised, refined, and gracious, Rhona didn't appear like a woman who'd ever had to learn to do anything on her own, and yet she cooked, made the fire, and kept the cottage tidy. Anne might have grown used to such things in the past year, but a woman as refined as Rhona . . . it didn't make sense.

"You have a rather faraway look in your eyes, Anne."

"I'm admiring you." Anne managed a smile for her cousin's wife. "You don't seem . . . I wouldn't have thought you could be so accomplished in domestic duties."

Rhona settled into one of the two chairs in the room. "I led a quiet life, and boredom is not something I tolerate well. I manage enough, but it is true, I have not had to do for myself." Rhona tilted her head slightly, an action Anne's mother once did whenever she was about to ask Anne a question. "Why did you not reach out to Charles sooner?"

Anne pulled inward, her back straightened, and her chin rose slightly. "About what?"

Rhona's reassuring smile deflated Anne's rigidness somewhat.

"About your family's difficulties. Every family has its challenges—this I know firsthand—but Charles would have helped after your father passed away, had he known of the circumstances. I hope you'll allow us to help now."

Anne looked into the flames and wondered how her life had veered so far off its original path. She could lay the sole blame of her family's current financial situation at her father's feet, God rest his soul. Kevan Doyle had done his best, but he did not possess the mind of a businessman. Her father's debt—now hers—was not something she wanted Charles to feel obligated to resolve.

She turned back to Rhona. "I know he would have helped financially. All it would have taken is one letter. However, I couldn't have my pride and family be a case for charity or pity." Anne stood and walked to stand by the window. A light and wet snow drifted down, each flake melting into the damp ground. "I couldn't bear the shame if Charles knew what had happened and how."

Crossing her arms over her chest, Anne leaned against the wall and looked at Rhona. Anne envied Rhona's calm manner. Anne always felt the need to move. If she remained still for too long, her world might collapse. "Our state of affairs has not always been distressed. Had this not . . . had I not seen what I did, I would have found a way. It doesn't matter now. Charles will know by now how far we've fallen."

Rhona left the chair and crossed the room. Anne didn't pull back when Rhona took her hands. "You've not fallen, Anne, you or your family. No matter what happens from here on, we are by your side."

Three

Laoch Nua
(A New Hero)

Northumberland, England

"Are you going to keep it?"

Devon's fingers glided over the balustrade, the polished wood smooth beneath his touch. "It's in the middle of bloody nowhere."

Tristan grinned and opened a door, to where he had no clue. "I should think that would appeal to you."

"It does, but it's of little use to me at the moment. I'm rarely at home." The plush carpets muffled Devon's footsteps as he walked from the parlor to the study, down the hall to the library and dining room, and back again. The great entrance hall could easily double as a ballroom—if Devon was the type to host a ball—and the staircase could manage a team of horses and the width of a coach.

"Your uncle was not a subtle man."

Devon laughed and leaned his head back so he could look at the two chandeliers. "No, he was not. I had no idea the old man even had such an estate. I'm told he refurbished after he purchased the property, but he lived in it for only six months."

Tristan brushed his ungloved hand across a table surface.

"Someone has been here."

Devon nodded. "My uncle's solicitor sent a small staff to clean the place before I arrived."

"I don't recall you ever speaking of an uncle before."

Devon shrugged and meandered down the hall. "He and my father argued long ago, and I rarely saw him in the ensuing years." Devon recognized a few of the paintings and wondered how his uncle managed to obtain them. The collection of art hanging in this one hall could have financed another three estates like Greyson Hall. "Uncle Wynton didn't believe in my father's work—he disliked solicitors—and my father didn't agree with Uncle Wynton's laissez-faire way of thinking."

Devon stepped closer to inspect one of many grand paintings. "I do believe this is an original Vermeer." Devon shook his head and stepped away. Pulling out his pocket watch, he noted the time and glanced out to the darkened sky. "I'll inspect the rest of the estate later. We won't beat the storm back to Claiborne Manor. I hope Alaina won't mind if you're late for the ball."

Tristan shrugged into his coat and reached for his hat. "I told her we might be delayed. How did my wife convince you to attend?"

Devon groaned. "No sane man with eyes and brain could turn down a request from your wife. I don't know how you ever say no."

Tristan grinned. "I don't." He opened the front door and asked, "Where did the servants go? One would expect them to have stayed on."

"I couldn't say. The solicitor said to expect a butler and maid, both of whom he sent before the holidays." Devon checked his umbrella before stepping through the massive front door. "At least we brought the coach. If we catch the train, we'll save ourselves some time. By the by, have you heard from Charles?"

Tristan waited while Devon turned the lock on the door. "A

telegram stated they'd arrived in Ireland. I imagine our friend has more important, and delightful, things on his mind."

Six hours later, the coach stopped in front of Claiborne Manor, Alaina's family estate which she and Tristan now occupied. When she married Tristan, he had many properties, but not one had he called home. Many would envy the mansion and massive estate Devon recently inherited, but it was the family within the walls of Claiborne Manor that Devon envied. He may not be ready to settle down with a wife—may never be—but he enjoyed the time spent with Tristan and his family.

The dance was well underway by the time they arrived. Tristan and Alaina's neighbor had overdone the candles and was too sparing with the drinks. Devon had promised Alaina an appearance but did not guarantee he'd stay long. To Devon's thinking, Alaina appeared tired, and no wonder with her expecting another child. She had insisted on attending the country ball, and he admired her ability to enjoy the company of so many at one time. However, he tried not to throttle the eager debutantes and their mothers.

King and country help me if one more hopeful mother and her chit come this way, I'll—

"It can't be all bad man." Tristan stepped up behind Devon and attempted a whisper, but he couldn't suppress the light laughter.

Devon scowled at Tristan, then turned a warm smile to Alaina. "You are lovelier than when I last saw you, Your Grace." He bowed his head briefly and winked at her. "You've brightened what has become a considerably dull evening."

"You scoundrel, you're worse than Tristan." Alaina laughed softly and leaned closer. "Why do you come, if these social affairs displease you?"

Devon raised a brow. "And refuse you? I am a weak man, my dear."

Alaina's laughter brightened her eyes. "You are not as weak as you are clever."

Tristan winked at Alaina. "If I did not enjoy dancing with my lovely wife, I would not attend either."

Alaina gently swatted Tristan's arm. "Don't believe a word he says, Devon. We could hardly turn down an invitation from one of our only neighbors, though we wouldn't want Lady Carlyle to know our reasons."

"Never fear, I rarely believe anything Tristan utters." Devon addressed Alaina's question. "As to my presence here, I believe I can rectify that immediately."

Tristan scanned the mass of wishful young women and single-minded men currently dancing. "Perhaps one of these young ladies—"

"If you value your life, good man, don't finish that sentence."

"Your Graces!" Lady Carlyle smiled brightly, and to Devon's horror, she escorted a homely young woman draped in a canary yellow gown with too many bows.

"Forgive me, my dear," Devon bent his head and kissed Alaina's hand, "but it's time for me to leave."

"You will stay at Claiborne Manor tonight."

Devon dazzled Alaina with a grin. "I gladly accept." Devon left the ballroom without drawing much notice and stepped out into the light drizzle. He shook his head at the driver and said, "I'm in need of a walk."

The next morning, Devon sat alone at breakfast when Tristan sauntered in. "Alaina won't be down and apologizes for not seeing you off."

Devon finished his meal and set aside his serviette. "It's a wonder she lasted as long as she did last night."

Tristan prepared a plate and sat down across from his friend. "She's not especially fond of formal affairs, but it's been almost a year since she's attended one. I thought I would have to carry her out of there over my shoulder."

Devon laughed. "That would have livened up the dance."

Ellington, Tristan's butler, entered the room wearing a stern expression. "You have a visitor, Your Grace."

Devon glanced at his friend. "Are you expecting someone?"

Tristan shook his head, and both men left the table to venture outside where a light drizzle fell upon the earth. The young man's clothes were ragged, but clean, and the horse he rode looked ready for retirement.

"Beg pardon, which of you is Mr. Clayton?"

Devon stepped forward. "I am. And you are?"

"Jimmy, sir. Here." Jimmy buckled forward after he handed a letter to Devon.

Tristan took pity on the boy and asked Ellington to see that he was given drink and a meal. He also instructed the butler to keep the boy inside until they had a chance to question him. Devon ignored them all and read the letter for the second time. He crumbled the paper. "It would seem London will have to wait. I'm headed for Ireland."

DEVON MOVED HIS HORSE off the country road one half mile from Brannon Cottage and backed behind an abandoned crofter's cottage. The surrounding area was quiet except for wild wind and the sound of the winter ocean as it crashed against the rocks and quay. A discernable stream of smoke drifted from the chimney of the cottage. He checked the area once more before he moved back onto the road and finally stopped outside.

The front door opened before he finished securing his horse to the post.

"Devon, thank goodness!"

"Rhona."

She rushed forward and grabbed his hands. "I've been mad with worry. Charles sent a young man to tell me all was well and he'd be home soon, but nothing else. If he's sent for you, something must have gone wrong."

Devon ushered her inside and closed the door. "Charles knows how to take care of himself. You, above all, should know that."

"I do, but this is different . . . Devon?"

He nodded, but his eyes remained fixed on the other woman. Charles spared the details in his letter, and Devon had not expected to meet anyone else.

"Oh, I'm sorry. Lady Anne Doyle, this is Devon Clayton, the friend of Charles's I told you about. Devon, this is Charles's cousin, Lady Anne. She's the reason we're all here."

Devon stared into Anne's eyes, entranced with the hidden secrets lurking in her gaze. Devon's purpose in life had been the unfolding of one mystery after another, and he wanted to uncover every secret Lady Anne possessed.

Devon mentally shook himself from the unexpected stupor and returned his attention to Rhona when she asked, "Charles sent for you?"

Devon nodded. "Tell me exactly what's happened and why Charles isn't here."

Rhona looked as confused as Devon felt. "He didn't tell you?"

Anne stepped forward, the first movement from her since he arrived. She said with some surprise, "You came here without knowing why?"

Devon glanced back at Anne. Her green eyes, the color of summer moss, narrowed in distrust. He wanted to destroy whatever man or circumstance caused such caution in one so innocent. "Of course I came. He asked me to. Details weren't important at the time, but they are now."

Rhona drew his attention once more. "Please, sit down, and I'll prepare some tea. You must be hungry."

Devon shook his head. "I'll take the tea, only if you have

nothing stronger, but I need you to tell me what's going on."

Anne lowered herself into a chair opposite Devon. "He's trying to rescue my family."

Charles and Rhona obviously trusted this man, but trust was a carefully guarded commodity in Anne's life. What kind of person would come when a friend summoned, no questions asked? Anne wondered if she was simply too jaded to remember the last true friend she had, or if she'd ever known such a bond.

His intense scrutiny seemed to penetrate deep into her heart and thoughts. She looked down just to be certain her clothes still covered what they should, and then she met his eyes. Trust or not, she had no choice. If anything happened to Charles because of her . . . "Will you go and help my cousin?"

Devon thanked Rhona for the brandy, though he continued to stare at Anne. Instead of answering her question, he asked one of his own. "Tell me what you know."

Anne shook her head. "There isn't time. Charles could now be in danger. I witnessed a murder and I ran. I knew Charles would be here, and I didn't know who else to turn to with this kind of information. We don't have a lawman in the village, and Charles gained my promise that I wouldn't leave the cottage."

"If you are now safe, why did Charles go to . . . where is he?"

"Ballinrock Castle, my family's home, or what's left of it."

"Why is he there?"

"My mother and sister are in residence. When I returned home the other night, I couldn't find them, and then I saw . . ." Anne watched Devon's brow raise and swore revulsion lurked in his eyes. "You believe I left them to save myself?" Anne stood and looked down at Devon. "I would never. Do not presume to know me, Mr. Clayton. I have to get them out of Ballinrock and back to England, away from danger."

Rhona had remained silent during the interchange. Anne's eyes briefly met Rhona's, and thankfully her new friend understood.

"Devon, none of this is Anne's fault."

"I didn't say it was, and don't presume to know my thoughts, Lady Anne."

Devon set his drink aside and stood, almost toe-to-toe with Anne. She wanted to step back, but the Irish resolve in her wouldn't back down.

"You may consider me an enemy, though I cannot imagine why, but I am here to help. If Charles sent me to you directly, I have to assume it's because he wants you and Rhona safely back in England and under my protection."

Rhona almost knocked over her chair with the force from standing so quickly. "I'm not going, not without Charles."

Anne was grateful for the solidarity. She had no intention to leave behind Charles or her mother and sister. "Neither am I."

Devon considered Anne's high color set against her alabaster skin, the determined stance, and how she struggled to hide a lot of fear. He would have smiled if he didn't think Anne would misinterpret the expression. He'd grown accustomed to Rhona's stubbornness on their last mission, and he admired her for it, even as he pitied Charles the task of dealing with a beautiful but obstinate wife. He and Tristan managed to bind themselves to women who were as unyielding and uncompromising as themselves. Fortunately, Devon had plenty of experience dealing with a variety of women. Unfortunately, charm was not going to work on either of them. One set of blue eyes, the other green, stared at him, waiting.

He wouldn't allow them to see his amusement, but he would admit defeat. He didn't doubt Rhona would go and look for Charles herself, and Anne was proving to be a match for his tenacity.

"Where's Ballinrock Castle?"

"Four miles northwest. I'll show you."

Devon studied Anne and the way her back straightened, an indication of determination, and the way she bit her lower lip, a sign of nervousness. Charles's cousin would make a horrible agent, but he didn't doubt she could take care of herself if the need arose. Sadly for her, Devon wasn't going to be swayed. "You'll stay here with Rhona." He held up a hand to quiet her when she opened her mouth to speak. "After I leave, Rhona can tell you what happens when distractions prevent us from doing our job. How do I get there?"

"Travel the road north three miles. It will veer left first for one quarter mile and soon after bend back to the right. You'll see Ballinrock before the turn. There are few cottages on the land, but only one of the farms is occupied, and it's on the north side. Unless they're watching, no one should see you arrive."

Devon admired Anne's tenacity and respected the trust she placed in a stranger. He slipped into his coat and checked his pistol before he stepped outside. Addressing both women, he said, "Lock this door and don't open it again until Charles or I return."

The rain dwindled until a thick mist covered the hills. Patches of green peeked through a light layer of snow. Devon rode the four miles down a maze of back roads until the castle came into view. The debilitated stone structure appeared more haunted than habitable. The grounds had been neglected to the point where he suspected the fields were fallow and the stables empty. No one came to the door when he rode up, which either meant no one was home, or Anne was mistaken in thinking someone would care about her absence.

He dismounted and led his horse around to the side and back again to the front. This time, someone leaned casually against one of the stone pillars at the base of the steps. "You're slowing in your old age, Devon. I expected you hours ago."

"I'm still a year younger and more handsome than you."

Devon grinned and embraced Charles. "Rhona is well and sends her love, but I suspect beneath her worry is a great deal of annoyance that you've not returned. No sensible man would leave behind a bride like Rhona. What in the bloody name of decency is going on?"

"Let's settle your horse into the stable. Better to speak outside."

Devon secured his stallion in one of the stalls, all empty save for the one occupied by Charles's horse and another one which currently sheltered a bedraggled mare. There was grain, but not much. He examined it before feeding the animal, and then followed Charles to the entrance of the stable where they watched the mist turn to rain.

"You intended for me to come and take Anne and Rhona back to England, didn't you?"

Charles nodded. "I knew they wouldn't listen, at least not Rhona, and knowing your inability to say no to women—"

Devon laughed and leaned back against one of the stable doors. "Any colder and this becomes snow. I'd as soon be back across the channel by then." He lifted the collar of his coat and bunched his black scarf beneath his chin for warmth.

"So would I. Unfortunately, the honeymoon will have to be delayed because now that you're here, I intend to get my wife and Anne, along with her family, out of Ireland until Gaspar is found."

Devon pushed away from the door. "Lord Gaspar? Marquess of Lochnabar? He's who has Anne so afraid?"

"How much did Anne tell you?"

"Your cousin wasn't cooperative. She did not reveal much."

Charles laughed. "Losing your charm with women?"

Devon scoffed at the idea. "Anne claims she witnessed a murder. Am I to assume Gaspar has a part in this, and by the by, how does she know him?"

"From what little I've learned here, Lord Gaspar, though he is unfit to carry the title, is a regular visitor to Ballinrock."

"One of the servants I've yet to see told you this?"

Charles smiled. "Not intentionally."

Despite the grim circumstances, Devon knew Charles loved this work as much as he did. The mystery of it all. Answering who and why, and bringing the culprits to justice. Charles gave up the work professionally, but only for Rhona. Devon hoped his friend could remain in retirement, but if Gaspar was involved, the situation might require a temporary reinstatement of both Charles and Tristan. When they went up against a member of the peerage, circumstances changed.

"Gaspar would not risk murder unless he believed that whatever he protected was far more important than a man's life. I could count him among my enemies, but he's a weak man, Charles. I would not be surprised to know he preys upon women and children, but faced with a man younger, and possibly stronger than he, or any man for that matter . . ." Devon shook his head. "A few years past, I heard of a lord who had beaten one of his servants to such a degree, the young man lost the use of his legs. The truth revealed Gaspar as the lord in question, but he did not conduct the beating. He hires men to handle matters which could further damage his already tarnished reputation. He's too cowardly to have done this alone."

Charles nodded. "Precisely why I wanted you here. You know the man better than Tristan or me. Speaking of Tristan . . ."

Despite the cold and gloom, Devon filled his lungs with the invigorating air. "He wanted to come."

"I'd rather he remain at home. With Alaina expecting another child, I didn't want him to venture far from Claiborne Manor or put him in harm's way. He spent so much time away from his family while helping me protect Rhona, he needs to be home."

"Lucky for you, I'm unencumbered and eager for a new case."

Devon lightly slapped his friend's back and stepped outside. The rain had once more resumed to a drizzle, and the pair made their way across the grounds to the house. Once inside, the footman arrived to take their coats. "My lord, Mrs. Keegan had to resolve an issue in the kitchen."

"Is everything all right?" Charles asked.

"Yes, my lord."

"My friend will stay the night. Please see that a room is prepared for him."

The footman's gaze darted between the two men, but he bowed and backed from the room.

Once alone in the parlor, with the fire blazing to ward off the chill, Charles poured them each two fingers of whiskey. "I don't know if this is a case or not."

Devon enjoyed the warmth from the whiskey as it coursed down his throat. "This is high quality. A bit out of place considering." He looked around the spacious room, complete with shabby drapes and bare shelves. Large pale sections of the walls indicated paintings or tapestries once graced the interior. Devon finished his drink and set the glass on the sideboard. "Charles, you've been here a few days and could have taken Anne's family away from here. It doesn't appear you would have met with any resistance from the servants, and I assume Gaspar isn't around. Why are you still here?"

Charles stared out the window and turned back to his friend. "Anne's mother, Kathryn, and her sister, young Claire, aren't here, or if they are, I haven't been able to find them, and it feels as though someone is always watching. The last thing I need is for Gaspar to get wind of what I'm doing here. Last night while I was searching the east wing, the housekeeper emerged from the shadows. Her stealth rivals ours."

"You suspect the servants?"

Charles shrugged. "I suspect everyone. The butler I once

knew is away, and I recognize no one else. Anne did warn me that most of the servants had left, but this skeleton of a staff is beyond what I had expected." Charles lowered his voice a notch. "I could demand someone tell me, but it's Kathryn and her daughter's safety for which I'm concerned. If someone here is suspect, and I dismiss them all, or speak to the wrong person—"

"They could harm Anne's mother and sister before you find them. No one has mentioned to you that Anne is missing?"

"No, they claim she is indisposed, but no matter. I'd rather they believe I don't know where she is or what she has told me, even though it's not much." Charles stepped toward the hall, and Devon realized that Charles wasn't experiencing paranoia. His friend believed without a doubt that someone spied on them both.

Charles stood close to Devon, his voice a whisper. "The past few days have been more fact-finding than any actual progress, but there aren't enough people here to watch us both. Once we find them, I need to understand what has happened and what the bloody Lord Gaspar has to do with all of this."

Alby, who had yet to make eye contact with Devon, announced that dinner was served in the dining room. "A formal dinner, Charles?"

"Appearances," Charles said in an aside as he walked with Devon to the dining room. They ate in silence and ate little. Charles dismissed Alby and the men returned to the study.

"Two of us shall make quicker work of another search." Devon stepped up beside Charles and glanced out into the hallway, which was as eerie as the rest of the place.

Charles nodded. "I would rather do this quietly so as not to arouse suspicions. These old castles have plenty of hidden passages and rooms, but as yet I've not found one. Even as a young man, those secrets were not revealed to me."

Devon understood the grim situation, but he preferred an

optimistic approach until proven otherwise. "Don't worry, Charles. We'll find them."

Four

Fothraigh is Rith
(Ruins and Run)

They resumed the search the following morning, and frustrations mounted. Devon closed the last door in the upstairs hallway that seemed to have no end. If a door was locked, he knocked or utilized his prodigious lock-picking skills. He was left disappointed every time. One empty room after another revealed the same thing—Ballinrock Castle was close to ruin, yet still habitable. Two doors didn't lock and another fell off the hinges when Devon opened it too quickly.

He walked to the closest window and looked down at the ground below. The side of the castle extended at least fifteen feet beyond where Devon stood, at the end of the hall. He glanced at the interior wall and then back outside. Checking behind him to ensure he was still alone, and reminded of his own childhood home, Devon ran his hands along the wall. Every so often he pressed forward or knocked against the worn paper. Nothing.

Devon opened the door to the last room in the east wing and once more entered, careful to secure it from the inside. He followed the same pattern on the interior of the bedroom until the wall yielded next to the scarred bureau. He moved the piece aside and pushed against the wall until it gave a bit more. One final heave and a section of the wall moved inward to reveal an antechamber with a stone staircase curving upward. The room was lit only by the dim sunlight through narrow windows. His soft-soled boots made little noise as he climbed the stairs. The higher he climbed, the warmer it became.

A faint glow showed beneath a strong oak door at the stop of the stairs. Devon listened to the soft murmurings, and what sounded like singing, coming from the other side. He knocked once and the voices stopped. Devon heard shuffling and finally a quiet voice telling him to enter.

He stepped onto the landing and pushed the door inward. A flurry of skirts frantically moved to the far end of the room.

Devon put a finger to his lips, asking them to keep quiet. "I'm not going to hurt you." He closed the door but didn't secure it until he saw another door on the other side of the chamber. "I'm a friend of Anne's."

The older woman inched forward, squinting her eyes. The resemblance to the young girl was apparent, and Devon realized this must be Anne's mother and sister, though none of Kathryn's physical features had passed to Anne, except perhaps her height. She stood tall and slender like her eldest daughter.

"I don't know you." Her brogue was thick and raspy. "A friend of my Anne? She's been a bad daughter and not come to see her mother. She must come and see us or I cannot return to my duties."

Devon studied her thoroughly, from her disheveled dark gray hair to the hem of her filthy skirts. This could not be Anne's doing, not with the fear and worry she had expressed for her family. "Lady Doyle, I've come to take both you and Lady Claire to see Anne."

She scrunched her eyes again and took another step forward. "To return to my duties?"

Devon slowly nodded, uncertain what was wrong with the woman, but something was indeed amiss. He should have pried more information out of Anne. "Yes, to return to your duties."

Kathryn motioned for the young girl to come forward. After some hesitation, Anne's younger sister stood beside her mother. Devon wondered why neither Anne nor Charles told him about the girl or at least what to expect. She was most certainly different, but barring those differences, she was as lovely as her sister. A child trapped in an unforgiving body. "Are you well, Lady Claire?"

The young girl tilted her head and instead of answering, walked toward him. With the innocence of an incorruptible soul, she reached out with her small hand. Devon knelt on the rug and waited while she ran her fingers over his face. Her touch was light, and her eyes were those of a pure and guileless heart. She stepped back and smiled. "I'm Claire. Who are you?"

Devon stood and returned her smile. "Devon. I'm a friend of your sister's. Would you like to see her?"

Claire nodded enthusiastically and turned to her mother. "We're going to see Anne."

Kathryn smoothed her hair back into the haphazard bun and pinched her cheeks. Her eyes appeared brighter now, and her cheeks filled with color. She didn't seem to notice the faint stench of uncleanliness in the air. Devon couldn't credit the sudden change in her demeanor, but he didn't question it. Now that he believed he had their cooperation, he would locate Charles and get them outside without incident.

"Hurry and gather your things." Devon walked to the other door opposite of where he entered and opened it. The narrow hallway was dark, but newer than the one by which he entered. "Where does this lead?"

Claire poked her head around him. "To mother."

He translated that to mean Kathryn's bedchamber was at the other end of the hall or at least he hoped so. She held a single bag, one of some expense, against her body. She smoothed her skirts and stood straight. Devon ignored his curious tendencies to ask about the bag and told them to stay directly behind him. He picked the lock to the door and entered the room before motioning them both inside. The bedchamber was not as sparse as the rest of the house. She seemed at ease when she set her bag down on a trunk and took a seat at the dressing table.

"My lady, we are to go and see Anne."

Kathryn looked into the stained mirror, turning from side to side while tucking in loose hairs. "I must be presentable for my guests first."

Devon almost reached for her but pulled back so as not to startle the woman. Hurried footsteps sounded in the hallway. He told them both to remain quiet and went to the door. The footsteps drew closer. The door handle turned but did not open. If it had been a servant, they would have a key.

Devon opened the door, and Charles turned back around. "Tell me you've found them." Devon nodded and Charles quickly came inside.

"Thank God. Gaspar's coach is wheeling up the drive."

Devon lowered his voice. "We have to get them out quietly. I believe Lady Doyle's touched or in a state after being locked up. You should have seen the conditions in the other chamber."

"A quiet departure. Anne can explain once we get them back, but if Kathryn and Claire were locked up, the servants must have known about it. They're in need of a bath, but they don't appear starved." Charles knelt down in front of Claire. "I'm your cousin Charles, and I'm going to help take you to your sister."

Claire hugged her own small bag. "Anne said we could go to the sea."

"Yes, we'll go to the sea."

It wasn't a lie. They would have to cross St. George's Channel to reach England, and Devon had a man waiting with a small ship ready to take them across whenever they arrived.

Devon held the door open less than two inches, his focus split between watching the hallway and listening to Charles convince Claire and Kathryn that they had to leave now.

While Claire seemed receptive to the idea, convincing Kathryn was proving to be more of a complication. Still at the mirror, she behaved as a woman set to resume whatever duties she imagined she still had. Charles's urgings to remain quiet did little to prevent the commotion she was about to cause. Claire finally spoke up and gave her mother a hug. She slipped her small hand into her mother's, and only then did Kathryn calm.

When Charles had finally gained their cooperation, convincing the lady that it was her who Anne needed most right now, they stepped out into the hall. Devon heard voices, faint but sounding from the direction in which they needed to go. He looked over his shoulder at Charles. "Do you know of any other way out of here?"

Charles replied in the negative. "Someone will see us on the servants' staircase."

Claire tugged on Devon's jacket. "I know a secret."

Devon glanced up at Charles and bent forward until he was closer. "What secret, Claire?"

She slipped her hand into Devon's and tugged once more until he followed. They returned to the bedroom where Claire continued to lead them back into the chamber where she and her mother had been kept.

Charles held them up once the door to the chamber closed behind them. "What is this?"

"It's where I found them." Devon nodded toward Claire. "You have every right to be here, Charles, but unless you want them caught in the middle of whatever is happening, I suggest we get them out of here now."

"Yes, you should."

Devon stopped again when Claire pulled on his arm. "You're

going to stay here and confront Lord Gaspar."

Charles nodded. "As you've said, I have every right to be here." He turned to Claire. "Devon will follow you now, Claire."

The little girl stepped close to Charles. "What about Papa?"

Kathryn's complexion paled. Devon ignored Claire for the moment and focused on the lady. Her eyes darted, not meeting his, and a steady hushing noise seeped through her lips. "Lady Doyle? Are you all right?"

"I'm not Lady Doyle . . . no, no, no." Her head shook violently, and Devon held Claire back while Charles attempted to calm the older woman again.

"Kathryn, look at me. It's Cousin Charles." Charles gently grabbed her chin and held her face straight. She looked straight at him but didn't appear to actually see him. "Kathryn?"

"It's Lady Gaspar to you."

Charles stepped back. "Claire, who is Lady Gaspar?"

"That's what the man calls Mama."

Devon leaned toward Charles. "How is that possible in Kathryn's delusional state? If Anne knew, she would have told you, wouldn't she?"

"I don't know, but if there's any truth to it, or if she believes it, this situation has just become much more complicated." Charles slid a wooden bar into place to barricade the door leading back into the narrow hall. "We're going now. You get them back to the cottage safely, Devon. Rhona will help Anne care for them."

Devon knew better than to argue. He would rather be the one to remain behind and deal with Lord Gaspar, but he had no legal right to the family or property. He leaned down to eye level of the eight-year-old. "Will you show us your secret now?"

The girl seemed delighted to help and once more gripped his hand as she led them back toward the staircase Devon had climbed up the first time. However, rather than going back through the same wall, Claire led them into what appeared like a dark corner but was in fact another staircase. This new passageway had smaller windows which allowed for little light to illuminate the dark walls. Kathryn became increasingly agitated. Claire seemed at ease, as though she'd walked these steps a hundred times. At the bottom landing, Devon lifted the girl aside and pushed open the heavy door. Late afternoon mist met them outside the castle walls.

Charles set his hand on Claire's shoulder. "Someday, dear cousin, you're going to have to tell me how you found that."

"They can't go on foot, Charles. You'll need to distract the household while I get them to the stables." Shouts echoed from somewhere inside the castle. "Change of plans."

Devon lifted Claire into his arms and had to hush the girl when she giggled. The seriousness of his tone must have reached her because she pushed her face against his shoulder. Kathryn fought Charles, but after he whispered something Devon didn't hear, she picked up the hems of her skirts so they didn't drag on the ground and followed them to the stables. Charles helped Devon saddle the old mare. Once the lady was seated on the horse, Devon set Claire on his stallion and swung up behind her.

Devon grinned at Charles. "Don't be too long, or I'll be the one answering to Rhona." He accepted the mare's reins from Charles and set the horses in motion.

Charles watched them ride away, and after a few minutes, the mist engulfed them, masking their getaway. He waited another minute, listening intently for any more shouts, and upon hearing silence, he walked back to the front door.

Inside, he started to remove his damp coat. Alby almost hurried past him. The younger man came to a stop and pulled on the edges of his coat. "My lord."

"I go on a walk and return to find the household in an uproar. Whose carriage is outside?"

The footman hesitated. "Lord Gaspar's, my lord. He's come to call."

Charles nodded and passed his coat to the footman. "Call on whom? Have my cousins returned and I wasn't informed?"

"Yes, I mean, no, my lord."

Mrs. Keegan walked hurriedly toward them. "I've been looking for you, my lord. Lord Gaspar has come to call."

Somewhat amused, and immensely curious, Charles nodded and walked toward the study. "So I've been told. Please send our guest into the study."

Charles poured himself a finger of brandy, no doubt from Gaspar's stock, and stood behind the desk. He didn't have long to wait before Gaspar stepped into the room. His step faltered momentarily, but Charles gave the man credit for a speedy recovery.

"Lord Blackwood. It has been a long time."

Charles finished his drink and set the glass aside. He noticed the tick in Gaspar's cheek and decided to see just how far he could press the man. He knew people revealed the most when they were trying to keep a secret. "Five years. You fought me in the House of Lords on many occasions. I do hope there are no hard feelings."

"None at all. What, may I ask, are you doing at Ballinrock Castle?"

Charles shuffled through papers, looking for what he didn't know, but it seemed to irritate the other man. "It was time to visit my cousins. Although, I should have sent word for none of them are here. Do you have business with Lady Doyle?"

Gaspar's tick quickened, and Charles didn't miss the tightening of the man's fists, suggesting he took exception to the "Lady Doyle."

"I do, in fact. May I call on her?"

Charles shook his head and shrugged. "I don't know when

she'll return. Unfortunate because I must return to England the day after tomorrow."

Gaspar cleared his throat. "The life of leisure."

Charles glanced up. "My burden to bear. Now, if you'll excuse me, I have some letters to draft. I will be certain to leave word for Lady Doyle that you called." When Gaspar didn't leave, Charles affected an even more casual air. "Unless I may help you."

Charles knew he had Gaspar in a difficult spot, and frankly, he enjoyed the man's discomfort. Gaspar no doubt expected to return to Ballinrock and find Kathryn and Claire in the locked chamber upstairs. Charles wanted answers, but they would have to wait until he could confirm that Kathryn was not in fact Lady Gaspar. However, if she was, would Gaspar not say something?

Charles shuffled a few more papers, showing Gaspar complete indifference. His eyes skimmed the top page of the stack of documents, and he looked back up. "Is there anything you need?"

"Not a thing. Please tell Lady Doyle I will return this evening."

Charles nodded once and didn't bother to ring for the footman. Gaspar didn't wait to be shown out, and instead, he turned and walked briskly from the room. Charles heard the front door open and close, and only then did he settle into the chair behind the desk. He picked up the top document, reading it with great care.

"Good God, Cousin Kathryn. What have you done?"

DEVON HAD BEEN IN sword fights, duels, and more than a few bouts of fisticuffs for he enjoyed the ring, but never had he endured a more grueling experience than riding alongside Kathryn. The four-mile ride from Ballinrock Castle to Brannon Cottage proved to be one of Devon's most trying ordeals. Once he assured himself that no one followed, he kept them off the road—a plan with which Lady Doyle did not agree—keeping to the trees where possible. Devon led them to the back of the cottage where he dismounted and lifted Claire to the ground. As he helped the lady down from the mare, the back door of the cottage opened.

"Where's Charles?"

"He'll be along soon," Devon told Rhona. He let go of Kathryn and waited while she smoothed her hair. She'd forced Devon to quiet her numerous times on what should have been a short ride, but now that they'd arrived, she would neither look at nor speak to Devon.

"Mother? Claire!" Anne rushed through the door and embraced her sister, kissed the top of her head, and then held her back as though to make sure Claire was unharmed. "Are you all right? I'm so sorry I left you behind." She looked up at Devon and next turned to her mother. "Mother, are you well?"

Kathryn smoothed down her skirts and nodded toward Devon without looking at him. "He wouldn't allow me to speak. You know how I enjoy good conversation while riding." She left Devon's side and moved sedately to her daughter. Curious as to which version of the woman they were all about to see, he watched the lady lean forward and kiss her daughter lightly on her cheek. "Why am I here, Anne? I should be at home with Asher."

Anne released her sister and gripped her mother's arms. "Who is Asher, Mother?"

Devon also caught the significance of what Kathryn had said, only he knew exactly who Asher was. He dropped the horses' reins and stepped over to stand beside Anne. Devon gently set his hand on Anne's arm until she freed her mother. "Asher is Lord Gaspar." He turned the lady's face gently, until he could see her eyes. "Is it true? You're wed to Lord Gaspar?"

Devon heard Anne's gasp but kept his eyes focused on the lady. "Tell me, now."

"You can't—"

"Come away, Claire."

Devon would thank Rhona later for distracting the young girl. He believed the woman to be delusional, but right now, he had to know the extent of the ramifications of what they'd just done. If Kathryn was married . . . "Is Lord Gaspar your husband?"

She spoke not a word, but the imperceptible nod was all Devon needed.

Devon stepped away and asked Rhona to take them all inside. Anne remained behind, stubborn in her refusal to follow. Rhona spared a quick glance at Devon, then guided Anne's mother and sister inside the small cottage.

"I don't believe this. I hadn't realized she . . . how did you know?"

Devon stepped closer, naturally drawn to her. "Claire said something, and it didn't make sense. I thought perhaps she didn't know what she was talking about, but I misjudged her."

"Most people do." Anne pulled on the edges of her shawl and burrowed into the heavy wool. "I don't admit this often, but I'm frightened. None of this makes any sense. Why my mother would do this, or why he'd want her to. I've always thought of Lord Gaspar as a rather pathetic man, but when I saw the knife drive into . . ."

Devon circled her with his arms and waited until she lowered her head on his shoulder. It should be Charles or Rhona comforting her, but Devon was oddly pleased he was there instead. "Gaspar is a weak man, at least for as long as I've known him."

"Charles said he's unworthy of the title he holds."

Devon scoffed. "And of everything else."

Anne drew away, leaving only a few inches between them. At her height, she didn't have to look too far up to meet his eyes. "That man who killed the village boy was not weak, Devon. He's a cold and heartless murderer."

Anne shivered beneath Devon's gentle touch, and he rubbed warmth into her arms. "He's a murderer, but he's still weak. Whatever Gaspar's reasons for any of his actions, he's not done it alone. How well did you know the boy who was killed?"

"Cillian Ó Fionnáin. His father is a tenant farmer at Ballinrock, one of the last few. I need to tell his family, Devon. I should have done so sooner, but I was selfishly worried about my own family. Cillian was a kind young man who never did harm to anyone. They had no reason—"

"What would Cillian have been doing in the house at that hour? Did he work there?"

"The crops haven't yielded much these past two years, and so I hired him to help out when he wasn't working the family's land. Sometimes he took it upon himself to check on the household when he knew I was away, and this time Haverly was visiting family." Anne looked up at Devon. "What could he have possibly seen to warrant what they did?"

"Don't try to make sense of it." Devon gently raised her chin up. "There is no sense in what they've done, but we will learn the truth."

Anne pushed away and walked to the horses, lifting their reins. "Come, we'll put them away before this weather turns worse."

Devon accepted that Anne had to sort out her thoughts on her own. He reached out and took the reins of his own stallion. "I expect Charles won't be long, and we have to be ready to leave quickly."

"He stayed behind so you could get them away. Was Lord Gaspar still there?"

Devon shook his head and secured the horses in the small one-room stable. "Not when I arrived, nor while Charles had been there. He arrived as we were leaving through Claire's secret passageway."

"What secret passage?"

"You didn't know? Someday you should ask her to show you. One of the entrances is through your mother's bedroom." Devon leaned up against his horse, running his hands over the long black mane. "What's wrong with your mother?"

"I don't know, but she's become gradually worse with each passing year. My father's death was difficult, and it changed her. At first, I thought it only grief, but she began to have fits, and her moods changed from day-to-day. Most days she's the mother I know, but other days I don't recognize her, and what she says makes little sense." Anne faced him, stepping closer. "If her mind is not sound, how could a marriage be legal, and to what end? Lord Gaspar can't have wanted to marry a woman whose mind is not entirely her own."

"It shouldn't be legal, but Gaspar might have paid an unscrupulous clergyman to perform the deed if, in fact, the marriage is legitimate. Has Lord Gaspar expressed interest in your mother before?"

"I thought he spent too much time at Ballinrock, but when he came, my mother appeared to enjoy his company, so I ignored his presence the best I could, but my mother has nothing to offer him if it's wealth he's after."

Devon shook his head. "As far as I know, Gaspar is a wealthy man in his own right. You said that most days your mother is lucid. It doesn't take long to perform a wedding and gain consent. Are you not with her often?"

"You mean, how could it have happened without me knowing?"

Devon nodded.

"Sometimes I am called away to help the sick or to look after an expecting mother. Last month, one of our farmers' wives was near her time and she was having difficulty. We cannot provide much for them, but I could be there while her husband worked. I spent every day there for almost two weeks."

"You care for these people like a nurse?"

Anne shook her head. "Like a healer. After the doctor told us that we could never do anything to help Claire's condition, I wanted to be able to help someone, even if it couldn't be my sister. An old woman in the village, a healer for many years, tutored me. And it was that duty that may have put my family in danger."

Anne turned and walked out of the stable, leaving Devon to follow. He caught up to her and stopped her with a hand on her shoulder. "I'm confused as to how all of this happened. You have family. Charles would have been here for you, and he has the means to take care of you and the estate. All you needed to do was ask."

"Charles barely knew my family. We're cousins, but distant. We knew each other a short time while we were children, and he asked to visit because he was going to be in Ireland. I believe he would have helped, but the debts are my father's which now makes them mine."

Stubborn Irish woman. She reminded him of an equally stubborn Scottish lass and English noblewoman. Devon removed his hat and pulled Anne back inside when the rain began. "Rhona will be out soon to check on you." He removed his outer coat and covered her.

"Wait." This time it was Anne who touched him. Her long fingers settled nicely on his arm. "I know I made a mistake. Charles did write occasionally to see how we were doing, and I always told him that all was well and that Father had left everything in order. I knew that for Charles, in his line of work, distractions could be . . . difficult, even dangerous. I allowed him to believe life was as prosperous as it had once been. Eventually, matters reached beyond my control. I was ashamed to ask for any kind of help until I had no choice."

Devon covered her hand with his. The yearning in her eyes wasn't for him but for understanding. She was without guile, and he did not doubt that she would give her life and freedom if that's what it took to correct the path on which she now found herself. Devon silently swore that he wasn't going to let that happen.

Anne almost diverted her eyes from Devon's gaze, but she saw something deep and dark behind the blue eyes. Their color changed and the emotion came in waves like the ocean off the Wexford coast. Stormy one moment and calm the next. Anne wondered if he realized how much those eyes revealed.

She reached beneath the edge of her bodice and withdrew a long silver chain. The pendant was a silver Celtic cross surrounded by a ring of gold, and at the center rested a polish pearl. She closed her eyes and held the pendant within her grasp, close to her heart. Exhaling, she lifted the chain over her head and gathered it into her palm. She knew Devon watched her, and she reached for his hand. Turning it over, she pressed the pendant into his palm. His questioning eyes sought hers out.

"This will be safer with you."

Devon held her treasure up to examine it. "This is rare and valuable." He lowered the pendant. "Where did you get it?"

"It was a gift from my father on my twenty-first birthday. Other than my family, it's the only thing I have of value."

"This pendant alone must be worth more than your father's debts."

Anne nodded. "Much more, but I can't sell it."

"Surely your father wouldn't expect you to hold onto—"

"I can't, Devon. Something in my father's eyes when he gave it to me said it was important." Anne ran her finger over the smooth stone as it sat in Devon's palm. "It was the last gift he ever gave me, and what danger could a pendant bring, or that's what I told myself. After what's happened, I don't know what to believe anymore. Please. If I believed I could keep it from falling into the wrong hands, I wouldn't ask this of you. If Charles trusts you, then I will also put my faith in you."

"Why me? You could give this to Charles or—"

"No." Anne pressed his hand closed over the pendant. "Please, Devon."

Devon lowered the silver chain over his head and slipped the heavy pendant beneath his clothes. "I'll have the rest of the story someday, Anne." Without any question or admonishment for keeping secrets, Devon pulled his coat up and over her head to protect against the wind and rain, then walked beside her back to the cottage.

Rhona met them at the door. Anne thanked Devon for the use of his coat and shook out her heavy shawl before looking around the room. Rhona stood between them and the fire, and from what Anne could see, she wasn't going to allow either of them to pass.

"Devon, I love you and I trust you, but what is going on? You were out there far longer than necessary." Rhona held up her hand when Devon would have spoken and refocused her attention. Anne suffered like a child whose nanny was about to reprimand her, but when Rhona spoke, her words echoed concern instead of anger or disappointment. "Anne, your sister is beside herself with fear, and your mother . . . she's not well."

Anne was used to the sudden swell of panic that came upon her whenever her mother drifted into whatever reality kept her company these days. Her moments of lucidity were becoming more and more rare. "Where are they?"

Rhona nodded over her shoulder. "Claire is reading while I heat water for a bath, and your mother is lying down. I gave her three fingers of whiskey." She shrugged unapologetically. "Your mother needed it."

Anne embraced Rhona. "Thank you. I know I've thrust you into a great deal of unpleasantness these past few days, and I won't ever be able to repay you for your kindness. Devon is not at fault for delaying us. I needed to speak with him, and I need to ask you not to question it." Anne looked toward the bedroom first and back to her sister who sat quietly before the fire with a book in her hands. "I've placed you all in danger, and if it had been only me . . ."

Rhona squeezed Anne's hands. The gesture was meant to comfort, but it was Rhona's small smile that gave Anne great relief. "Don't mistake my worry for displeasure in you. I have put Charles and Devon through far worse, and we all lived to tell the story."

Anne caught the look shared between Devon and Rhona and wondered at the bond between two people who had nothing between them save for respect and the kind of love reserved for friendship. She looked up at Devon. "Charles should be here now, shouldn't he?"

"He will be, Anne, I promise." Devon walked past them and stood by the fire. Anne watched as he knelt beside Claire. She couldn't hear what he said, but her sister's sweet smile was all she needed to see.

"You know Devon well." Anne stared at Rhona. "How well?"

Rhona smiled. "I love him. Not as I do Charles, of course, but you see, Devon saved my life."

Anne slowly exhaled. "I've trusted him with something valuable, and by doing so, I may have put my life in his hands. For my mother and sister I willingly did this. Tell me I was not mistaken."

"Other than my husband, there is no one I trust more than Devon and Tristan." Rhona's arm draped over Anne's shoulder, and for a few seconds, Anne was comforted in her decision.

"I pray you are right, cousin." Anne's close regard did not waver from Devon and her sister. Claire's smile brightened an intolerable and dreary day. How long would that smile last? Her family was safe, but Anne could not quiet the unease within. Devon moved, a slight shift in his body, but it was enough for Anne to see that he no longer listened to Claire's chatter. His body slowly extended until he stood. Claire quieted, but Devon offered her a brief smile and walked to the windows by the front door. He readied his pistol and held it flush with his leg, drawing back the curtain.

"Devon?" Anne hurried to her sister's side and drew her up and close.

Devon faced them, his lips turned up into a smile to reveal two small hollows in his cheeks. It was an unexpected response to what Anne believed might have been a dangerous situation, but certainly no man would behave with such aloofness if a true threat existed.

"Charles is here." Devon secured his pistol and nodded toward the back of the cottage. Rhona didn't wait for anyone but raced down the narrow hallway and thrust open the door.

"How did you know?"

Devon shrugged. "I've been doing this a long time." He walked over to them, but it wasn't Anne who received his attention but Claire. "Would you help me with something important, Claire?"

Eager to please, Claire nodded.

"Good. Will you stay with your mother while she rests and keep watch over her?"

Claire considered, peering up at Devon. "Then will we go to the sea?"

Devon's soft chuckle brought out a responding grin from Claire. "Yes, we'll go to the sea."

With the promise delivered, Claire skipped to the larger of the two bedrooms, Anne smiling at her retreating back. "I envy her at times. Not knowing would be far easier than carrying the burden of this cruel world."

"She's lucky to have you. They both are."

"If anything should happen, Devon—"

"Nothing is going to."

Anne lowered her voice, though the distance between them was slight. "If anything should happen, promise me you'll help Charles get my family to safety and keep them safe."

"What do you believe is going to happen?" Devon's eyes narrowed, penetrating the first barrier that encased her secrets. "You're still not telling us everything. Of course, you haven't really told us much, and we're uncovering facts as we go along. I knew it before I went to Ballinrock, and I was even more certain once I'd arrived. I know Gaspar, and he is a coward. What is it he wants from your family that he would deceive your mother and lock her and your sister in a secret room? What does he want that's worth a man's life?"

Anne pulled away as disbelief clouded her thoughts. "I swear to you, I don't know anything else about Lord Gaspar. I only know what was right there before my eyes."

A door closed, breaking Anne away from the conversation. Charles and Rhona appeared, and it was only seconds before Charles was beside her. "Gaspar backed down without argument. Either the man is deranged—and not the coward Devon believes—or he did not recently murder anyone."

Anne stepped back a few paces, putting distance between her and everyone else. "I saw what I saw."

"I'm not saying you didn't, cousin, which is why it's my assumption that he is severely deranged."

"No." Devon stood by his assessment of Gaspar. "Diabolical, perhaps, but his mind is sound. I'm sure of it. He knows what he's doing."

Anne caught the unmistakable look of "we'll talk later" Charles sent Devon. "In either case, the man is unpredictable, and we can't risk keeping you here. We leave for England in the morning. Tonight we rest. Devon and I will share the watch, and we'll be gone at first light."

"My mother and sister will go with you, but I must return home. I promise, I won't be far behind."

All eyes stared at Anne. Charles's expression was one that clearly stated she had no say in whether she remained behind or left with them. Devon's lips twitched as though he wanted to smile.

Anne had yet to figure out what the man always found so bloody amusing. Since her father passed and her mother's mind faded in and out of sensibility, Anne had become her own mistress. Relinquishing that control would not come easily now, if ever.

Devon said, "There are people here in Wexford I know. I'll contact them before we leave, and they can look after—"

"It's not the castle itself that concerns me. As you've already seen, it's in a dire state of repair, and Haverly, our butler, should return soon." Anne reached for the pendant out of habit, only to recall that she'd given it to Devon for safekeeping. "There are papers hidden in my father's study, and I cannot risk anyone finding them. I won't risk anyone else, and now that my family is safe—"

"You think Gaspar won't harm you? Whatever his secret, he undoubtedly knows by now that you either saw what happened or are a threat to him. Our goal is to get you and your family to safety without bloodshed. We have to keep up the farce, at least for now."

"Charles is right, Anne," Devon interjected. "We're playing a game, and no matter what impression he gave Charles, or how weak of a man he is, Gaspar is not a fool, and whoever is working with him should not be underestimated."

When Charles spoke, his words, though soft, resounded with such authority that Anne knew she would not win this argument. "Where in the study?"

Anne was outnumbered. "There's a panel in the wall behind the middle bookcase, about level with my eyes,"

Devon nodded. "I'll return for them in the morning, and I'll be waiting at the ship when you arrive. I promise, there will be no difficulties."

Anne shook her head at the man's arrogance. "No man is a ghost, Mr. Clayton. They'll see you, and if Gaspar could kill a boy, he won't hesitate to kill you."

"And have you met many ghosts, Lady Anne?"

"Who is to say what ghosts we carry with us. We cannot escape them, nor they us. Promise me, no matter what happens, don't leave anything behind."

Five

Trasna na d'Tonnta
(Across the Sea)

The following morning, Devon and Charles harnessed the carriage horses to the small coach Charles and Rhona had used when they first arrived in Ireland. The ride to the harbor was not long, but the weather required shelter for the short journey. Devon swung up on the back of his own horse, but Charles's hands gripped the stallion's bridle. His friend's concern was apparent. "What's troubling you, Charles?"

"Anne spoke with you, told you something she doesn't wish us to know?"

Devon wasn't going to deny the conversation he had with Charles's emerald-eyed cousin, but he could reassure his friend with the truth. "Yes, she spoke to me. I believe she's beginning to trust me, though I don't think she likes it or even trusts herself. She's unsure of everything right now, and I don't believe she wishes to burden you."

"She's not a burden."

Devon nodded. "Give her time to come to terms with that. I made her a promise, and I don't wish to betray her trust unless necessary."

"I wouldn't want that, but you'll—"

MK MCCLINTOCK

"I'll tell you when it becomes necessary."

Charles released the horse. "I'm grateful to you for what you're doing. I don't know how long this will take or what might happen. This isn't official."

"You know that doesn't matter, Charles." Devon studied his friend and recognized the signs of guilt. When it came to personal responsibility, Charles purposely carried an unnecessary burden, especially when it concerned family. "Talk to her. Anne doesn't blame you for not knowing their situation and admitted that she lied to protect you, in her own way. Your cousin is of the notion that she alone is responsible for her family's situation, and I believe that if she did not fear for her mother and sister, she would have tried to face everything on her own." Devon leaned forward and grinned. "Stubbornness is a family trait."

"That's what worries me."

Devon's good spirits returned. His stallion exuded power, and Devon wanted to run as much as the great animal. "When we return to England, I'll contact my brothers. If there's been recent talk within the agency about Lord Gaspar, they might know."

"You believe there's enough for an official agency investigation?"

"Not with what we have. We've investigated peerage before, but this is different. Despite Gaspar's odious qualities, he has managed to gain a few influential friends, including our own agency's director."

Devon nodded. "It's not a well-known association, for obvious reasons, but I've seen them together on more than one occasion. No matter. We have no proof yet, but when has that ever stopped us from trying?" Devon smiled and without another word, turned the horse and set a course for Ballinrock.

They covered the four miles in quick time. The stallion slowed with a gentle tug on the reins, his warm breath released into the cold air, and the animal remained as alert as its rider as they approached the back of the castle. Charles had told him that Gaspar left shortly after their encounter in the study, but the Marquess's coach was in front of the entrance. "Well boy, nothing like catching our foe unawares."

Devon dismounted, and knowing a stable boy or footman was not going to appear to care for his horse, he secured the animal to an iron post and rail before ascending the steps to the front door. Despite its battered form and unkempt appearance, he could clearly see again that Ballinrock had once been a grand home and estate. He lifted the heavy iron ring and knocked three times. To his surprise, the door opened immediately.

Mrs. Keegan stood before him, her pinched lips and narrow eyes attesting to her annoyance at seeing him there. Devon grinned and stepped inside, moving past the startled housekeeper. "Forgive me, Mrs. Keegan, but I have left behind a satchel and must retrieve it before I leave the county."

"Is Lord Blackwood here as well?"

Devon wondered if that was hope he heard in her voice or mere curiosity. "He is not. It is not common knowledge, but Lord Blackwood is here on honeymoon with his bride and did not wish to be apart from her any longer." He removed his hat and gloves but kept his coat in place. "I won't be long."

Seeming taken aback, Mrs. Keegan peered up at him and asked him where he needed to look—perhaps she could assist. Devon had no qualms about lying to the woman, and the sooner she thought him not a threat, the sooner he could fulfill Anne's request and be on the boat. "Either in the study or upstairs. I would be grateful if someone checked the bedroom I used." The housekeeper wavered, but nodded and told him she would return shortly.

Once out of sight, Devon checked the rooms close by and waited for any sound to indicate he might not be alone or that Gaspar was still there. He entered the study, quietly closed the door, and went to the bookshelf. Following Anne's instructions, Devon maneuvered the bookcase, and as she promised, he found the loose wall panel. Without glancing at the contents, he transferred all of the papers and a small box Anne had not mentioned, into the empty satchel he carried beneath his coat. He methodically replaced the bookshelf and after a few heartbeats and continued silence, Devon walked from the room.

Devon's carefully honed ability to interpret a person's glance or translate what they say into what they actually mean had proven useful in his long career as an agent in one of the crown's most clandestine agencies. Gathering information from people who didn't wish to divulge it was one of his specialties. Devon had not intentionally studied Gaspar's life, but the lord was an obnoxious man who had crossed paths with Devon more than a few times. Had it not been for the fact that Devon detested the weak man, he might not have bothered. As it happened, Devon knew more about Gaspar than the lord realized and little of it was flattering.

Devon had always come around to one conclusion—Gaspar was an ineffectual man with a big voice and no courage to follow through. Lord Gaspar appeared only slightly surprised to see Devon in the hallway. He was no doubt informed of Devon's presence by Mrs. Keegan, though what hold the man had on the staff at Ballinrock to allow him entry had yet to be determined.

"I didn't know you were in Ireland, Mr. Clayton."

Except that Mrs. Keegan or that young footman had likely confessed all by now. Devon hid his amusement behind a look of boredom. "I have business in Belfast, but when I visited Lord Blackwood earlier, I left behind my satchel."

Devon watched as one of the man's feet inched forward, but he stopped himself—a wise choice considering Devon was five inches taller and his fondness for boxing was well-known in certain London circles. Gaspar's eyes shifted downward to the polished leather bag secured over his shoulder yet made no other move toward Devon.

"I haven't seen you in London of late."

Have you been watching for me? Devon wondered, and shrugged. "Business takes me farther afield these days, and I have grown weary of London's stagnant stench."

Gaspar noticeably flinched and licked his lips once before returning his attention to Devon's bag. As much as Devon enjoyed playing the man for a fool, he had a boat to catch.

"I'm sorry I can't stay for a longer visit, but I have to catch a northbound train."

"Yes, yes, I understand." Gaspar looked around, most likely seeking out a member of the small staff and faced Devon once more. "I'll show you out."

Show me out of a house that is not yours? Devon stopped at the door, half in, half out, and turned to Gaspar. "By the by, I was under the impression that this home belongs to family of Lord Blackwood's. Quite unwelcoming for them to leave their guest playing host."

Gaspar cleared his throat. "Not at all. I'm an old family friend. In fact, I saw Lord Blackwood only yesterday and mentioned that I would return to call on Lady Doyle again."

Devon smiled. "Well, please give his family my best." He set his hat in place. "Perhaps we'll meet in London again soon." A pair of eyes seemed to bore into Devon's back as he mounted the stallion and turned the animal west—in the opposite direction he needed to go.

THE COACH AMBLED ALONG the back roads, battling with fierce winds and a harsh rain that pummeled the vehicle. When they reached Wexford Harbour, Claire clapped her hands and laughed, pointing to the sea. Kathryn proved to be more difficult.

"Manannán will destroy us." Kathryn shook her head and her

whole body moved side to side. "He'll kill us if we go!"

"Mother, look at me." Anne pulled her mother close to her side, so she could look directly at her. "Manannán is not going to destroy anyone today." Anne prayed she spoke the truth. She grew up with the legends and folklore of the islands, and her father took great joy in sharing the tales of sea monsters, dragons, and ancient deities, especially when Anne begged to cross the sea with him. With time, she had learned that a tale was merely a tale, but her mother's mind often wandered into another world, and of late, that world blended reality with fiction.

When the coach stopped, Charles assisted Rhona and Claire and waited for Anne and Kathryn who continued her ranting. "I'm not going, Anne, do you hear? The sea will swallow us."

Anne pulled back slightly. Her mother was prone to fits, more and more of late, but never quite to this extent. Claire huddled against the seat, staring wide-eyed at their mother. "Claire cannot go alone, Mother. Do you want her to cross the sea and face Manannán alone? She needs you to protect her."

Kathryn's shaking ebbed and she raised wide, green eyes to her daughter. "Claire."

"Yes, Mother."

Her back straightened. "I mustn't leave Claire. Where is my shawl?"

Anne didn't bother to tell her mother that she did not need a shawl with the heavy cloak she wore but instead reached into her own bag and removed a paisley shawl. Anne waited as her mother secured the garment over her shoulders, and then leaned toward the open door. "She's ready now." Charles helped Kathryn out of the coach. When Anne set foot on the ground, she whispered aside to her cousin. "She's getting worse. We have to get her on the ship before she falls into another fit."

"Take care of Claire, and I'll help your mother."

Anne had no difficulty with her young sister for Claire's

excitement grew with each step closer to the small sailing vessel. Claire twirled twice, and before she managed a third time, Anne placed her hands firmly on her sister's shoulders, but the young girl jumped up and down. "Horse!"

Everyone turned to look where Claire pointed. Approaching fast on the road was a horse and rider, unmistakably Devon. Anne exhaled slowly to calm the pounding in her chest. He was safe, and she hoped successful. Devon drew his horse to a stop near the coach, and Anne watched Charles break away from the small group to greet his friend. Anxious to know what they were saying, Anne waited impatiently with the others. Rhona kept a gentle hold on Kathryn, and Claire seemed more interested in a new distraction than in the ship and sea behind them.

Drat that man and his smiles. Anne couldn't tell if things went well or not, for one second Devon grinned and the next moment he looked somber. They finally returned to the women, but when Anne attempted to speak with Devon, he placed a finger to his lips, nodded once, and urged her to join the others as they walked up the plank to the small ship. It wasn't until Devon had secured his horse, and the others escorted away from the cargo area of the boat, that Anne approached him.

"You have them?"

How did he manage to unsettle her with a mere glance? Devon soothed his horse, his soft words calming the animal as the vessel glided through the water. "I do. They're safe," he added with a wink before Anne could ask.

"I'd like to see them, Devon."

"When we're safely ashore again."

Devon turned to her, one hand on the stallion's back. "What's in the box?"

"You didn't open it?"

"It wasn't my place, but if what I took is of such great importance, you need to at least tell Charles. You didn't give him a chance to help when he could have, and he deserves to know everything, and I mean everything. Trust him, if no one else."

Anne smoothed her hands over the stallion's flanks, his beautiful black coat shimmering in the lantern light. "You both deserve to be told the full story. Charles is family, but you've placed yourself at risk for no other reason except that he asked."

As though he understood what she was trying to say, Devon's hand reached for his chest where she knew the pendant hung beneath his clothes. "Your fear is understandable."

"I'm not afraid for my own life."

Devon stepped closer. "There is a deeper secret here. Charles told me about the night you showed up at the cottage, desperately seeking his help to rescue your mother and sister, after witnessing a horrific murder of a young man you knew, and then learning about your mother, possibly a wife to a ghastly man. You possess more control than anyone under such circumstances should."

"Anyone? Including you and my cousin?" Anne regretted her tone once the words left her lips. Devon's blue eyes revealed nothing, but still he answered.

"We've witnessed worse in our line of work; some of us are more hardened than others."

"I'm sorry. I didn't have the right to sound accusing. My father once imbibed too much while I was in his company, and he spoke of our brave cousin who helped save England from the wretches of the world. My father always wanted a son." Anne's hand came close to touching Devon's where they met on the horse's back. "I've never told anyone about Charles's secret life, nor will I ever about you."

"I don't doubt your sincerity. We live our lives between the worlds of black and white, and our identities fall somewhere in between. There are people who know, but who say nothing. There are others who would exploit the truth if found out, for we've made our share of enemies."

Anne moved away from Devon and the horse when she heard voices just above them. "Does Lord Gaspar know about you? Have I put you and Charles in far greater danger than I realized?"

"He suspects I am more than who I say, but not because of you. He and I have crossed paths before, each encounter barely civil."

Heavy footsteps on the wooden steps bade them both into silence, and when Charles walked toward them, Anne met him partway. "Thank you, cousin. I cannot repay what you've all done for us."

Charles embraced her, and his comforting arms swept away the dread and hollowness. Devon was right. Charles deserved to know all she did. He guided her back to where Devon waited and shared a glance with his friend that clearly said they knew what the other was thinking. Anne crossed her arms and stared at them both. "You and Devon have already done so much for me and my family, but I beg for your patience a little while longer until I can sort matters out in my own mind and heart."

"You have to trust us now. In this strange web of riddles and secrets, a lack of information, as Rhona has already told you, can be dangerous for all of us."

"An absence of trust is not at the center of my reluctance. Is not incorrect information just as dangerous as the lack of it?"

Devon and Charles exchanged another glance, then both nodded.

"And if what I told you now was not true, or could not be proven, what happens?"

Charles narrowed his eyes. "We're not speaking about the murder any longer here, are we?"

"Not entirely. At least, I don't know how everything is connected." Anne looked to Devon. "Where is it?"

Without a word, Devon removed his satchel from a leather

case strapped to his horse's saddle and handed it to her. Anne knelt down and reached into the bag. She pulled out only the small box and handed it to her cousin.

He opened the lid on the ornately carved and gold-etched box. Charles and Devon both looked up from the box to her, and in a smooth tone that belied his rigid jaw, Charles said, "Start talking."

Six

Dúnmharú agus Rúin
(Murder and Secrets)

Devon rode alongside the rented coach, fascinated with the woman within. They were still half a day's journey from Blackwood Crossing, Charles's estate, where they would rest before secreting Anne and her family into seclusion. Anne did not realize the power of the information she possessed or the true value of the ring tucked within the wooden box. The most pressing mystery for Devon was how Anne, or anyone in her family, came to have the jewel. A ring believed to have been lost with the man who wore it when his ship sank into the Irish Sea.

The implications that her possession of the ring introduced were far more dangerous than witnessing the murder of a tenant farmer's son. The death of the English duke had been deemed a tragic accident. No one could have predicted the storm that would sweep the Irish Sea and rival that of any other in this century. The Royal Charter Storm of 1859 had claimed the lives of more than 450 souls, including the 4th Duke of Hambleton— or so it had been believed.

There was little likelihood that a possible murderer from more than three decades ago would still be alive, or if he was, that he would worry about the truth surfacing now. Devon didn't relish approaching his supervisor, Agent Patrick Ashford, with a possible thirty-year old crime, but if Hambleton had been murdered, the ramifications for certain political parties could be catastrophic.

Charles continued to ride behind the carriage. Devon held back and followed suit.

"I don't want Patrick to know what we've learned or found."

Devon nodded, for he'd reached the same conclusion. Patrick had been their supervisor at the agency since they first joined, but they had to keep their circle of trust small. The fewer people who knew the better; his brothers—both agents—would follow their lead. It would not be the first time they'd successfully unearthed secrets that took place when they were barely from the womb, and this investigation could be more challenging than most. Once it was believed that the duke went down with the ship, a proper investigation was not started, let alone evidence gathered or suspects questioned. "Tristan has met the current Duke of Hambleton, and his father also knew Hambleton. He may know of someone who was intimate or at least friendly with the duke."

"Perhaps. Right now I'm willing to exhaust all possibilities, even if it means we start at the beginning." Charles looked at Devon. "I've asked much of you, friend. Had it not been for you, Rhona would not be alive, and now I must ask both you and Tristan for your help once more."

"You don't have to ask. I would have given my life for Rhona, and I will gladly offer it now for Anne."

Charles reached over and grasped hands with Devon. "Let's hope it doesn't come to that."

The moon rose when the party drove past the gates of Blackwood Crossing. One third of the house was closed off from the devastating fire that had almost consumed them all. Rhona's family may have helped destroy part of Charles's home, but they could not shatter the bond that had bound Charles and Rhona together for eternity. Looking up at the stately mansion, Devon saw not a damaged structure, but a home and legacy built on a foundation that would not crumble.

Kathryn and Claire had to be roused from sleep, though Devon thought Anne could have used a few hours rest as well. Rhona immediately took over as hostess, despite how exhausted she must have been, and escorted them into the house.

Anne held back, speaking in hushed tones with her cousin. Charles glanced up and gave Devon a measured look, but nodded once in consent to whatever Anne had said or asked. When Devon followed his wife and the others inside, Charles handed the horses off to a stable boy and walked to Anne.

"How are you, Anne?"

"I honestly don't know. After what you and Devon told me about the ring, I wished I hadn't kept my father's secret." Anne's eyes showed a hint of moisture, and her body was more relaxed than it had been since their reunion. "If I had known . . ."

"It's not your fault." Charles pulled her gently into his arms. "Your father asked you to tell no one or risk your family's life."

Anne settled her head against her cousin's shoulder. "Yes. I wonder if he was somehow involved, but even as I think it, I pray with all my heart he's as innocent as Gaspar's other victims."

Charles gently set her away a few inches. "I didn't know your father well after boyhood, but he wasn't a foolish man who would keep such evidence of his crime. No, Kevan Doyle was not weak-minded. A man can make mistakes, but those errors in judgment don't always define him."

This time Anne stepped back, and Charles's arms dropped at his sides. "With my family safe now, can we not destroy the ring and allow the secret to remain buried?"

"In your heart, you know we can't do that. We'll get justice for young Cillian, but this other matter with the ring . . . we must at least try to discover the truth. Did your father tell you how he came into possession of the ring?"

"No, he didn't. Do you believe he had something to do with the duke's disappearance, Charles? I want a straight answer."

"After the Tories' victory during the 1859 British election, there were many unhappy politicians and citizens alike who were eager to see the duke gone. Any number of them could have hired someone or done the deed themselves. That you father had the ring makes him suspect, but until I have proof otherwise, he's innocent."

"A clandestine investigation may go unnoticed, or it could further risk my mother and sister. All for a man who died more than three decades ago."

Charles knew Anne couldn't understand his obligations to his country and the truth. He would forsake them both if the life of someone he loved hung in the balance, but short of that eventuality, his honor meant something to him. He'd walked away from the agency for Rhona, but the work was still a part of him. "If what happened thirty-three years ago is linked to events today, we owe it to the truth to learn all we can."

Anne threw up her hands and walked up the steps and into the mansion. Devon stood in the foyer, and Charles soon joined them. To Anne, Devon looked like a man who knew exactly what she and Charles had discussed. These men shared a bond she didn't understand, and their wives seemed just as intricately involved with each other and their secrets. "What do you intend to do, Charles? Confront the politicians? Accuse the current duke of murdering his father? How far will you go?"

Devon waited while Anne gave into her emotions before she managed to suppress her fiery temper. Anne had proved to have an agile mind and a keen-edged tongue. Her animated eyes, the color of England's most beautiful green hills, radiated with excitement. Her hair, when touched by the light, shone like the autumn leaves of the elm trees which dotted the landscape around his childhood home. Devon found her fascinating, and though she'd made strides in trusting him, he sensed her uncertainty.

Anne would do well in Rhona and Alaina's company. They'd been through similar experiences, but they too possessed strength, stubbornness, and a duty to something greater than themselves. Devon counted on their influence to help Anne see what she may not see in herself—that despite her misgivings about what must be done, she was endowed with her own sense of justice. Charles would also need their assistance when it came time to leave Anne behind while they pursued the investigation.

The sky darkened while they stood in the foyer with Anne's back to them. "I'm sorry."

"You don't ever have to apologize to me, but I appreciate the words." Charles approached Anne from the side. "To answer your question, we'll go as far as we must. I promise you, we will do everything in our power to keep you safe."

"I'm not worried about me, but Mother and Claire are so fragile."

Devon had heard those words more than once from her lips. Devon smiled, for he knew how to gain her cooperation—to remain behind and out of harm's way.

When she turned around, a lock of her lovely amber hair fell over her shoulder, and she caught sight of his smile. "Do you realize your amusement is revealed at the most unusual times?"

"I'm not amused, but I am pleased."

Devon seemed to find hilarity in the most curious situations. Regardless of what he might believe, she was aware of her precarious position. Suspicion wouldn't fall on her regardless of her possession of the ring. She was not yet a thought in the mind of her parents when the Duke of Hambleton went missing. However, suspicion could fall on her father, ruining his good name and her family's. That eventuality wasn't acceptable to her—not if Kevan Doyle proved innocent. And yet, what if the investigation proved he was guilty? She vanished the question from her mind before doubt took root. Her father was many things but not a murderer. She believed that as much now as when she defended him to Devon and Charles.

"Pleased about what?"

"That you'll be safe and you'll do as Charles asks. Your mother and sister need you with them, especially Claire."

"I'm not staying behind while either of you risk your lives over this matter. There must be something I can do to help."

"Don't ask us to put you in danger. It's an argument you won't win," Charles said.

"I'm not."

Anne swore she heard Devon's sigh over the sound of the breeze, speaking in tandem with Charles. "You are."

Anne's hands went to her hips, and she refused to back down. "If Cillian's death is linked to this chaos—I don't have proof— then my family may be in even greater danger. It's my duty to protect them. I realize that I don't have the same physical abilities or experience as you or Charles, but I can do my part."

Devon grinned. After a few seconds, his smile softened and she sensed great concern in his voice and a gentle pleading in his eyes. "You will protect your mother and sister by watching over them while we're out there doing what we do. Greyson Hall is secluded and unconnected to you or Charles, and it's the safest place right now. Your duty is to your mother and sister, but how can you fulfill that duty if you leave them?"

Anne was not used to compromise. Since her father's death, she had made every decision concerning her family and the estate. She'd managed to pay off one third of her father's debts, but a mountain of creditors still loomed over her, and she could not till coins from the earth.

"I ache for Cillian's family and feel responsible for his death. If the Duke of Hambleton's death is related to what's happening now, and if you and Charles refuse to walk away, then I must see this through."

"How do you reconcile Gaspar's actions as your doing?"

Anne glanced at Charles. "Lord Gaspar had offered to purchase the land and allow my family to remain in the castle. He was there the day of Cillian's death because I had invited him to discuss his proposal. He arrived early, otherwise I would have been there. The offer was generous and included paying all debts, but I wasn't going to accept. I didn't trust his eagerness."

Anne's head snapped up as a new idea dawned. "If he was legally married to mother, he would not need to buy Ballinrock. My father bequeathed the estate to me, but a provision ensures that my mother and Claire would always have a home there."

"If something happened to you, who would inherit?" Charles asked.

"Claire."

"Does your mother know?" Charles asked.

"She was present when the will was read, but she doesn't know about Claire. My father left me a private letter, but it all matters little. Ballinrock, if sold, wouldn't cover the debts. What could he possibly want with a dilapidated castle?"

"You've asked one of many questions," Devon remarked. "When did he make the first offer?"

"A few months after my father died."

Rhona walked into the foyer, but not alone. A beautiful woman with hair the color of spun gold and eyes of sapphire came into the grand entrance holding a child's hand. Rhona separated from the pair, moved to her husband's side, and slipped her arm through his.

Devon revealed another side of himself when the women entered. He moved forward and kissed the smaller one on each cheek. He took the time to lift the young boy into his arms, causing the child to release a fit of giggles. Devon reluctantly handed the boy back to his mother.

"Her Grace, the Duchess of Wadebrooke, may I introduce Lady Anne Doyle." Devon stepped aside so Anne faced the petite woman.

Aware of her disheveled appearance, Anne smoothed her hair and skirts, and with a slight curtsy, said, "Your Grace."

"Please, call me Alaina. This scoundrel here knows I prefer my given name." Alaina spoke aside to a young woman who materialized from the shadows and who Anne assumed was the nanny. The servant escorted the smiling child away after receiving a kiss from his mother. "When Tristan received Charles's message, we hurried to meet you here."

Devon asked, "Has Tristan explained the situation?"

Alaina shook her head. "He's in the study waiting for you and Charles."

Charles pressed a loving kiss to his wife's cheek, whispered something in her ear, and then said to Devon, "Let us go and see Tristan. Anne, you'll follow?"

Anne nodded and watched Devon and Charles disappear into another room. She thought of Tristan, a university friend of Charles, and a man who she knew worked closely with her cousin. Yet another loyal confidant who was bound by brotherhood to risk his life for her family, and this one with a wife and child. "Alaina, I'm uncomfortable adding this burden to your husband. I didn't intend to endanger the lives of so many."

Anne watched Alaina and Rhona exchanged a sly glance of their own. To Anne's surprise, they both smiled. "Our husbands don't need to be asked. You are Charles's family, therefore our family, and we protect our own." Alaina leaned slightly up and kissed Anne on the cheek.

When Alaina stepped back, Rhona linked her arm with Anne's. "Let us go in and see what trouble we can find ourselves. After all, Alaina and I are in need of a good adventure, are we not?"

"Most certainly," Alaina said. "I was left out of the last one." She patted her stomach and looked at Anne with sparkling eyes. "And with another on the way, I daresay Tristan won't allow me any real fun."

Rhona's throaty laughter filled the air when she caught sight of Anne's wide eyes. "Careful, Alaina, else Anne will believe us preposterous."

Alaina's response was a wink to Anne. "We've learned to find pleasure in the simplest of moments, my dear. You'd be wise to do the same."

Alaina linked her arm with Anne's on the opposite side, both women flanking Anne and guiding her toward the study. Inside, Charles stood next to Devon and another man with soft brown hair and amber eyes. He stood a couple of inches taller than Charles and bore the regal bearing of nobility. Alaina guided Anne to her husband. "Tristan, may I present Lady Anne Doyle."

"Your Grace." Anne might have curtsied had Alaina not been holding her arm.

"Tristan, please. You'll find among family, we prefer to dispense with formalities."

Charles asked them all to get comfortable for they had much to discuss. Anne studied her cousin as he gained command of everyone's attention. He spoke to the men as though they were brothers and to the women as though he respected them above all others. Anne saw that she had found herself in the center of an intimate group of people who loved, trusted, and respected one another. She now understood what Alaina had meant about their loyalty to each other and offering their assistance no matter how dangerous the situation.

Before Charles began, Anne respectfully interrupted. "Pardon me, but my mother and sister?"

Charles smiled and sat down beside her. "They're resting. I've sent for the local doctor to see your mother. She's well enough in health, but I'd like a professional opinion on her mental state."

Anne thanked Charles and Rhona, inclined her head, and succumbed to weariness. She leaned against the back of the sofa and looked at each one of them in turn. "I wish to thank everyone for more help and support than I've had in as long as I can remember. I appreciate the risks you've taken and may take on my behalf. If there was a way to convince you not to pursue any of this, I would try, but I've been assured that it will make no difference. It would seem the matter is no longer in my hands."

"A wise change of heart, cousin," Charles said.

Anne missed the brief glance he exchanged with Devon.

"You're tired, but if you can manage it, I'd like for you to tell all of us everything. Start at the beginning. There may be details you'd forgotten but now recall."

Anne mustered what little energy she had left and sat forward. For Tristan's benefit, she summarized what she'd told Devon and Charles in the foyer. "Lord Gaspar offered to purchase Ballinrock and all of the land. I did not believe it relevant, but now I don't know what is or isn't important. Lord Gaspar said my family could continue to live on the estate, but almost as I said it, I realized if he had in fact married my mother as we believe—as she believes—he would not have pursued me about the purchase."

Charles scooted to the edge of the sofa and faced Anne. "After you turned him down the first time, did he ask again?"

"I refused him many times, but recently . . . I asked him for an audience on the day I witnessed Cillian's death." Anne quickly looked to Tristan and the women. "This must all be confusing."

Tristan said, "Charles caught me up with some of it, but why don't you start from the beginning?"

Anne took in a restorative breath and looked to Devon. His kind smile bolstered her strength, and she proceeded to relay everything that she had told Charles and Devon in Ireland. With some embarrassment, Anne discussed her father's debts and how she had lied to Charles about needing his help. "When my father gave me the pendant on my twenty-first birthday . . ." She reached for the jewelry only to remember again that she didn't wear it. Devon removed the chain from around his neck and handed it to her. "When you and Devon returned from Ballinrock, I asked him to keep this safe, though at this moment I can't explain the panic I endured when I thought something might happen to it." She passed the pendant to Charles. "I don't know its significance, only that my father told me to keep it safe."

Charles palmed the pendant and smoothed a finger over the pearl. "This is exquisite and valuable. Your father offered no further explanation about its importance?"

Anne shook her head. "I considered it once, when I first learned how difficult our situation had become, but my father was most sincere about the pendant's importance. When I saw . . . when events began to unfold, I didn't trust my ability to keep it safe."

Tristan asked, "Do you believe the pendant is connected to what's happening?"

"Perhaps not, but I won't risk it. My father had his reasons for giving it to me."

"But he didn't share those reasons with you. If the pendant was a threat, why did he not destroy it?" Alaina asked.

Anne stared down at the pendant for a moment, uncertain and disconcerted. "I don't know." She looked up at Charles. "I've overreacted, haven't I? Alaina's right. If there was a danger, why keep it?"

"We don't yet understand the pendant's significance, but it mattered to your father, and that's where we start."

"Did your father ever ask you to return the pendant?"

Anne glanced at Tristan. "No, but my father also planned to return home. I don't know what he may or may not have done had he lived."

"Where were you for the days leading up to Lord Gaspar's arrival?" Rhona asked.

"I was in the village, caring for a sick child. The little girl has no mother and her father couldn't spare the days away from his crops." A dull pain began between Anne's eyes as she remembered what came next. She excluded the gruesome details of Cillian's murder, and Charles and Devon filled in gaps of information she had overlooked.

An hour later, the story was told and the room quiet. Tristan had stood and paced in front of a window during the last few minutes of the telling. Devon was the first to break through the silence.

"Tristan, you know the current Duke of Hambleton."

"Not well enough to know if he had a part in this, but I have my doubts. His father's political beliefs differed from his own . . . there are those in his political circles who would have preferred to silence the former duke—he was quite vocal about Ireland's state of affairs. Harlan—the former duke—believed in an independent Ireland. The current duke has financial interests in Ireland, though I can't say what those are, but a free state would no doubt be distressing to those interests."

"Did your father ever speak of the duke, of Harlan?" Charles asked.

"A few times, and I gathered that he and my father were close friends, a rarity for my father as you know."

Anne listened in fascination as the men continued to ask questions and relay thoughts off one another. Alaina and Rhona even voiced their opinions, and Anne paid close attention when Charles asked Devon if he'd given their previous conversation further thought. "Conversation about what?" Anne asked.

Charles said, "For you and your family to stay at Devon's estate rather than Blackwood Crossing."

Anne stood and moved past Charles to stand before the group. "Why would we not remain here? At least here, with Rhona, I would be kept abreast of any developments." Exhausted, she asked Devon, "Is your estate close?"

Devon rose from the chair and casually went to the sideboard to pour himself a drink and asked the others if they would like anything. The delay gave Anne time to calm her temper, and it wasn't until he handed her a glass that she realized the delay had been intentional. "If you are still in danger, they may look for you here. Blackwood Crossing is not a difficult place to find. As to my own home, I do have one nearby, but Charles speaks of an estate I was recently bequeathed. No one would think to look for you there."

"And where is it?"

"Northumberland."

Anne took a drink of the amber liquid and choked at the burning sensation. She coughed once to clear her throat and handed the glass back to Devon.

He said, "I promise you will know any progress we make. I will deliver any news and updates myself, if necessary."

Rhona smiled, and said, "I feel quite left out. What is this new place you've inherited?"

Devon finished his drink and set both glasses on a tray at the desk. "Greyson Hall. It belonged to an uncle. It's secluded and far from anywhere someone might look."

"It sounds perfect," Rhona said.

"Quite perfect," Alaina added.

Anne looked from face to face and admitted defeat. She would rather have remained at Charles's home, and that was her intention when she agreed to the plan, but once again she was compelled to compromise. Anne thought of what Devon said about protecting her mother and sister by staying with them. She looked once more to Devon. "Your offer is most gracious. When do we leave?"

Seven

I bhFolach
(In Hiding)

A sea of snow-covered heather and low-rolling hills spread out on either side of the coach. Behind them was more of the same, and had been since passing the small village of Rothbury. The landscape offered an almost desolate beauty. Winter trees, groves, and stone walls scattered the countryside, but it had been miles since she'd seen sign of human life. A ruined castle stood in the distance, a reminder that even the most stalwart of places and people could fall.

Tristan and two men Anne didn't know had ridden with them for the first day to Claiborne Manor, Tristan and Alaina's home, where Anne was told they would stop and rest. To the unknowing eye, they were a vanguard of wealthy travelers and nothing more. When the small caravan departed Claiborne Manor two days later, Tristan and the others were nowhere to be seen. In their place was a smaller coach carrying a footman and maid from Tristan's own staff. The driver, Fairley, was the only servant to remain with them since they left Blackwood Crossing. Anne was told that Fairley had once been an informant for Charles, and her cousin had saved the older man's son.

Anne spent the day between comfortable silence and answering her sister's questions about where they were going. "An adventure" is what Anne kept calling it, for what else could she say? If there was one thing to remain intact during the ordeal, Anne swore it would be Claire's innocence.

At times, Anne envied Claire's naiveté and her ability to see the world through untarnished eyes. She was the reason Anne had agreed to this plan of seclusion when in truth, she would have preferred to be back in Ireland, caring for Cillian's family and assuring them that the man responsible would be brought to justice.

Anne watched Devon as he passed by the small window. He occasionally rode ahead, but he always returned to ride alongside them. Devon's focus was unlike anything she'd ever seen. Gone was the charming man who grinned without reason, and in his place was a man who she found equally focused, fascinating, and disturbing.

"Did Mr. Clayton send word to Asher where he could find me? I must not be apart from him for too long."

Anne dropped the curtain back in place and looked across to her mother. She glanced at Claire who was still asleep and then back to her mother. "Lord Gaspar will find you when the time is right."

Her mother seemed to accept this as an affirmative to her question and returned to her needlepoint. Anne had long since abandoned the copy of *Jane Eyre* Rhona had lent to her for the journey. Jane Eyre's evocative and melodramatic words suited Anne's mood, and yet, she could concentrate on little more than the man outside.

Devon behaved as a man who did this same thing every day. He didn't question any request and even seemed eager to fulfill any task or accept any risk. Anne had discovered that Alaina had known Devon for a few years, and when asked, Alaina echoed

Rhona's words. "I would not be here now had it not been for Devon." Of course, Alaina admitted that each of the men had risen to the task of saving her not long after they'd come into her life. It was plain to see that Alaina loved these men dearly and valued Devon and Charles's friendship and loyalty, just as Rhona valued Devon and Tristan.

"Will Devon ever retire like the others?" Anne had asked them. Rhona and Alaina had both agreed that it was unlikely Devon would leave behind the adventure offered by the agency.

"He thrives on the excitement and danger," Rhona had added. "But our Devon is often full of surprises."

Anne lifted the curtain once more thinking on the women's words and gentle advice that she accept she was not alone. Anne understood any decision she made from this point forward might affect the actions Charles, Devon, and Tristan took on her behalf. Charles remained behind at Blackwood Crossing while the women accompanied the others on the first day of their journey. It was decided Rhona would remain at Claiborne Manor with Alaina, and Charles's home would remain the unofficial headquarters for what they'd taken to call the Gaspar Investigation.

As the only official agent among the three, Devon decided not to contact his supervisor until Anne was safely at Greyson Hall and they'd had the time to uncover any evidence which suggested foul play. Anne had readily agreed with the decision, for she did not wish anyone else's involvement yet, even if they did work with Devon. She was uncertain of her ability to trust anyone else.

Anne sat forward when she glimpsed a massive structure in the distance, and it wasn't long before the coach came to a stop in front of a stately mansion twice again the size of Ballinrock Castle.

The coach door opened and Devon swept an arm wide. "Welcome to Greyson Hall." He helped Kathryn down and then patiently waited while Claire was roused from sleep. He motioned Anne toward him, and after he helped her down, Devon gathered Claire into his arms and waited until she'd woken fully before setting her down by the wide stone steps.

"We're here!" Claire's excitement became contagious and Anne found herself smiling. "Is this our new home? Are there horses?"

Anne laid a gentle hand on her sister's shoulder. "Calm yourself, Claire. There will be time to explore later."

Devon leaned close to her, his warmth radiating through her layers of wool. "It's good that she is excited because I don't know how long you'll be here."

Anne watched her sister enthusiastically point to something in the distance while their mother smiled at her youngest daughter. "Perhaps it will be good for my mother as well. She mentioned Lord Gaspar again and asked if he was told where to find her." Anne faced him and lowered her voice. "She cannot be allowed to send any letters."

Devon nodded. "I'll let the others know. It could be a few weeks, which means at some point your mother may become frustrated."

"A few weeks? So long?"

"I hope not. We tend to work quickly, but I want to be prepared. If they are looking for you, they'll likely be watching Charles, so he won't come until he's certain no one suspects his involvement."

"And if they do suspect?"

"Then you won't see him for a while."

Anne nodded and turned back to watch her sister and mother, both of whom stood before the great house with admiration. Walls of enclosed gardens, though covered in snow, added a desolate beauty to the landscape. A great oak, bare of leaves, its branches exposed to the elements, stood tall in the midst of the barren hills. Anne closed her eyes and filled her lungs with the wintry air. In the distance beyond, castle ruins lay in crumbles, unforgotten like the people who had once protected this land with strongholds from the wild wars which plagued England and Scotland. Yet, it was here and not in Charles's home where she experienced a moment of solace and hope.

"Even when life was at its most difficult, I at least knew my family was safe at home, but even the sense of security has been taken from us. You and Charles were right to send us here." Anne soaked in her surroundings, comforted in seclusion and by Devon's presence. "Thank you for allowing us to come."

Devon wrapped an arm around her back and turned her to face him once more. She shouldn't have allowed such familiarity, but from the beginning it had felt natural. Anne did not dare hope that when this tribulation was over, she would have a chance to discover what else might transpire between them. Until then, she would take comfort in knowing he was close, he would protect her family, and she'd found a new friend.

Devon lifted her chin and looked into her eyes. "If I can make no other promise to you, on my honor we will see this through."

SNOW BLEW ACROSS THE grass-covered hills, sheltering the earth during the season of hibernation. Devon stared out the window of his new study and watched the sun set behind the hills while his thoughts drifted upward to the woman in the room down the hall from his own. He would see her again soon when she joined him for dinner, a light supper of cold meats, cheese, and bread Rhona had her cook pack and send with them. Kathryn had requested a tray in her suite, but Claire was eager to join them downstairs. It was just as well that her ladyship would not be there to dampen the evening with her moods.

Charles's doctor had given Kathryn a positive report on her health but said her mind was quite a mystery. She was not senile or insane, but her moments of lucidity were puzzling. He firmly believed she suffered from some sort of dementia. Whether it was caused by age or a traumatic event, he could not be certain. The doctor instructed them to keep her close at all times. Devon couldn't risk hiring an unknown servant while Anne and her family were there, and his own small staff was not well-known to him. He rarely visited his modest residence in Austwick and had not been there in two months. He could not trust even them.

They would make do. Devon had yet to tell anyone, including Patrick, about the new estate, but it wouldn't be long before someone attempted to reach him. He narrowed his eyes and studied the dark objects in the distance. Devon smiled when he recognized the two riders and rushed from the room. With no butler and only the one footman, Devon opened the door himself and grinned at the two men dismounting from their impressive and travel-weary horses.

"I didn't expect you until morning." Devon walked down the wide stone steps and embraced first one and then the other. "Took you less time than I thought it would to find us."

"Your message was more cryptic than usual, but it happens that I've been here before." Zachary looked around. "No stable man?"

Devon laughed. "Not anyone tonight." He looked to Zachary. "What do you mean you've been here?"

"Not to this estate, but Northumberland, on my first solo case. I remember hearing about a massive estate having been abandoned up here, but I had no idea it belonged to Uncle Wynton."

Devon shrugged. "I didn't know until recently, when I'd learned I inherited the place." At his brothers surprised looks, he grinned and motioned them to follow him. "Come, we'll stable the horses and I'll give you the full story." He stepped in beside Derek and Zachary and led them around the house to the stables.

It was a bit of a walk, and the night air hovered just below freezing, but the wind had mellowed to a calm breeze, which kept the temperatures from dropping to a biting cold.

Devon helped settle in the horses, but instead of immediately heading back to the house, he checked on his stallion and delayed their return. Devon had always confided in Charles and Tristan and knew he could count on them for anything. They'd been through enough danger together to cement their bond as friends and brothers. His brothers by birth, Zachary and Derek had been shipped off to boarding schools at a young age, and it wasn't until later in life when Devon had formed a true bond of friendship. It wasn't long before the other Clayton brothers had also proven themselves to Tristan and Charles.

Zachary, the most even-tempered among the brothers, stood two inches below Devon. His hair, a shade lighter than the midnight black of Devon and Derek, blew riotously in the wind. Zachary's greatest strength was his analytical mind, while Derek and Devon shared a love for athleticism. Derek, who stood barely an inch shorter than Devon, resembled him in both looks and personality. They both craved the next adventure and thrived on the excitement hidden beneath danger.

Together, Zachary and Derek made an impressive team, and one the agency had learned to use to their advantage, much as they had Devon, Charles, and Tristan. Zachary and Derek had joined the agency immediately after university, both eager to follow their brother's path. Devon, Charles, and Tristan all had a part in their training, but it wasn't long before they'd proven their worth and honed their own unique set of talents. It was those talents on which Devon would now rely.

Derek ran a hand over the muzzle of Devon's horse and asked, "Who is she?"

Devon's head snapped up, but he shouldn't have been surprised that his brothers had figured out a woman was involved. He had kept the information out of his correspondence to them, but the last time he'd requested their assistance, the mission had concerned Rhona. The time before, it had been Alaina.

"Charles's cousin, Lady Anne Doyle. We brought her and her family—her mother and sister—from Ireland." Devon leaned back against the stall door. "It was the only place we could think of that no one would know about. I've just inherited, and other than Uncle Wynton's solicitor, no one else outside of our circle knows about Greyson Hall."

"Including us." Derek sent his brother a teasing smile.

"You've both been mysteriously absent since Charles's wedding. A new case?"

Zachary nodded. "Resolved yesterday, but we only just returned from France, and there was your message. We're here for as long as you need us."

Devon pushed away from the stall and walked to the stable's main doors. "I don't want Patrick, or anyone else at the agency, to know where you are or why you're here."

Derek hurried to reassure his brother. "No one knows."

Devon slowly nodded and opened the doors. "There's a lot more to tell, but I need to get back. Anne may come downstairs, and I don't want her to worry." Frigid air swept through the open doors, and all three stepped outside. Devon secured the door and once again stepped in beside his brothers as they followed the same path through the snow back to the main house.

Devon retold the story, and beginning with his arrival in Ireland, he repeated everything Anne had told them. He told his brothers about Lord Gaspar, a man both of them had also met, and a man for whom they had no admiration. Devon even showed them the pendant Anne had given him to keep safe, but it was the revelation about the ring and the Duke of Hambleton's possible murder which gave them the greatest shock. Like others in the agency, they'd learned not to show emotion when working a case, but when among friends and family, their expressions revealed their surprise.

"How long do you plan to keep Patrick on the outskirts of this case?" Derek asked.

Devon tucked the pendant back beneath his shirt. "For as long as we can. We'll need to make this official if there's going to be an arrest, but I can't go to Patrick without solid evidence. We're going to handle this as two separate cases and see where, or if, they meet. Derek, I'd like you to go to Ireland with Charles and look into the death of the farmer's son, a young lad named Cillian Ó Fionnáin. Anne witnessed his murder, and she is Charles's first priority."

"Of course. Do I meet Charles in Ireland or at Blackwood Crossing?"

"Ireland. He'll be at Brannon Cottage in Wexford."

Derek nodded. "I'll leave in the morning."

Devon turned to his other brother. "Zachary, I'd like you to stay here and watch over Anne and her family while I'm out there investigating with Charles. I won't be gone for too long at a time, but I have contacts I need to meet with who know Gaspar better than I do. Tristan is going to make discreet contacts and connect with us periodically. Charles wishes to keep him away from the fire as much as possible."

"Contacts who won't send word to him?"

Devon leaned back, his expression grim. "Men who would like to see him hanged, drawn, and quartered and would fight to bring back the law just to see the deed done."

Devon and his brothers spent another hour discussing their plans, after which Devon showed them to the west wing upstairs where half a dozen empty rooms waited for occupants. They settled in and told him they'd clean up before dinner, but like Devon and the others, Zachary and Derek traveled with what they could carry on their horses. Alone again in the study his uncle had used for only a short time, Devon admired the extensive collection of books on the shelves and expensive paintings on the walls. He wondered what prompted his uncle to hold onto the mansion when he could have easily sold it.

Other than a little dust, there was nothing about the estate's appearance to suggest someone had been in residence all these years. Servants came in to clean for a few days at a time but did not live there. Though more grandiose than Devon needed, Greyson Hall had the feel of a home, a home that needed a family, and a family was something Devon had avoided all these years. What kind of life could he give to a wife and children when he rarely knew where he'd be from one day to the next? He had his friends and his brothers—what more did he need?

Devon's hand instinctively reached for the knife he kept in a scabbard at his waist when he heard footsteps in the hall, but after a few minutes, he dropped his hand. No need to be so guarded, for no one unfamiliar had found their way into Greyson Hall. He'd checked every room before he'd escorted the women upstairs, and once they were settled, Devon had inspected the servants' quarters, below stairs, and every room on the main levels before he was satisfied. He and his brothers made another sweep of the house after they returned from the stables. Perhaps he was overly cautious, but it would be the way of things for the foreseeable future.

His body relaxed when he saw her in the doorway, and he knew that it wasn't only a duty to his friend that drove him to protect this woman.

"I didn't mean to disturb you." Anne walked quietly into the room. She had changed from her traveling clothes into a simple gown, but there was nothing simple about the way she seemed to glow, the wine color of her dress accentuating her brilliant green eyes and luminous skin. His eyes roamed from her lush hair to the hem of her skirts, and he took no small amount of pleasure at the soft blush rising in her cheeks.

"You didn't disturb me." Devon welcomed her in and offered her a seat. "Would you like something to drink? I could ring for tea." Although Devon was used to doing for himself, the large kitchen and its massive ovens below stairs were a bit beyond his abilities. It turned out that the footman was a fair hand in the kitchen and therefore placed in charge of the meals. Devon had pulled the maid aside upon their arrival and instructed her to watch after Kathryn and Claire. He didn't expect miracles to be wrought with a staff of only two and a house as grand as Balmoral Castle.

"No, I'm fine." Anne lowered herself into one of the chairs. "I heard other voices in the hall earlier." Her shoulders raised in a brief shrug. "I wandered the halls while my mother and Claire rested. They're still sleeping."

Devon set his glass on the sideboard and walked toward her to occupy the chair beside her. "My brothers are here."

"You have brothers? Why have you not mentioned them before now?"

Devon had been honest with her thus far and wasn't going to risk her trust by lying to her now. "I couldn't risk your mother or sister learning about them and accidentally saying something. I had hoped not to draw them in because their involvement may raise some suspicions."

"Then why now?"

"Like me, they're still active in the agency, and I'll need their help out there, and here with you."

Anne rose from the chair and stood directly in front of him. If Devon reached out, he could pull her onto his lap, but he doubted she would appreciate the action or the direction his thoughts had momentarily taken. "I knew you'd be leaving, but I don't know them, Devon. I don't know how my mother will fare with more strangers."

Devon remained sitting, allowing her the advantage of looking down at him. "Not strangers. My brothers. I know you didn't want anyone else involved, and our circle of trusted is small, but it does include my brothers. To trust me is to trust them."

Anne stepped away and walked to the window where he had stood before she had come into the room. "Will you leave soon?"

"In a day or two. You'll meet them both tonight." Devon stood and walked up behind her. His first instinct was to wrap his arms around her and draw her body against his, but he resisted the temptation and instead leaned against the wall beside the window. "We've taken over your life, it seems."

Anne nodded, but the slight upturn of her lips told him she wasn't angry. What he did see in her eyes was a mixture of worry and exhaustion. He wondered if she had slept at all since their arrival.

"I can hardly be upset. I came to Charles, and after what I've seen and learned, I don't expect anything to be easy right now. I can't promise I won't fight to be a part of this, but I won't purposely endanger my family."

Devon stared out the window at the wintery landscape. From where the house stood, he could see the miles of open hills and valleys which surrounded Greyson Hall. When he first visited the estate, he thought it would be too isolated, but now he appreciated the safety the solitude afforded. "Don't make a promise to yourself you may not be able to keep. There is only one absolute truth in the work we do—no one can predict the outcome of any situation."

"And yet, isn't that what you do? Investigate, fight if necessary, and force the outcome in the direction you choose."

Devon smiled and stepped closer to her. Their warm breath mingled, and they were close enough to the window to cause the glass to fog. "It is, but until the conclusion of an event, we don't know what will happen. It's why we work alone and live alone."

Anne tilted her head, a lock of her hair falling over her shoulder. "Charles and Tristan do not live alone."

"They retired when they married, or at least as much as any of us can." Devon stepped away, the closeness to Anne stirring him in a way he couldn't allow. She was his friend's cousin, and had it not been for that fact alone, he would have seduced her by now—innocence be damned. A woman like Anne deserved more than what he could currently offer, and he'd do well to remember the circumstances which had brought them together. "My brothers will be down soon. I'd like to introduce you to them and discuss our plans."

Devon did not mistake Anne's sudden surprise when she asked, "Am I then to be a part of these decisions?"

"Of course." Devon expressed surprise of his own. "I promised that I'd be honest with you and keep you informed. Much of what must be done will require your cooperation, and I'd like your input."

Anne's features softened even more. "Thank you." This time she closed the distance between them. Devon had managed to bring his thoughts and body under control and remained where he stood when she approached. He should have suspected that she was not thinking what he was thinking.

"Are Charles and Tristan in danger?"

Eight

Baol agus Bás
(Danger and Death)

lames flickered and danced in the hearth while laughter and conversation filled the air. Anne delighted in the camaraderie among the brothers. She didn't know the likes of such a familial relationship. Her own sister was the dearest soul to Anne's heart, but her mind was forever young. Anne envied her sister who would likely never know the chaos and ugliness of the world. She and Kathryn had loved as mother and daughter, but Anne had always been the stronger of the two. It was only her father in whom she had confided, and he had confided in her, but those days went away with her father's senseless sacrifice to a foolish war.

Zachary and Derek Clayton possessed the same charm their older brother exuded, and when called for, used to their advantage. Zachary's image almost mirrored Devon's, down to the black hair and sea-blue eyes. Derek's hair was lighter, but only by slight degrees. His eyes were more hazel than blue, but their piercing gaze was just as lethal as Devon's. They all stood well above six feet tall and were all devilishly handsome, but Devon was the only one who drew her constant notice. He was the only one who caused her stomach to clench and her breath to quicken.

Devon had assured her that Charles and Tristan were not in any danger and Charles would be in contact once he'd gleaned information pertinent to their investigation. She'd go slowly mad if she did not find something to occupy her time and thoughts.

They asked her opinion on each step of their plan, and once the particulars were discussed, the brothers spoke of their latest adventures, though Anne sensed they left out a good deal of information. Despite their willingness to include her, Anne couldn't help but suspect they left out some details. She wondered how Rhona and Alaina handled the secrecy.

"I'd like to meet your mother and sister." Zachary captured her full attention. "They'll need to get used to seeing me around."

Anne agreed. "Claire is always delighted to meet new people, and don't concern yourself too much with my mother. She can be difficult." Anne glanced at Devon and back to Zachary. If he was going to spend any amount of time with her mother, he should know what to expect.

"Devon explained the situation."

Anne looked over at Devon, a silent "thank you" in her eyes. To Zachary she said, "I'm grateful for all you're doing." To them all she asked, "Are we to remain confined indoors?"

"Of course not," Devon said. "You are as safe outside as you are in. We can see for miles, and other than the small staff who readied the place, no one has been here in a year."

Anne studied the variety of paintings and tapestries which graced the walls. The plush and gently worn carpet beneath her feet could alone finance half the farmsteads at Ballinrock. Leather-bound books and gleaming furniture told her someone had once cherished this room. Would Devon remain here when his present duty to her cousin was completed, or would it once again remain empty while he returned to the danger and death of his adventurous existence?

After another hour of jovial conversation, Zachary and Derek excused themselves for the evening. Anne wanted to check on her mother and sister, but she acquiesced to Devon's quietly spoken request that she remain behind.

"You've been far away tonight." Devon settled into the place next to her on the sofa. He'd been casual and friendly while his brothers were in the room, but now they were once again alone, and propriety seemed to be of little concern to him.

"You don't care much for rules, do you?"

Devon cocked his head and asked, "What do you mean?"

"When we're alone, you forget we shouldn't be, or that your best friend is my cousin, or—"

"I don't forget." Devon's lips twitched, and Anne sensed another grin coming about. "My dear, Anne. We would be having an entirely different conversation if I allowed myself to forget who you are."

Heat creeped into Anne's cheeks and she cleared her throat. "Yes, well, please forget I said anything."

"I'd rather not."

Anne's eyes narrowed and she smiled, matching Devon grin for grin. "I haven't known you long, but I believe I can without prejudice say you're incorrigible."

Devon's deep laughter filled the air. "Many would say you're right." His laughter subsided and he reached out to touch her arm. A gentle touch, reassuring her once again that she wasn't alone. "What were you thinking of tonight?"

"I pinch myself to make sure I'm not dreaming. I look out the window to remind myself that I'm too far away from home to help young Cillian's family or to look after my home." Anne stood and wandered to the window, which had become her porthole to the outside world since her arrival. "I can do more.

I've agreed to stay with my family, but I can do more." She swung around to find he'd approached her from behind. "I need to do more."

"Anne, you promised."

Frustration mounted and she reached for his arms, hoping he'd feel the urgency of her words. "I won't break my promise, but I am asking you to release me from it."

Her sapphire eyes sparkled with fire and temper, unease and desperation.

How could Devon deny her request? Did she not realize that if she begged, he would do anything for her . . . anything in his power and right?

"You promised Charles."

Anne dropped her hands back to her side, the loss of her warmth on his arms immediate.

Devon knew what Charles would say, and Charles would be right. Instead of saying what he should, Devon asked, "What would you do if you were to leave here? What would your family do? They count on you."

"My mother and sister are safe here, and I will forever be in your debt and your brothers' debts for keeping them from harm."

Devon watched her carefully and saw the change from desperation to determination.

"Use me to draw him out."

Devon swore and stepped away from her. Unfortunately for him, Charles's cousin had to think like one of them. What happened to the frightened damsels and weak ladies history lauded, for all he'd known these last few years were women like Rhona and Alaina, and now to his chagrin, Anne. Of course drawing out Gaspar and whoever was working with him was the perfect plan, the most effective plan, but they didn't intentionally use women.

Less than a month ago, Devon found himself saving Rhona because she believed she was capable of saving her father and brother from prison, or worse, death. What Anne proposed was far more perilous.

"Only danger and death await you out there. Forget that Charles will consider garroting too civil for me if I allow anything to happen to you."

"But he won't. This is my idea and if you could only see—"

"I do." Devon swiped a hand through his hair and stared at her. "Not considering everything that will go wrong, there's little chance Charles will allow this."

"How long will it take to send word to him?"

Reluctantly, Devon admitted it wouldn't take long. "Derek is to leave in the morning and meet up with Charles at his home. From there, they will go to Ireland."

"I'm not asking you to take me back to Ireland. To be honest, I'm not certain I want to return to Ballinrock after what's happened. Take me to Blackwood Crossing. I can remain relatively safe, and you all agreed that if Lord Gaspar, or someone working for him, was going to search me out, they would look there."

Devon contemplated the security risks. With Zachary here and Derek with Charles, they would be one man short of a proper defense. Devon couldn't very well leave Anne alone, even if it was at Charles's home. Anne's plan had merit.

"I'll send the request with Derek in the morning, but so help me, Anne, if Charles doesn't agree, you must promise to remain here."

Anne's smile was so brilliant it could have dazed a blind man. "I promise."

The next morning, Derek set out for Keswick with Anne's request. She had wanted to pen the letter herself, but Devon refused. When she read the unusual note, she understood why.

It gave away nothing about her or her location. In fact, if Anne didn't know better, she'd surmise it was merely an invitation to dine in London in a week's time.

Anne waited at the top of the front steps, watching with Devon and Zachary as Derek's silhouette faded into the distance. Zachary left them alone, telling them he planned to acquaint himself with the grounds and outbuildings. Devon remained by her side, his casual stance and the quiet around them prompting her to break the silence first.

"He won't agree, will he?"

Devon briefly raised his shoulders and leaned against one of the pillars by the front door. "I couldn't say."

"If you were in his position?"

His eyes bore into her, and Anne once again experienced the feeling of someone seeing into her soul, breaking past all barriers, and knowing what was in her thoughts.

"I would agree."

The chill of the morning air forgotten, Anne faced him. "You would?"

"Yes." Devon continued to stare at her with such concentration, she wondered how he managed it without blinking. "However, I would be wrong."

"Yet, you would still do it. Why?" Anne shifted her focus to the snow-coated hills. A heavy mist began to settle, blocking the view into the far distance.

"The quickest methods are not always the best, Anne, but without your help, this investigation could last weeks or months. The longer it takes, the greater the chance of the agency finding out what I'm doing, and the greater the danger for you. Short of retiring, I cannot remain silent with my headquarters for long."

His focus drifted away from her and he stood straighter. What he saw out there in the mist, Anne could not say, but his silence told her there was no danger.

"Will you ever retire as Charles has done?"

Devon's eyes flicked back to her briefly. "It's not in my nature." Without warning, Devon sauntered down the steps and looked back up at her. "I'm going to join Zachary for a walk on the grounds before the weather worsens."

Anne watched him walk away, not entirely certain what had happened or what she might have said to cause Devon's sudden departure.

Almost an hour later, Devon walked into the study where Anne waited with an open volume of Henry James's *Portrait of a Lady* on her lap. He left the door open and walked to the liquor cabinet where he poured himself two fingers of whiskey and set the glass aside without drinking. "A messenger arrived with a telegram not ten minutes ago. Charles has already left Blackwood Crossing."

Anne tempered the rising panic. If Charles wasn't there, then her request to aid them would go unanswered, at least until Derek arrived in Ireland, and she'd have to wait until Charles could send a messenger which could take days longer. "What about Derek?"

"Charles would have left instructions for him." Devon came to her, his hands settling on her arms. His touch, no matter how light or brief always managed to comfort her.

"What will we do?"

Nine

Gealltanais
(Promises)

D evon roamed the quiet halls, listening for a creak, a cry, or any other sign that he was not the only one unable to find solace in dreams. He passed Anne's dark and silent room where she no doubt slept peacefully despite the storm raging outside. Devon paused at Claire's room when he heard a faint whimper. He pressed the door open and listened. Claire whimpered again, then turned on her side and sighed. Devon smiled and backed out of the room. He continued down the hall, stopping in front of Kathryn's room. No sound came from the other side of the door, but a dim light crept into the hall. He knocked once, twice, and a third time with more vigor. Silence.

The handle gave beneath his grip. Once inside, Devon scanned the room, expecting to find Anne's mother safe in bed. The rumpled bedding told him she had been there, yet now the room was empty. Devon strode to the adjoining bath, and this time the handle did not give.

"Lady Doyle?"

Devon pulled up and down on the handle again. "Kathryn? If

you're in there, say something."

The continued absence of sound spurred him to pound on the door in rapid succession.

Anne approached from behind. "Devon?"

He nodded toward the locked door. "Perhaps you can get through to her."

Anne didn't hesitate to cross the room and stand beside him. Devon inhaled the light floral fragrance wafting from what he supposed had been an evening bath. Her hair hung down in a loose braid, soft curls sweeping her shoulders. The heavy robe and long nightgown gave nothing away, and yet she was more alluring to him than ever before. He cleared his mind and listened to Anne's gentle pleadings to her mother.

"Is there a key?"

Devon had a ring of keys, but finding the one that fit would take too long, as would the delay to go down and fetch them. "Step back, Anne."

"What are you—"

The cracking of wood as the door splintered away from its frame followed Anne's gasp. Devon bounded through the broken door. "Good God." He propelled himself forward, his long arms reaching into the water.

"Mother!" Anne hurried over and lifted her mother's head while Devon carried her limp form to the chaise. "She's not . . ."

Devon held his hand over Kathryn's mouth hoping for any sign that she still breathed. "Stand back, Anne." He raised Kathryn's arms above her head and pressed his hands against her chest over and over until she sputtered. Devon gently shifted her to her side and held her while water escaped her lungs. Her body convulsed a few times before settling again. Anne smoothed her mother's hair away from her face and whispered in her ear. "Is breá liom tú, máthair."

Devon moved away and gave them a few moments of privacy.

He walked into the bedroom to where the bell pull hung beside a curtain. It didn't take long for the maid, Rozalyn, to make her way upstairs. She was immediately dispatched to help the lady into dry clothes. Anne refused to leave her mother's side until she was in bed and sleeping comfortably. Rozalyn was instructed to remain by the lady's side until someone came to relieve her.

A reluctant Anne followed Devon into the hall, but when they closed the door, both saw they weren't alone. Zachary leaned against the wall beside Claire's door. "She woke up when the commotion began. What's happened?" Anne stepped toward the door, but Zachary held up a hand to stop her. "She's sleeping."

Devon leaned closed to Anne and whispered, "Let her rest. Nothing can be done or learned until your mother awakens in the morning." To Zachary he said, "I'll relieve Rozalyn in two hours, and I'll ask you to take the shift after that."

"I can sit with her."

"Anne, you'll need your sleep. Claire and your mother will need you in the morning." Devon's eyes met his brothers over Anne's head. He nodded once, and Devon guided Anne away from the door and down the hall to her own room. Once inside, he reached into his pocket and pulled out a small amber bottle. "Is this the laudanum the doctor gave her?"

Anne lifted the empty bottle from his hand. "No. I have the bottle in my satchel."

"Could she have obtained it before we left Ireland?"

Anne turned the bottle over to examine the label. "I don't believe so." She moved to the dressing table and lowered herself into the chair. "There wasn't time to pack her belongings. Except . . . she did have her moneybag with her when we left—always does—but you found her and Claire locked away. She couldn't have obtained the medicine between the time I left and Charles arrived."

"Your staff at Ballinrock, how long have they been with you?

There was no butler, but your young housekeeper, Mrs. Keegan . . ." Devon watched Anne's eyes widen and her fist clench around the bottle.

"Winston Haverly, the butler, is away in Cork visiting his ailing brother." Anne rose, her eyes unblinking, her back stiff. "But Devon, Mrs. Keegan is years older than my mother. She left a year ago to live with her sister's family in Donegal."

Devon described "Mrs. Keegan" in detail, but Anne could not recollect ever seeing such a woman at Ballinrock or even in the neighboring village.

"Noleen Keegan was the head housekeeper at Ballinrock for a decade, but when I had to let most of the servants go, she went north, not wishing to be a burden. There is a cook who comes in daily. Was she there?"

"If I suggested you calm yourself, would it help?" Devon knew the matter was grim, but he needed Anne to remain levelheaded.

"No, but I'll do it just the same." Anne once more found her seat. "They're my responsibility, Devon. Once my mother and sister were safe, I should have returned. I agreed to hide myself away up here, but I shouldn't have."

Devon feared he knew what was coming, and yet he doubted preemptive tactics would do any good. "Before you say anything, I have an idea." He walked back to the door and asked Zachary to come in from the hall.

"What's happened?"

"I'm going back to Ireland," Devon held up a hand to deter what he suspected would have been an objection from Anne, "and I'm taking Anne with me. I need you to stay and look after her family."

Zachary's eyes darted from his brother to Anne and back again. "You're certain you know what you're doing?"

"No." Devon looked to Anne. "Charles will have my head, but you're right, this is your fight and you have a right to see it through."

Anne stood, her expression one of concern and relief. "The maid, Rozalyn. Can she be trusted to look after my mother and Claire?"

Devon nodded. "Tristan said she can be trusted or she wouldn't be here, and she's the niece of Alaina's butler. Zachary will be here to see that they are safe."

Zachary said, "I can locate a doctor and ask him to look in on your mother a few times per week."

Anne cast a nervous glance toward Devon. "Words alone could not express my gratitude if a doctor were to visit, but you said we couldn't allow anyone else from the outside."

"If we remained, it is still a risk I would willingly take. Your mother is ill, Anne. You would rest easier knowing she is looked after."

Zachary walked to the window where a view of the road and hills beyond was masked by a curtain of falling snow. "Horses or coach?"

"Coach. It will be less suspect, and Uncle Wynton's crested coach is still in the stable. That will leave you without a driver, but once we reach the train station, I'll send Fairley back with the coach. You'll need him to take the doctor back and forth from the village." Devon glanced at his brother. "I need a few minutes with Anne."

Zachary hesitated and the action did not go unnoticed. Devon had breached propriety more than once with his inordinate familiarity with Anne. Here at Greyson Hall where gossip did not reach beyond the walls, there was little chance of issues arising. However, Charles and Rhona had already noticed and commented on his rapid friendship with their cousin. Devon did not concern himself with the outdated opinions of society, but he did care about Anne and her reputation. Charles may not react with the anger with which he had allowed Anne to believe, but his disapproval was another matter.

Instead of waiting for his brother to leave, Devon walked Zachary to the door. His whispered words did not reach beyond them. "The alternative is to leave her, and she won't stand that."

"You could give her no choice, Devon. I know you, brother, and I realize she is safe with you, but this is like Alaina all over again. She insisted on taking part in the investigation, and you recall what happened to her."

"Kidnapped, three times." Devon grinned with the memory. "I understand your point, but it doesn't change Anne's desire to be a part of the resolution or to protect her family. She has the right, Zachary." Devon's fingers played through his thick, black hair. "Our instinct is to protect, but sometimes I wonder if we stifle in the process. Anne is strong and smart—she can do this. We'll leave in the morning under the mask of darkness."

Zachary looked back over his brother's shoulder. "Something else is troubling her."

"Charles and I met a woman at Ballinrock who claimed to be her old housekeeper, Mrs. Keegan. I've just learned that Mrs. Keegan now lives with a sister in Donegal."

"I have an idea. Wait here a moment with Anne." Zachary hurried down the hall and Devon returned to Anne's side. When his brother entered the room again, he carried a large notebook and charcoal. Zachary settled down in one of the chairs near the hearth and asked Devon and Anne to join him.

"I didn't know you still sketched, brother."

"I haven't in some time, but it can't hurt to try." Zachary leaned against the back of the chair and looked at Anne, the chalk poised above the clean sheets of bound paper. "I'm going to attempt to create a likeness of the woman who claimed to be Mrs. Keegan."

"You can do that?"

"We'll see." Zachary kept his eyes on the paper but spoke to his brother. "Start with her features, the shape of her face."

The young "Mrs. Keegan" was not someone easily forgotten considering Devon's ability to recall details.

Zachary listened carefully to Devon's description as he moved the charcoal skillfully over the paper while Anne waited in silence.

"May I see that drawing, Zachary?" Anne rose and paced the area in front of the hearth, staring at the face of the woman. "I've not seen her before."

Devon peered at the sketch. "That's a good likeness, Zachary."

Zachary set down the charcoal and extra paper on the seat he vacated. "If I'm not mistaken, that's Lady Berkes, though it's not her real name."

Devon and Anne both stared at Zachary. "You know this woman?"

"I met her once a social function in London. I was on assignment and she was doing her best to gain my interest, but she didn't look like that when I met her."

"Was she there with anyone?"

"I turned her away and went about my work, Devon."

Anne handed the sketch back to Zachary. "It doesn't matter anymore. She's gone now, and we have to be ready early." Anne moved to the door, leaving behind a discernable sigh and two men who desperately wanted to help. "I'm going to try to get some sleep. Good night, Devon, Zachary."

Devon's gaze followed Anne from the room until his brother's words broke through his thoughts.

"Do you believe 'Lady Berkes' is gone?"

Devon turned his attention away from the empty doorway and back to his brother. "Yes, I do. She's not a threat, and she served her purpose."

"To replace the housekeeper."

Devon nodded. "It's the smartest way to gain access to the entire house. Charles's unexpected visit obviously interrupted their plans."

Zachary held up the sketch. "What do you want done with this?"

Devon slipped the drawing from his brother's hand, the paper crumbling inch by inch before it was thrown into the fire. "We're going to catch these bastards, and heaven help anyone who stands in the way."

CLAIRE'S LIGHT BROWN HAIR splayed over her shoulders with each stroke of the bristled brush. Anne went through the motions of brushing and smoothing her sister's hair while Claire played with the small doll Alaina had given her. The ache of guilt filled the slight hollow in Anne's heart over what her sister was going through. Her mother would sleep or imagine her way through the situation, but Anne couldn't help but feel that she had somehow failed to do right by her sister.

Although Claire's mind would always be like a child's, her heart was purer than the fresh snow falling from the heavens. Anne may harbor some guilt about Claire's present circumstances, but the young girl behaved as though life in a new place was as grand as home. Anne's eyes scanned the opulent bedroom, from the bed large enough to sleep three to the glowing fire in a hearth that had no chips or sign of great wear. The heavy curtains draped over the windows were of the finest fabric, and the adjoining bath boasted a lavish tub and dressing table. No suite of rooms in Ballinrock had ever been as luxurious.

Anne could not help but wonder at the type of man who would care for such a glorious place, yet rarely visit. She was not eager to return to Ballinrock yet, but when their troubles ended, they would leave this behind and return to Ireland. A more beautiful place Anne had never known. Ireland, her home and her heart, called to her now, and her anticipation mounted as the minutes ticked by.

Anne set the brush aside and began to braid Claire's hair. Her sister's giggle had her leaning over to see what Claire found so amusing.

Claire smoothed down the doll's skirts and fixed the coiffed red hair. "Lady Ballinrock has met her knight."

Anne's lips curved upward, her fingers nimbly interweaving locks of hair. "And what does the lady's knight look like?"

"He's handsome and tall, and he rides a great black steed." Claire giggled again. "He looks like Mr. Clayton, but he said I could call him Devon." Claire twisted back and looked up at her sister. "May I call him Devon? He said I could."

Anne straightened her sister's head so she could finish the braid. "If he gave you permission then it's allowed, but only here at the house. When others are present, you must call him Mr. Clayton." Anne paused in what she was doing. What cause would Claire ever have to again see Devon outside of this house or beyond the resolution of the case?

"May I ride a horse tomorrow?"

Anne set aside the brush and tapped her sister on the shoulder. "All done." Claire shifted and turned on the bedcovers until she sat cross-legged facing her sister.

"May I?"

"I will ask Zachary." Anne smoothed a hand over the doll's hair. "You remember Zachary from the meeting today?"

Claire bobbed her head. "Devon's brother."

"That's right. He's going to stay here and watch over you and Mother."

Claire's pale green and quizzical eyes shifted away from the doll and focused on her sister. "Are you leaving again?"

An invisible vice clinched Anne's heart, and she pulled her sister close. "Only because I must. You will be safe here with

Zachary and Mother. You may go riding and play in the great big house." Anne heard faint sniffles and hugged Claire closer. "I promise to return for you, and then we'll go home to Ireland."

Claire sat up and wiped her eyes with the sleeve of nightgown. Anne reached into her pocket and passed her sister a handkerchief.

"Can we stay here?"

Surprised, Anne asked, "You don't want to go home?"

Claire's narrow shoulders rose and fell before she returned her attention back to the doll.

"We'll talk of this more when I return."

"When will you come back?"

Anne squeezed Claire's hand. "I don't know, but it won't be for too long. Do you remember when I was away to look after the farmer's wife who had the baby?"

Claire nodded.

"It will be like that."

"Will you help people?"

Anne managed a smile, though grim. In truth, she would be helping people. She would be saving her family. "Yes."

"Then it's all right." Claire curled up, laid her head on Anne's lap, and tucked her doll beneath her chin. Anne leaned against the mahogany headboard, her back molding to the feather pillows. She tucked the covers around her sister's resting form. "Rest now, sweet one. Tomorrow, new adventures await you." Anne prayed her words rang true for she could not bear to see disappointment mar her sister's smile.

On wings of the wind o'er the dark rolling deep,
Angels are coming to watch over thy sleep;
Angels are coming to watch over thee,
So list to the wind coming over the sea.

Like an old friend, the lullaby comforted and soothed Anne. She continued to sing, her soft and lyrical voice wafting through the air.

Devon stood transfixed outside of Claire's door, opened only enough for the music to escape. The silky voice mesmerized him, and he halted with his hand on the handle. Devon wanted to step inside, but he dared not disturb them.

Hear the wind blow, love, hear the wind blow,
Hang your head o'er and hear the wind blow.
Hear the wind blow, love, hear the wind blow,
Hang your head o'er, love, and hear the wind blow.

The unfamiliar song ended and silence ensued. Devon nudged the door a few inches and walked into the spacious room with the intent of speaking with Anne, but the words never left his parted lips. Anne lay against the headboard, her soft curls draping her shoulders. Claire lay with her head on Anne's lap, and her sister's arm wrapped around her. Devon's eyes drifted to Anne's lips, the source of the soothing melody, and up to her closed eyes. He stepped closer. Anne's chest rose and fell with each silent breath.

Devon would swear later that he watched her for hours, her alabaster skin touched by the moonlight. When he managed to look away from her face, Devon left the room as quietly as he'd come. In the hall, he pressed his forehead against the door and pulled it closed until he heard the soft click. His life had changed the moment Anne had entered it. As pure and wonderful as a person's soul could be, Anne was the light Devon didn't know he'd been seeking.

With his back now to the door, he moved on powerful legs down the hall and retreated to the study. He should be sleeping, for in the early hours of morning, he and Anne would depart

Greyson Hall and enter the throes of the investigation. With renewed energy, Devon crossed the room to the desk where he had locked away Anne's secrets.

He lifted the satchel containing the documents and ring. The small piece of jewelry weighed heavy in his hands. If Kevan Doyle had possession of the ring when or after the Duke of Hambleton died, he either killed the man or had discovered who did. Devon would bet on the latter because a guilty man would have destroyed the evidence. What little Devon knew of Anne's father was that he had died in a skirmish, which was part of the larger battle surrounding Ireland's freedom from England. And yet, if the true murderer had discovered Doyle's knowledge, they would have risked much to see the man disappear.

"You've wandered into the dark abyss of your mind again."

Devon waved his brother into the study.

"How is Lady Doyle?"

"Sleeping. The maid returned, claiming she couldn't sleep. I believe she worries for her ladyship."

Devon nodded. "Tristan knew what he was about when he sent Rozalyn." He rose from the desk and held the ring up for Zachary to see. "If you had masterminded the murder of a duke, what would be your first concern?"

Zachary closed the distance and lifted the ring from his brother's hand. "I would ensure that all evidence to suggest a murder was no longer in existence."

"Precisely." Devon held up the stack of papers. "I have read through these half a dozen times and have found nothing of importance to these cases, nothing to link Anne's father with any of this, or to explain the ring. They are mostly legal documents, including a will naming Anne as his sole heir."

"An unusual arrangement." Zachary set the ring down and picked up the documents.

"Unless he knew something we have figured out yet. It's all

legal from the looks of the will, but that particular matter is between Charles and Anne. The ring is my primary concern, as is this." Devon removed the pendant from around his neck. "Somewhere in the recesses of my memory lies the answer to this."

"You've seen it?"

"I would swear to it. Despite the fact that selling the piece would wipe out all of her family's debts, Anne keeps it safe. I believe she suspects there was something more behind the pendant than a simple gift, for no one would keep their family in poverty to save a pretty trinket."

Zachary wrapped the chain around his hand and smoothed a finger over the pearl. "This is no trinket, Devon. This rivals the jewels our own mother once wore, and Father spared no expense on those. I'd wager this was created for a king's ransom, or at least—"

"A duke's?"

Devon watched his brother set the jewel back on the desk, but Devon made no move to pick it up again. He studied the pearl within the cross, surrounded by gold that shined in defiance of the years. His gaze snapped up to meet his brother's. "How familiar are you with the higher echelon of society?"

"Derek is more so, but I've made the rounds between cases. What are you thinking?"

Devon lowered the pendant back over his head and hid it once more beneath his clothes. "A woman who would now be in her forties, still handsome. Tall, with hair like spun gold and eyes . . ." Devon closed his eyes, imploring the memory to surface. "Lady Whitley Alexander."

Zachary's eyes shadowed and his expression became bleak. "By all accounts, Lady Alexander is a recluse. I know only what the gossips have told me, but it's said the lady has not left her country home in half a decade, refuses to show herself in London, or even to receive visitors. She will in all likelihood take her secrets to the grave."

Undaunted by the revelation, Devon set his own plan in motion. Anne's compliance with the new arrangement would be essential, and with any luck, keep her out of danger's path a while longer. He took an empty leather pouch from the desk and dropped the ring inside.

"You're taking it with you?"

Devon nodded and handed his brother the key to the desk. "You can secure the documents in the drawer once you've read through them. You were a far better pupil of the law than I. If you discover anything, find a messenger in the village and send word to Charles's home. We'll get it once we arrive."

"You're going to seek out Lady Alexander."

"Yes, and she will see us. By the by, where does she live?"

Resolved, Zachary answered, "Near Keswick. An estate they call Brickstead."

"Brilliant. We won't be too delayed from our original destination." Devon left his brother standing alone in the study and bounded up the stairs. He checked first in Claire's room, but Anne was no longer beside her sister. The young girl slept in peace. He reached Anne's door and knocked once before the portal opened.

"Has something happened to my mother? Claire?" Anne moved to walk past him. Devon held onto her arms and reassured her that they both slept.

"May I come in? I won't stay long."

Anne opened the door and stepped aside. Devon spun around. "I know it's late, but I have an idea, and I need your support."

"Will it matter if I object?"

Devon hesitated but pressed forward. "It will matter, but I hope you see the value of this plan."

"Then by all means." Anne offered him one of the chairs by the hearth and settled down across from him. "What is the grand new plan of yours? Does it take us to Ireland?"

"I'm certain it will." Devon leaned forward and lowered his voice. "I believe your pendant belonged to a Lady Whitley Alexander, who, if I'm not mistaken, was mistress to the Duke of Hambleton after her husband, Lord Alexander passed away."

"Owner of the ring."

"Correct." Devon inched closer to the edge of his seat even as Anne leaned closer to him. "According to London gossip, by way of Zachary, Lady Alexander has been in seclusion for these past five years, but I want to go to her. If I'm right about the pendant belonging to her, then perhaps we've found our connection to the Duke and the ring."

"Yes, but what does any of this have to do with now, or with the murder I witnessed? That pendant, as Alaina mentioned, could mean nothing."

"It's a clue, Anne, and we must follow the clues, piecing them together as we go."

Anne leaned back against the chair, her frustration unmistakable. "I used to imagine Charles embarking on great adventures, bringing about justice, and seeing the world, but this is most tedious. You ought to consider another line of work, Devon." Seeming determined to cooperate, she asked, "How do you plan to present this to Lady Alexander?"

"Trust me, she will see us. Whether she believes it matters not, so long as we gain the information we need." He rose and walked to the door.

"You'll tell me nothing more?"

Devon left his chair and to his own surprise, reached for her hand, his lips pressing a gentle kiss upon her soft skin. "There's nothing more to tell. Rest now for we leave before the sun rises."

"Wait." Anne moved forward, but stopped short of following

him to the door. "Is it unsafe to leave now?"

Devon released the door handle and returned to her. "Why now?"

"The night is more than half over. If we leave now, we will reach our destination soon after sunrise, correct?"

"Traveling in the dark is treacherous, and we cannot rush the animals for risk of ice on the roads."

"Yes, but if we stay to the main roads . . ."

Devon considered her rigid stance and the determination he saw flare in her eyes. "This is that important to you?"

"I must do something. I cannot sleep or sit idle this night, not when I know what tomorrow will bring."

He saw in her an echo of weariness, but she seemed determined to ignore it.

"It's too dangerous, and might I add unnecessary, to leave now. We will be on the road before the sun rises, and I promise, I will get you to Ireland."

Ten

Leideanna agus Ceisteanna
(Clues and Questions)

Determined to cooperate, Anne didn't object immediately. After all, Devon was the one protecting her, sacrificing his time and possibly his life, for her. She rose from the chair and paced in front of the hearth, the warmth from the fire a comfort. She glanced at Devon more than once as she considered his promise. She did not want to be difficult, nor did she wish to cause Devon and his brothers, or anyone else, more trouble than they already had on her behalf.

"Very well." Anne returned to the chair. "What role am I to play in this plan of yours?"

Devon grinned and revealed two rows of straight white teeth. Anne noticed his blue eyes lightened to the palest version of a clear Irish sky when he smiled, which in itself was a phenomenon. "Lady Alexander has no reason to see me alone. I am not of her social ranking, and I do not attend the same functions, at least not when she was active. However, she may see you."

"I couldn't know why."

"Your father's custody of both the ring and the pendant

cannot be insignificant. There is a chance, a marginal one, that she may recognize your name, or at least your father's."

"You're leaving much to chance. Is this how you often work?"

Devon's shoulders rose and fell once before he leaned back against the chair. "A Frenchman I once met when on a case in Paris used to say, 'Chance favors only the prepared mind.' I have come to learn that too much planning can be as detrimental as not enough."

"Do Charles and Tristan share your philosophy?"

"Sometimes."

Devon leaned forward, almost lazily, but Anne knew better. She'd been making a study of him since they first met and knew each one of his movements was deliberate. Every thought, action, and outcome seemed to be precise in execution and result.

"Anne, when you presented the notion to become bait for Gaspar and whoever is working with him, how did you see your plan developing?"

Anne's eyes narrowed in suspicion, for surely he would not allow her to move forward with her scheme. He said it was a good plan, but she'd heard nothing of it since, nor did she believe he'd allow it. For the plan to work, Gaspar would have to know she moved to Charles's home, and Anne didn't know how they would go about that task. And yet, since he asked, the thought must still be a possibility.

"I didn't. I don't know how it would work, but it could." Anne wondered how a more aggressive woman of the world might use charm and seduction to lure a man into her way of thinking, but Anne did not possess those skills. "Lord Gaspar would have to be told, but how without it appearing like a ruse?"

Devon smiled and stood, holding out a hand for her. Without pause, Anne accepted his help and rose to stand in front of him.

"My dear lady. We do not have to tell Gaspar anything. We have at our disposal the quickest means of communication since the beginning of time."

Amused, Anne crossed her arms and smiled up at him. "Pray tell, what is that?"

"No letter, messenger, or telegram can deliver news as quickly as a nobleman's servant."

THE WEATHER WARMED THE farther they ventured from Northumberland but not by much. Their greatest consolation had been the brilliant sunshine throughout their journey. Anne kept the curtain on the coach window secured back for most of the drive, enjoying scenery she'd been too worried to appreciate on the trip to Devon's home. Pristine snow covered the hills and mountains, and the sun glistened on the surface of the surrounding lakes.

The carriage rolled to a halt in front of Blackwood Crossing, and Anne sighed with some relief because the plan was in motion. All they had left to accomplish was to gain Charles's cooperation. Much to Anne's dismay, Devon had stopped at the nearest telegraph office and sent a message to Charles in Ireland. When Anne asked why a private messenger wasn't used in this instance, Devon explained, "The sooner Charles knows, the better. Besides, servants aren't the only communication networks with leaks."

Ellis, Charles's butler, met them at the door. "His Grace, the Duke of Wadebrooke, is waiting for you in the study."

Anne's hand halted in midair, and Ellis took the liberty of taking the hat from her. She turned to Devon. "Tristan is here? I thought he was at home with Alaina."

Devon thanked Ellis and guided Anne toward the study. "Our plans change from time to time, but we eventually catch up with one another. If it had been more important, Tristan would have sent word."

They walked into the study where Tristan sat in one of the

plush chairs, a drink in his hand. He stood when they entered, offering Anne a genuine smile and a kiss on her hand. "I have ordered tea and light repast for you, my dear. I dare hope the journey was not too taxing."

"Not in the least."

"Brilliant." Tristan turned to Devon. "Tell me, old friend. Have you become reckless?"

Devon escorted Anne to her seat and availed himself of a glass of whiskey from the sideboard. "Not to my knowledge." He swirled the liquid twice before sipping.

Anne spoke up in Devon's defense. "The journey was my idea—"

Conversation halted when Ellis entered with the tea. Devon waved away Anne's concern. "Don't worry, Ellis knows everything, don't you?"

Ellis bowed once. "Quite right, sir."

Devon smirked and occupied the seat next to Anne. Once the butler had exited, Anne continued. "It was my idea to leave Greyson Hall, not Devon's." She looked to Devon for confirmation, but he appeared entertained by what she'd said. Anne glanced at Tristan whose expression conveyed great amusement and a touch of doubt.

Devon responded on his friend's behalf. "Tristan is simply overcome with appreciation for any woman who would deny me, especially when he knows there is not a soul on earth who could ever make me do anything."

"It's risky, and Charles won't like it," Tristan argued.

Devon nodded. "I know, but hear us out. Anne's plan is smart, and it's nothing we wouldn't consider had she not been Charles's cousin."

Tristan retook his seat. "So, we let the cat come to the cream."

"That is the idea." Devon set his glass aside and leaned forward. "But first, Anne and I have a social visit to make upon one Lady Alexander."

Tristan's glass stopped halfway to his lips.

Anne observed him with a careful eye, and his reaction was unmistakable.

"You know her?"

"No, but my father did."

Tristan eyed Devon.

"It was rumored that Lady Alexander was Hambleton's mistress. I remembered why Anne's pendant looked so familiar. Only one like it was ever made, and it was quite distinctive. A painting of the lady wearing the pendant was commissioned by Hambleton, and in it she wore the pendant. I don't recall where I saw the painting, but it disappeared, believed to have been destroyed in a house fire in London. The pendant is the same."

"Good God, man." Tristan leaned forward and set his glass on the tray next to Devon's. Anne's tea had gone untouched for she was engrossed with the story.

Devon had told Anne the tale on their trek across England, but he left out the part about the fire. She said, "If the painting has been destroyed, perhaps few people remember the pendant. And when one considers that Lady Alexander has lived in seclusion all of these years, why would she or the necklace, be considered a threat?"

Tristan smiled at her. "Impressive deduction, Anne."

Devon cast her a grin and a wink. "Anne has a mind for these things, and it will get her into trouble one of these days. In the meantime, it could be of use. Anne and I will go to Brickstead in the morning to prevail upon the lady for information."

Anne asked, "What if we don't get in?"

Devon shrugged. "Then we return the next day."

Tristan agreed. "I wager Charles has received your telegram by now."

"Oh dear. He'll be cross with me."

Devon reassured her with a pat to her hand. "He'll be cross with me, but what's done is done."

Tristan stood, motioning Anne and Devon to remain seated. "I'm going to set the other part of your ingenious, albeit foolish, plan in place."

Anne waited until Tristan had left the room before asking, "What is he doing?"

"He'll ask Ellis who among the servants has a penchant for gossip."

The next morning, Devon and Anne left for Brickstead after the morning meal. Anne watched the clock through her morning bath and through breakfast, eager to be on their way. Her unsettled nerves had kept her awake most of the night. Before dinner the night before, a message arrived from Charles with a cryptic directive like the ones Devon was so fond of sending. Devon translated it to say there were new developments, Charles would be home soon, and he wasn't to let her out of his sight. Devon remained true to Charles's directive, though Anne suspected Devon would have remained by her side regardless.

Brickstead was a modest manor house of weathered gray stone surrounded by extensive gardens, now barren for the winter. The country home reminded Anne a little of Ballinrock, except her beloved home was near to ruins. She accepted Devon's assistance from the carriage and welcomed his escort into the house where they were greeted by a staid butler old enough to be her grandfather.

Devon handed his card to the butler who studied it and raised narrow eyes on them. "Her ladyship does not receive callers."

"Please tell her ladyship that Lady Anne Doyle of Ireland is here, and the matter is of some urgency."

The butler waited a few more seconds and said, "Wait here."

Anne released the breath she'd been holding. "He doesn't like us, and he didn't take our coats. I don't believe he expects us to be received."

Devon's light laughter helped to ease some of her worry. "Of course he doesn't like us. It's in the job description of an English butler to dislike everyone until told otherwise. And she will see us."

After ten minutes of waiting in the foyer, the butler returned wearing a look of some astonishment. "Her ladyship will see you." The butler divested them of their outer garments and escorted them to a cozy parlor where a fire flickered and warmed the room. Situated beneath blankets in the only chair in the room sat Lady Whitley Alexander.

"Please, be seated. Tea will be along shortly, though I can't imagine you will be here long enough to enjoy it." Lady Alexander set aside her book and lorgnette and offered them a seat. Anne's eyes remained fixed on the lady. Devon had not exaggerated in his memory of her, for she was still a handsome and regal woman.

Anne and Devon settled onto the sofa. "Why have you agreed to see us?" Anne hadn't meant to ask the question, and Devon's light touch on her arm suggested she remain quiet, but she ignored him. Lady Alexander's unexpected smile surprised Anne, as did her next words.

"You have the look of your father, Lady Anne."

"You knew him?"

Lady Alexander nodded once. "Not well, but we met on two occasions when I visited Ireland. Your parents were kind enough to host me at their home, but that was before you were born. Harlan trusted your father and visited him on a few occasions." The lady's studied eyes moved from Anne to Devon. "I once knew of a solicitor named Marcus Clayton."

Devon nodded. "He was my father."

"I have not left this estate in more than five years, and I have not received callers for almost as long. However, your visit intrigues me." Lady Alexander remained quiet while a tea service was brought in. Once the butler departed, she asked, "What does the son of a solicitor and the daughter of an old acquaintance want from me?"

"Information." Devon removed the pendant from around his neck and handed it to the lady. Anne watched the woman's eyes widen and then soften before tears began to fall.

"How . . . where did you find this?"

Devon gave Anne a smile of encouragement and her hand a gentle squeeze. She looked to the lady, hoping her words would not bring too much sadness. "My father gave me the necklace on my twenty-first birthday. I couldn't part with it. Recent events, and I regret to say, tragedies, have led us to you." Anne told her everything that had happened from the moment of Cillian's murder to how they discovered she was the original owner of the pendant. Devon offered additional details about the painting and what little he knew of the Duke of Hambleton and her relationship with him.

Devon said, "I know it is a great deal to ask, my lady, but if you're willing to help us, we can find the duke's killer."

Lady Alexander remained silent for several minutes, staring at them. Anne tried to ignore the guilt which consumed her for bringing this woman such pain, but the lady soon proved to be a woman of great strength.

"You are certain of his death, Mr. Clayton?"

"Certain, but I cannot offer you proof at this time, my lady."

"I met Harlan soon after my husband passed away, and he was my first and greatest love. When word reached me that he had gone down with the ship, I didn't want to believe it. He wasn't supposed to be there, but they swore they saw him walk aboard."

"Who's 'they'?" Devon asked.

"I don't know their names. They delivered the message,

nothing more. The letter was unsigned, and when I inquired about its author, the messenger could tell me nothing."

Anne sympathized with the woman and noticed her body had become wearied during the short time they had been there. Justice is something they both wanted, but Anne had doubts they would solve a mystery more than thirty years old. Anne said, "I, too, had believed my father's death was an accident, a result of his fight for Ireland's freedom, but after all I've learned, I wonder if he was not killed by the same people for what he knew."

Lady Alexander asked, "Do you know how your father came to possess my pendant?"

Anne shook her head. "We had hoped you might know."

Devon asked, "When did you last see it?"

"Before the duke died. We were together in Ireland, but I returned early and he remained behind to conduct further business. I always believed I had accidentally left behind the pendant and it went down with the ship."

"There was a ring in my father's possession, one I've since learned belonged to the duke."

Lady Alexander raised misty eyes to look at Anne. "His father's ring, and his grandfather's. He never took it off in all the years I knew him, swearing that if anything ever happened to him, people would know him by the ring alone. You have it?"

Anne nodded. "You said he trusted my father. Enough for him to have given my father the ring and pendant? If so, why?"

Lady Alexander sat quietly for a moment and stared at the pendant. "Harlan was a suspicious man. He possessed great wealth and influence, and he garnered a few enemies. Harlan was different during our last holiday in Ireland. Normally, I went with him to all social engagements, but he left me behind twice, and each time he came back he looked so weary. But he always had a smile for me." Lady Alexander's own smile did little to brighten her handsome face. "Your father, Mr. Clayton, was in

Ireland during our last visit."

Devon inched forward on the seat. "Do you know for what purpose?"

"He was at a dinner party we attended, but beyond that I could not tell you." Lady Alexander picked up a thick, leather-bound book from the table beside her chair. "I started this journal a few months before I met the duke, and I have continued to write in it, year after year. There are some gaps, but it remembers more than my memories. I pray it will be of some use to you. If Harlan gave your father the pendant and ring for safekeeping, then his worries were greater than I had realized."

Lady Alexander held the journal out in front of her, and Devon rose to accept it. "I will keep it safe and return it to you, my lady."

Anne saw a soft and almost indiscernible tilt of the lady's lips. The woman's tired eyes tugged at Anne's heart but not as much as the lady's next words.

"I tried to go on after Harlan died, and I did for many years, but I could not love or marry another."

Anne asked, "Is there anything I can get for you?"

"There is, my dear. You can find his killer."

Eleven

Crógacht agus dul sa seans
(Bravery and Risk)

To catch a killer was always easier to request than to accomplish. Devon, Charles, and Tristan had one of the highest case-closing rates in the agency. Devon continued reaping success, sometimes with the help of others, but often alone. He had to remind himself that this case was not his, but rather Charles's, and he was merely helping. Devon admired Anne's form and face from the seat opposite her, and he knew no matter how this case had started out, he would treat it as his own.

They needed to regroup and talk through every clue, question, and answer. Each of them worked well alone, but they were most successful when working together. Their combined talents made them truly great, and they needed their joined gifts in order to solve this mystery.

Devon held the journal close, his desire to bend the spine and read the words strong. The words of a woman who had lost the most important person in her life and continued on despite her misery. What clues did these pages hold? What secrets would be revealed when Devon delved into the most intimate recesses of the author's mind? He needed answers, they all did, and he hoped the pages of the journal would divulge the key to solving these murders.

Back at Charles's house, Anne begged Devon's indulgence while she went to her room and said she'd be down for dinner. Devon watched her ascend the stairs before veering off to the library. Ellis appeared in the doorway before Devon had sat down.

"Shall I order tea, sir?"

"No, thank you, Ellis."

"Very good, sir. His Grace has gone to the village but is expected to return shortly."

"Thank you." Devon walked to the window which offered a view of the road. It wasn't long ago when he stood in this place working with Charles and Tristan to protect Rhona. Such was their life.

The hours passed and the earth was engulfed in twilight when Devon heard the unmistakable sounds of horses running. He set aside the journal and walked into the hall. Moments later, Charles and Tristan strode toward him.

Devon noticed the grimness of Charles's features and set his fears at rest. "She's resting. She'll be down for dinner."

Charles nodded. "Tristan mentioned the other part of your plan, but I'd like the details."

Tristan said, "Had it not been for a loose shoe on my horse, I would have returned an hour ago. As it happens, all Charles knows is that you paid a call upon Lady Alexander."

"We did, with success I might add, and I have something to show you." They followed Devon into Charles's study where neither he nor Tristan bothered with refreshment. Devon lifted the thick volume and handed it to Charles. "Lady Alexander kept a journal. I've spent the afternoon reading through it, and although most of it is useless for our purposes, there are some entries around the time of the duke's death which may be of help."

Charles took the seat at the desk and opened the journal. Devon stood beside him and turned the pages until he reached the entry dated one week before the duke's death. "She couldn't have known the significance of what she wrote at the time."

Charles read while Tristan looked over his shoulder. It took them both only seconds to discover what Devon had. Tristan said, "Lady Berkes? The woman who impersonated Mrs. Keegan?"

"The same," Charles said, and looked up at Devon who now stood across the desk. "Turn to five days later."

This time, Charles stood and left the reading to Tristan, who flipped through the worn pages. "She describes a man who looks remarkably like Gaspar but calls him Bartley, no title or surname. And it seems our Lady Berkes is niece to this Bartley."

Devon nodded. "If he was at that dinner party, Lady Alexander might know him better than she realizes."

Charles asked, "Will you call upon her again?"

"I promised to return the journal. I've made notes on anything seemingly relevant." Devon moved to the sideboard, if for no other reason than to do something with his hands. He fixed Charles a drink and handed it to his friend. "What did you learn in Ireland?"

Charles stared at the amber liquid and swallowed. "Brannon Cottage was ransacked. Rhona loved that cottage. Thankfully, the Brannons are in America for an extended holiday. Obviously, our culprits found nothing, but I'd wager it was not Gaspar's doing, at least not alone. They left nothing behind except a mess and this." Charles pulled a short dagger from his waistband and set it on the desk. "With Anne and her family safe, I returned to Ballinrock, intent on seeing after the remaining tenants. No one else was there except for the butler, Haverly, who had returned from the south."

Tristan settled into one of the chairs, nursing his own glass of brandy. "Did he know anything?"

Charles shook his head. "Nothing. The imposters claiming to be the housekeeper and footman were both gone. Haverly calmed once I promised him the family was safe. I was in the process of searching through the rest of the house when your telegram arrived." He glanced at Devon. "I saw Derek at the port. He's taking over the search, and I'll need to return, but the fight isn't there. There was no sign of Gaspar or anyone else out of place. Haverly will keep watch, and Derek will continue to search the house and the area."

Devon watched as Charles turned his back and walked to the window, as was their habit. It was their nature to know what was coming and to be ready for it, but they'd learned a deadly and valuable lesson one night in Scotland, many years ago. They could plan and anticipate every scenario, but such diligence did not guarantee success. The deception of Alaina's aunt and Rhona's family had proven that truth.

A footman knocked and entered, carrying a silver tray with an envelope. He walked directly to Tristan. "Your Grace, a messenger has just delivered this."

Tristan opened and read the letter, then looked up at the footman. "Is the messenger still here?"

"Yes, Your Grace."

"Please ask him to wait while I write a reply." When the footman left, Tristan said, "It's from Alaina. She doesn't like to be parted for long these days. I'll return shortly."

Charles turned to look at Devon when their friend walked from the room. "Tristan shouldn't be here."

"He won't leave but we'll do our best to end this and get him to Alaina sooner." Devon walked to his friend. Not a day, month, or year passed when they hadn't relied on each other. Since their days at Oxford, the trio had been bound by friendship and their duty to country. Later, when they'd witnessed the depravities which some people forced upon one another, they were bound to mete out justice upon the corrupt. They stood together when Tristan fought to save Alaina and again when Rhona's life depended upon them. Now, Charles was faced with risking another close to him.

"The things we do for the women in our lives." Charles managed a smile. "I don't know Anne well, but it doesn't take long to see the strength and stubbornness beneath her gentle soul. She wants to be the bait that ensnares the snake, then so be it."

Devon had expected many reactions, perhaps even an argument to Anne's plan. It couldn't be this easy. "Your conditions?"

Charles turned away from the window. "One of us is always with her when she leaves this house. It doesn't matter if she is riding or walking, but she isn't to be left alone."

"Agreed."

Charles sighed and grinned at his friend. "I once pitied Tristan and the trouble Alaina found herself in, and then Rhona came back into my life, and I nearly lost her. You, Tristan, and your brothers helped save her life, and I will be indebted to you all beyond the grave."

"Does Rhona know you've returned?"

"No." Charles laughed. "She did slip a letter into my bag before I left, letting me know she would not be kept away for long."

Devon grinned because he knew Rhona would keep her promise. "It's good she's with Alaina. Tristan worries for his wife, carrying their second child. Rhona will be a comfort to her while Tristan is away."

"It's a bloody mess, Devon. Tristan should be with Alaina, and if I could convince him of it, he would leave tonight." Charles's eyes carried the strain of guilt. "Alaina had confessed to Rhona that this pregnancy was more difficult, but she didn't tell Tristan, not wishing to make him choose."

Devon studied his friend, sensing the frustration. He didn't have the burden of love to worry him. He didn't leave behind a wife or children when a case called him away. Devon tried, but he could not fully understand what it must be like to be torn between the love for a woman and the oath he took to protect his country.

Devon took three steps away and spun around. "Tristan could take Alaina and Rhona to Greyson Hall. There, he could watch over Anne's mother and sister and be with his wife. They're safer there than anywhere else right now."

Charles seemed to consider the idea. "And Zachary?"

"Send him to London. If Gaspar is no longer in Ireland, and we haven't seen him around, he may try to hide in the city among the crowds."

"Tristan may not agree."

Devon cocked his head and shrugged. "We'll give him no choice."

As it happened, Tristan did agree, though not without reservations. Anne was the one who convinced him the plan not only had merit, but that she would be in his debt. The more people with her family, especially women to keep them company, the greater at ease she would be. Devon had not given Anne enough credit for her power to employ her wishes on the opposite sex. He had believed only himself afflicted with an intense desire to please her, yet Tristan proved to be just as susceptible.

Tristan would leave at first light for Claiborne Manor, and

from there, north to Greyson Hall. For this night though, they would enjoy the company of friends. The men did their best to keep Anne from thinking of what lay ahead, though Devon sensed her mounting impatience. Portraying the prey was often a long and unexciting process.

The meal over, the foursome convened in the parlor. Devon expected Anne to retire soon but she surprised them all by lingering. When she refused the second offer for an evening drink, Devon decided to enjoy what he believed was about to happen.

"I should be doing more."

There it was. Devon found a comfortable position in the chair and smirked. Charles sat across from Tristan at a small table where they moved carved ivory chess pieces across a marble board.

Without looking up, Charles said dryly, "You are doing something. Breathing, and I have every intention to see you keep on breathing."

Anne tapped her foot on the floor and glanced at Devon. He suspected she was silently asking him for assistance, but he shook his head. He might disagree with Charles from time to time, but he agreed with his friend on this point. Besides, he wanted to see how far she would go.

"Why would Lord Gaspar come here when he must know by now you have me surrounded?"

This time Charles looked up and stared at his cousin. "What would you suggest we do? Derek is in Ireland, Zachary will soon be in London, and Tristan will leave tomorrow and stay with your mother and Claire. That will leave only two of us." Charles stood and crossed the room. "Do you have any idea the danger you could be in, even with Devon and me here to watch over you? There is no man on earth more capable than Devon to keep you safe, and yet, it's not enough."

Devon watched Anne closely. She didn't shrivel like a wilted flower beneath Charles's stormy gaze, but he saw an understanding creep into her eyes. Charles continued, though not in anger. Devon knew he only wanted Anne to grasp the seriousness of what she suggested, but Devon saw she already had. It was not disrespect that caused her to question their lack of action but a sense of duty.

"We have lost people we've cared about, loved, and did everything in our power to keep safe, but still we lost them. I am not going to lose you." Charles swore and turned away. Anne, in her youthful and naïve wisdom, rose and laid a hand on her cousin's arm until he faced her once more.

"This is not your fault, Charles. I lied to you. The letters I sent saying all was well and refusing your offer to spend time in Ireland or for us to come here . . . those are my doing. If there is any one person to blame in all of this, it is me, and I will not hear anything to the contrary." She stepped back so she could look at everyone. Tristan and Devon both stood, Devon mesmerized by Anne's strength.

"I am not of your world. I have not been on great adventures like Alaina or Rhona nor have I lived through the dangers they've experienced because I'm still living it. That, too, is my doing. I am naïve and inexperienced, but do not believe I cannot fight alongside you if necessary." Anne steadied her gaze on each one of them before settling it fully on Charles. "I cannot repay you for what you've already done, and what I know you will do. I cannot change the circumstances which forced my hand and brought me back into your life, but I have accepted them. I will do whatever I must. Let me play my part, Charles."

Devon, no longer content to remain silent, stepped up beside Anne. "She can do this."

Charles fixed his stare on Devon. "I know she can. Just as Alaina could, and Rhona. We nearly lost them both."

Tristan set a hand on Charles's shoulder but looked to Anne. "These matters cannot be expedited without risking lives, yet your passion suggests you have a plan of your own."

Anne looked to Devon who nodded. He knew what she was asking, and he would stand beside her, no matter how foolish or perilous her plan. She exhaled deeply, and if Devon had not been standing beside her, he would not have known she trembled.

"You won't like it, cousin."

Charles closed his eyes for a few seconds and looked upward, as though he prayed to the heavens for the strength to deal with this impetuous woman. When his eyes opened, a brilliant green much like Anne's, his wry half-smile told Devon that Charles was resigned, at least for the moment.

"No, cousin, I don't believe I will like it."

ANNE ONCE AGAIN SAT across from Lady Alexander, who held the returned journal close to her heart. "I hope it was of some help."

"It was, and we're grateful. It could not have been easy to allow us into this intimate part of your life."

The lady smiled softly. "The most important memories are still with me, and the rest no longer matter." She set the journal on the small table by her chair. "Will you find his killer?"

Devon said, "I will do everything I can to bring the man or woman to justice, if they still live."

Anne watched sorrow fill the other woman's eyes, but it mixed with hope. They visited through tea and then took their leave, with a promise from Anne to visit again when it was all over. She remained quiet on the coach ride back to Charles's house, but Devon was persistent.

"You don't have to go through with this plan of yours."

Anne looked across the way at him. "You agreed to it, as did the others, though I know Charles is not pleased with the idea."

"You're no longer the bait. You wish to become the hunter in this game."

"A game? How is this a game when so many lives are at risk?"

"It is not our game, but theirs. We're forced to play it. The difference is, whether or not we play by their rules or ours."

"And that is how you solve cases?"

"It can help to separate the emotions from the work. We are duty-bound to serve our country but that doesn't always mean we feel nothing for the people involved." Devon moved to the seat next to her and reached for her gloved hand. "In '87, we were on a case in Scotland. Charles, Tristan, and I were three years with the agency at the time. The man we were meant to bring in chose not to come willingly. He used his wife for a shield, and his partner used the man's child. Both mother and son died. Their screams haunt me to this day, haunt all of us. Our fear is not that the plan won't work, but that it will."

Anne saw a tear drop on their joined hands, a tear from her own eye. She reached up and wiped away the others before her eyes met Devon's. The warmth from his bare hands reached through her gloves. "Will Charles pull back?"

Devon shook his head. "He'll want to, but he heard you, Anne. You're in a unique position to make your own decisions, much as Rhona was, and I imagine he sees some similarities."

Resolve and confidence welled up within her. "I can do this."

"I know you can, and I'll see you're ready."

"I already know what must be—"

Devon grinned. "There's knowing and there is doing."

He sobered, and Anne saw a fierceness in his eyes which appeared for a fleeting moment. "I will not let any harm come to you, Anne, if it's in my power."

Such a declaration from anyone would have offered her comfort, but from Devon, it bolstered her spirit until she believed she could accomplish anything with him by her side. And yet, he wouldn't be by her side once this plan was set in motion, but he would be watching. Somehow, she knew he would always be watching.

Twelve

Rogha na nGaiscíoch
(Choice of the Brave)

Shivers wracked her body, but she ignored them. Despair filled her heart, but she forced the pain away. Helplessness overcame her thoughts, but then her mind turned to Devon. Anne took in a deep breath, the Irish air filled her lungs, and a sense of calm suffused her body and mind.

Home. Odd, but Ballinrock no longer offered her the comfort it once had when she played hide-and-seek with her sister in the great halls or when her father told her stories while they sat before the hearth in his study. Haunted memories and personal ghosts now called Ballinrock their home. Death and sorrow waited for her beyond the crumbling stone walls. The farmland stretched out for miles, wild and unyielding to the farmers who had fought to keep their homes and families on this land. For generations, people had counted on the Doyles, and it was the Doyles who let them down. Anne closed her eyes and conjured the memories of long ago when the rich soil yielded crops aplenty, when horses and livestock grazed upon the green grass and children played along the river, while the older ones told tales of their generation.

The land was quiet now. The driver opened the coach door

and helped Anne down. Her gaze locked onto the front door, as though it opened to a life she barely recalled. No matter how little comfort the castle provided, this was her home, and no one would keep her away. She walked up the few stone steps, chipped away at the edges, and to her great relief, Derek walked outside, Haverly close behind him.

Anne held back the tears. She could do this. She was strong enough, but when Devon had become a fading memory from the coach window, Anne allowed herself a single moment of doubt. Derek was not his brother, but her courage was once again boosted by his presence and by the familiar face behind him. She greeted Derek and nodded when he said they needed to talk. Anne stood before Haverly, and propriety be damned, she embraced him.

"You are such a comfort to me, Haverly. I worried for you dearly."

Haverly held her close and in his heavy Irish brogue, said, "There, young one. You are home now, and we are safe."

Anne pulled back and looked up at the butler. His towering height matched Devon's. "I'm grateful you weren't here. These men who are helping us will find justice for our Cillian."

The butler looked over her head to Derek, and Anne caught Derek's indication for the butler to remain quiet. She turned around. "What's happened, Derek?"

"Come inside with me, Anne. We have much to discuss."

Anne followed Derek with some reluctance, divesting of her outer clothing before they reached the small library. Derek left her to find her own seat and poured her a drink. She saw from the bottle that it was one of her father's finest, and favorite, whiskey. Anne was not partial to strong libations, but Derek held it in front of her until she accepted. Sensing he would not leave her be until she drank, she swallowed the entire contents of the glass and handed him the empty glass.

"Lady Anne, it's not my place to instruct you, but have you thought about the danger you'll be in—the danger you'll put the others in—if you move forward with your plans?"

Anne stood and walked to the window. The walls of her home suddenly crowded her, and she longed to be back in England with her mother and sister. She reminded herself they were alive and safe. "Devon has told you of the plan?"

Derek remained across the room, but he had stood and watched her. "Charles did."

Anne spun around. "Charles is here?" She remembered the conversation with her cousin. He was to remain at Blackwood Crossing until she sent word.

"He's close. Lady Anne—"

"Please, just Anne."

Derek bowed his head once. "A telegram arrived from London. Zachary has said that Gaspar has not been seen for three days, but he was in London. If Gaspar is there, he's hiding, but it's possible he's learned that you have returned here. I am to ask you once again if you're certain you want to do this."

Anne smiled. "Devon told you to ask me?"

It was Derek's turn to grin, an expression that nearly matched his brother's. "Charles. Devon told me not to bother."

"Your brother is right, but you have concerns as well?"

Derek nodded. "I've seen the extent to which my brother, Charles, and Tristan will go for those they love—we all would—but it's nearly cost them their lives more than once. They could do this without you."

"I don't doubt that, but I have to see this through. If I can deflect some of the attention away from Devon and the others, then I need to try."

"We'll never let that happen, Anne."

Anne knew he meant that no matter what she tried, someone would be there to stand between her and Gaspar or anyone working with him. A slow burning formed behind Anne's eyes. Exhaustion was something she could not afford, but she had not slept since Devon left her side and barely before on the channel crossing. "If you don't mind, I believe I'll retire early tonight."

Anne saw the concern and disappointment etched on Derek's face, but he said nothing more about it. "Of course. Haverly and I will keep watch in shifts tonight, so one of us will always be about if you need anything."

"Thank you, Derek." Anne started for the door but looked back. "Have you been seen by anyone from the grounds or village?"

Derek nodded but was quick to assure her. "I paid a visit to Cillian's family. Charles had me deliver a letter and funds to them. As far as they are concerned, I am Charles's solicitor from London here to get affairs in order. It is easy enough since I studied law before joining the agency, as did Zachary." He smiled and continued. "For good measure, I went to the village myself to pay balances on your accounts—Charles's instructions—and they, too, believe I am here as his solicitor. No one has reason to suspect anything."

"Then we wait." Anne said good night, and passing Haverly in the hall, told him she would not be down for supper and to see that Derek was looked after.

"Of course, my lady. Your cousin, Lord Blackwood, hired Cillian's sister as the new cook. He assured me you would not mind."

"I don't mind at all. I should have done so myself." Anne laid a hand gently on the butler's arm and thanked him. "Try to rest, Haverly." She made her way through the house and up the stairs. Charles had not only been trying to keep her alive and her family safe, but he had managed to handle mundane household affairs. She should have been the one to make restitution to Cillian's family, to give his sister a position, and to pay the family's debts in the village.

It did not matter now, for although she inherited Ballinrock, Anne did not have the resources or ability to do what Charles could. She had waged a private war with her pride for long enough. All that mattered now was justice, truth, and the future of her family.

Anne reached the landing where she had not stood since that fateful night when her nightmares began. Without thought as to why curiosity compelled her, Anne walked down the hall opposite of her bedroom and stood in front of the door to the room where innocent life had been lost. The room no longer smelled of copper, but a dark stain marred the carpet. She pushed away from the room and pressed against the tapestry that had once aided in her escape.

Her legs managed to carry her back down the hall to her bedroom. Anne underestimated the difficulty she would have in returning to where it all began. The rooms within the castle had once been a place of hope and laughter, but those memories had since vanished. She stared at the fire burning in her bedroom hearth but could not bring herself to make use of the large bed. Her body was weary, but her mind would not shut off.

Anne lit the wick of a lantern and left the room, walking down the hall, shadows dancing around her. The portraits which had once graced the walls had since been sold. Inside her mother's room, she searched until she found the door Devon had told her about, a door she hadn't known existed. The light of her lantern did little to remove the darkness of the short passageway, and she was soon in the chamber where her mother and sister had been held.

How did Gaspar know about this room? Her mother had never mentioned it, nor had her father. The room wasn't on the castle drawings tucked away with the history of the estate. Anne knew old houses and castles often contained secret rooms and passages, but the question still remained—how did Lord Gaspar know about it?

Anne walked the length of the room, searching every crevice and corner she could find. A large bed and a trunk dominated the room, and it was in front of the trunk where she knelt, setting the lantern on the floor. The heavy lid did not budge the first time, and with extra strength, Anne managed to raise it. Empty. Her slender fingers deftly moved along the edges, searching and finding. Something nicked and stung her skin. She pulled her hand back to stare at the thin white line across the tip of her finger.

Peering over the edge of the trunk, she retraced the edges until she felt it again. Her finger barely fit into the corner to loosen whatever was trapped. Holding up her discovery, she studied the scrap of paper. The markings on the torn square looked somehow familiar.

How is this possible? The question rang through her thoughts over and over. Anne closed the trunk and with one last look around, quickly left the chamber and secured the door to the passage. She stopped in the hallway, debating her next choice. Was this something of consequence? She shook her head. Devon said they followed clues, no matter how insignificant the clue might seem. Anne blew out the lantern and hurried down the stairs in search of Derek.

"I'm not mistaken, am I?"

Derek held the scrap of paper up to the dim light. "No, you're not, but something about this isn't quite right." He set the paper down and looked at her. "This was all you found?"

"Yes, and it was only by chance." Anne picked up the scrap of what they'd deduced was a £2 British note. "It's possible my father hid money in there, but it makes no sense."

Derek shook his head and pulled a £2 note out of his own pocketbook. "The note is current, not like what your father would have had. Where did you find this?"

"In the room where my mother and sister were kept." Anne stared at him. "What does it mean?"

"I don't know yet, but I'll go back and search the room."

"Lord Gaspar?"

Derek shrugged, an affectation he shared with his brother and said, "Leave this with me and I'll have answers for you tomorrow." Derek slipped the torn banknote into his pocket.

DEVON AND CHARLES STOOD across from Derek in a large room attached to the old stable. The dank surroundings offered them privacy but little protection from the elements.

"She wasn't pleased."

Devon glanced from the banknote to his brother. "You'll get used to it."

Charles added, "Better alive and upset than curious and dead." He held the note closer to the lantern. "You're right about this note, Derek. Although similar and current, this here in the corner shouldn't be there."

Derek said, "Forgery."

Charles nodded and looked to Devon. "We've dealt with minor forgery cases in the past, but I've heard nothing recent."

"There is one that Patrick brought to my attention after your wedding. Apparently, one of our recently retired agents was working on a forgery that dates back more than thirty years. The man never made any real progress, and whoever was behind it managed to elude the authorities. Whenever someone was caught, another simply took his place. They couldn't find the person at the top."

Charles asked, "Can you find out more about this case?"

"Not without risking Patrick's interest in what I'm doing. I am supposed to be on an extended holiday." Devon nodded toward his brother. "Derek, what does Patrick think you and

Zachary are doing right now?"

"A well-deserved break but that will be over if I approach him with this."

"We'll risk it." Devon walked to the window next to the short wooden door. Wind and rain battered the stone while water dripped through the turf and thatch.

Charles spoke up with another idea. "I'll go. Derek's cover is in place here, and I currently have no official capacity with the agency."

Devon said, "Patrick is going to wonder what interest you have in a case when you should be on your honeymoon."

"Which is why I'm going to give him part of the truth."

Devon walked back to the center of the room, where the glow from the single lantern reached only a few feet. "What do you want me to tell Anne?"

"You'll know what to say." Charles moved toward the door and with his hand pressed against the wood, he said over his shoulder, "Keep her safe, Devon."

Devon watched as his friend mounted his horse and rode off into the storm toward the port, where a private ship waited.

Derek stepped up beside his brother. "You're going to tell her everything, aren't you?"

"I made her a promise." Devon nodded toward the house. "I'll come up tonight after I know it's safe."

THE KNIFE HOVERED OVER her heart; blood trickled from the hilt to the tip of the blade. Moonlight filtered into the room, but the face above her was masked. Her body lay numb, unable to move beneath the weight. She urged her mind to tell her body to fight back, but she remained helpless. The blade cut through the white linen at her throat, cold metal sliding across her flesh.

"Anne."

Her breath quickened and her lips moved, but no sound

emerged.

"Anne."

The knife moved away and warmth caressed her neck where the steel had once been. Her eyes fluttered.

"That's right, love. Open your eyes."

Above her was no masked man, but Devon, strong and safe and beautiful. He held her in his arms while she calmed her racing heart.

"Thank God it's you." She leaned back. "What are you doing here?"

"I didn't intend to stay away. I've been keeping watch with Charles, but I needed to see you."

Anne resettled herself beneath the bedcovers. Her nightgown clung to her damp body, and it was then she noticed the open window. The cold wind from outside swept through the room, offering minor relief. Devon hurried over to close and latch the windows before he returned to her side.

"It was open when I came in, but your moans and cries worried me more than the cold." Devon smoothed a hand over her damp brow. "What nightmares haunt you?"

Anne didn't want to relive the nightmare from which she escaped. What it meant, she didn't know, but if it was a foretelling of her future, she didn't have long to live. She leaned against the pillows and stared into his eyes, the same blue as a turbulent sea. She'd never known a man with eyes so changeable, and she wondered if anyone else ever noticed.

"Death is at my door, Devon. I won't turn back, but I'm not ignorant of what could happen."

Devon entwined his hand with hers. "You aren't dying today or any other day, at least not in the next thirty years if I can help it."

Anne drew comfort from his strength and managed a smile at his arrogance. "I believe you. What really brought you here tonight?"

"Charles has left for the port. He'll return to England in the morning."

"For what purpose?"

"To speak with Patrick about the banknote you found." Devon went on to relay the conversation that had taken place earlier.

"Money." Anne slid out of bed and into her robe. She watched the low blaze of the fire as it warmed her. "What a horrible motive to kill someone. I can understand protecting yourself or your loved ones, justice, or even revenge, but I cannot tolerate murder for money."

"It happens often."

Devon followed her to the hearth but kept some distance between them. It didn't matter how close or how far away he was, if he was in the same room, his energy surrounded her.

"What now?"

"The plan hasn't changed. It will be a few days before we hear from Charles, and Tristan promised to send a telegram when he reached Greyson Hall. We wait. You're a liability to them."

Somehow, that truth did not motivate her fear. Anne was awash with a sense of calm and duty. Is this what it meant to sacrifice yourself, your own wants, for the good of others? Motivated primarily by the safety of her family, Anne realized whatever they accomplished would be for a greater good.

Her father had taught Anne many lessons while he was on this earth, but none of them more important than fortitude. She drew on that strength now when it was needed most. "Then we wait." She looked up at Devon. "Where will you be?"

"Close."

This time it was Anne who reached out to Devon, their hands interlaced. "Let this happen, Devon." She raised herself up and pressed her lips gently to his. A kiss meant to silence but also to reassure. "I'm no longer afraid of what comes to pass. Promise me you will help Charles see that I alone made this choice."

Thirteen

Sna Scáthanna
(In the Shadows)

Devon's vigil over Anne and Ballinrock lasted two more days and nights, but she'd seen only glimpses of him since their arrival. Embers burned low in the hearth. Anne huddled beneath the covers and stared at the ceiling. Another nightmare had crept into her much-needed slumber, and for two hours she lay awake wishing for dawn to come. She closed her eyes, almost willing her mind to shut down, but Devon, her family, and the case kept her thoughts astir.

Anne pushed away the bedcovers and lowered her feet to the worn rug covering the cold floor. She slipped into her robe and padded in stockinged feet to the hearth where she set more peat on the fire and stirred the embers until they flamed. Satisfied the fire would soon take away the evening chill, she settled at her small desk, lit the lantern, and with pen and paper set to her task. A timeline of events soon formed. Along with her own thoughts and recounting of her conversations with Devon, Charles, Derek, and Lady Alexander, Anne quickly filled five sheets from her dwindling and precious supply of paper.

None of it helped. Anne set the pen aside and pushed away

from her desk. The single clock on her mantel told her she'd been occupied for nearly two hours. She refueled the fire and walked to the window to stare out into the darkness. When she couldn't fall asleep as a child, her father would tell her stories of how the strong winds brought fairies across the seas, carrying them to young children to keep away the demons and monsters who haunted their sleep. Though Anne had known the truth long before adulthood that the storms brought rain and cold instead of magic and wishes, the fierce winds still brought her comfort.

With memories of times passed, Anne sought comfort once more in sleep. It did not take long before Caer Ibormeith swept her away into dreams with her captivating music.

DEVON HAD WAITED LONGER than two days to catch elusive prey, but his patience waned. Devon had not returned to the castle, relying on daily reports from his brother. On the third day, the winds weakened and a damp frost covered the green hills and valleys. Derek once more left the castle, stopping at the old stable on his return.

"Telegram today. All is well at Greyson Hall. Zachary also sent word from London to inform us Gaspar is there." Derek shook the rain off his coat and looked around the old stable. "Where have you been sleeping?"

"There's a room above that appears not to have been used in a while. I've stayed in worse." Devon accepted the bag his brother held out. "I found more documents in Lord Doyle's desk. The man took deplorable care with his finances and the estate as a whole. From what I can tell, the only time he hired a solicitor was to draw up his last will."

Devon spread the documents out on an old table he'd found in the corner. Like many things at Ballinrock Castle, it was in need of repair. "Have you learned anything new about the will?"

"Not much. It was an odd arrangement." Derek removed his

sodden hat and rubbed the corners of his eyes.

"Tired, brother?"

Derek shrugged off Devon's concern. "Not as tired as you, I'd wager. I have Haverly to share in the shifts. Do you even sleep?"

"Enough." Devon grinned at his brother. "A few more years at this, and sleep will be remembered as a luxury. It is odd that Doyle left Anne the estate."

"Not just the estate, Devon—everything. Doyle had no sons, and Charles was the closest living male relative. Under normal circumstances, he would have inherited, but I can find no entail for generations back, let alone now. Perhaps Doyle knew that Charles would not contest the will, but the next logical choice would have been Lady Doyle, not Anne."

Devon leaned back on his heels. "Anne said her mother's condition did not manifest itself until after her father died, so the question is, why did Lord Doyle bypass his wife in favor of his daughter?"

"I haven't found the answer . . . yet. I'll continue to look. Doyle's finances weren't the only things in disarray. I'd wager the man never cleaned out his study, or he preferred chaos. Either way, I should be done tomorrow."

Devon nodded. "I'll study these documents tonight after I walk the grounds."

"Only one document seemed odd. A letter from a bank in England. He doesn't appear to have done any business or kept any accounts at this bank."

"Did you ask Anne about it?"

Derek shook his head. "I will tomorrow. She's been restless and asked if she could visit Cillian's family. Giving Nessa, Cillian's sister, the cook position has helped the family, but Anne would like to do more and to pay her respects."

Devon considered Anne's safety. No one could accompany her without drawing suspicion. Gaspar may still be in London, but they all knew he wasn't working alone. There could be men now watching the castle, waiting to find Anne alone. But isn't that what they wanted? To lure them in? Devon smiled because Anne likely hadn't considered any of that. She would want to go because she possessed an inherent goodness toward others. "She should go."

Derek stared at his brother for a few seconds and nodded. "I'll let her know. Sleep tonight, Devon. You're no good to her if you don't rest."

Rest was an extravagance he could ill afford, not until this was over. "I'll try." It was all he could promise. Unfortunately, it was a promise he could not keep. Dusk settled over the land while Devon finished reading through the papers Derek had provided. The bank letter appeared to have been a reply to an inquiry Lord Doyle sent them, but without the original letter, they could only guess at the context.

Frustrated at their current lack of information, Devon walked to the window to do what he did most nights—watch the castle and think of the woman within. He hoped Charles made more progress in London with Patrick. Devon looked up at the moon, shrouded in dark clouds offering enough cover for him to walk the property as he did every night. Careful to keep the lantern low and away from windows, Devon blew out the flame and made his way down the narrow wooden steps to the stable below.

THE DOOR CREAKED, BUT not enough to signal anyone who might be near. Devon stepped outside into the cold and halted. She should be safely inside her room, but there she walked along the edges of the castle. Moonlight shined upon her every time she weaved in and out of the shadows. The edges of her cape flew around in the wind, giving the illusion of flight. He caught a glimpse of her pale skin and long hair that escaped the cape's hood before she entered the castle through the servants' entrance.

"Bloody hell." Devon's long legs carried him swiftly over the wet ground, ignoring the force of the wind as it attempted to slow his progress. He entered through the long hall leading into the kitchen and stopped. Silence. He bounded up the servants' staircase to the main floor. Above him, a shadow and movement passed somewhere beyond his vision. Whoever it was moved without sound. Devon rushed upstairs to the landing where he turned to the left, but to his right, he heard footsteps.

"What are you doing here?" Derek lowered the pistol he carried. "I thought you—"

Devon held up his hand to quiet his brother. "You did hear someone. Anne's room." He hurried ahead of his brother to reach Anne's door, but it wouldn't open. "It's locked." Devon pounded on the door, shouting her name.

Coughing, struggles, and then the sweetest sound he'd ever heard.

"Devon!"

The brothers stood back and together charged the heavy oak door.

ANNE COULDN'T BREATHE. HER eyes wouldn't open, her fingers clawed and pulled, but the air wouldn't come into her lungs. Pounding in her head? Or was it? Her mind dimmed and the struggles eased. Was this supposed to happen? Her name. Who said it?

"Anne!"

Devon. Anne kicked, but the covers trapped her legs. With every bit of strength in mind and body she still possessed, Anne shoved and rolled across the bed. Her breath came in gasps, and she couldn't call out. The knife struck her body before the pain registered. Whoever was in the room stood between her and freedom. Anne backed against the wall and reached for the lantern beside the bed, holding it above her.

A shadow moved across the room, smaller than Anne had imagined from the strength of the arms holding her down. The shadow moved closer, darkness swarming around it—no, her.

"Devon!"

The shadow lunged, and Anne swung down bringing the oil lamp heavy upon the intruder's head. The door burst open, and there he stood. Anne's last thought was of him before everything dimmed.

"ANNE?"

Her eyes fluttered open. Was that she who groaned? Anne tried to move her arm, but the excruciating pain sliced through her shoulder.

"Devon. Is she gone?" It hurt to speak.

"You're safe now." Devon's familiar touch caressed her cheek and brow, and then he came into focus. "I'm so sorry we didn't get to you sooner."

Anne tried to shift, but her body preferred to remain still. "It wasn't your fault. I didn't even hear her come into my room. She moved so fast, and she was strong."

"That's not all she is." Devon helped her to sit up and moved the other pillows behind her back. "She's tied up downstairs, but you'll want to see her."

Anne tried to reach behind her shoulder. "She cut me."

"Across your shoulder and back."

"You stitched the wound?"

Devon's smile in the midst of such seriousness gave her great comfort. "I've learned a few things about healing, too. You won't be able to move your arm much for a few days, and it may be longer still before the pain ebbs, but the wound wasn't too deep."

Anne struggled to keep her eyes open. "Where is she?"

"Downstairs. Derek has attempted to get her to talk for two

days now."

"Two days?" Anne once more tried to get out of bed, but Devon gently pressed her backed into the pillows.

"She's not going anywhere."

"Devon, I'm sore, but more than that, I'm angry. This woman, whoever she is, came into my home and tried to kill me." Anne reached up to massage her throat. "My bag?"

Devon pulled it from the trunk at the base of the bed and handed it to her.

"Is the water in that teapot still warm?"

Devon nodded and handed it to her. Anne mixed a ground powder in with the water and drank slowly. "Thank you."

"What is that?"

"Herba Scabiosa. Devil's Bit. An unfortunate name for a healing herb. It's for my throat."

"Better?"

Anne nodded. "Well enough to give my assassin in-kind treatment. She surprised me, and I don't like surprises."

"You thought it would be Gaspar."

Anne scowled, knowing he was right. Had it been Gaspar or one of his men, she might not have lived, but then a man may not have so easily entered her room with such stealth. "A woman, Devon. They sent a woman. She made no sound when she moved."

"A woman assassin is unexpected, but not unheard of, and it was smart. I almost didn't see her."

"I want to speak with her." Anne sat up, this time pushing away Devon's hands. "I promise not to overdo, and you and Derek can be in the room, but there must have been a reason they sent her."

Devon stood and handed her the robe draped at the bottom of the bed. "A woman assassin is clever, but once you see, you'll know their other reason."

Anne slipped one arm into her robe, and Devon wrapped the other side of the garment over her wounded shoulder. "Cryptic words, Devon."

"You'll understand better when you see her in the light."

Anne walked down the stairs with the aid of Devon's arm around her waist. It was the first time in a year she was grateful the house was empty of a full staff. "Charles isn't going to be happy about this."

Devon held her close and gingerly guided her down the final steps. "No, but you'll soon be back in England, and he'll feel better with you closer."

Anne stopped in the hallway outside of the study. "What do you mean?"

Devon glanced toward the closed door and lowered his voice before speaking. "We leave in two days. Charles sent word yesterday. He has discovered a link between what's happened here and the Duke of Hambleton's death."

"Then it is about money forgery?"

Devon nodded and said, "Be careful of what you say. She won't get away from us, but I'd rather she not know any more than necessary."

Anne took a deep breath and immediately regretted it. "I believe she damaged more than my shoulder."

"You have some bruises along your rib cage. It will take a while for the tenderness and discoloration to fade."

Devon reached for the handle, but Anne stopped him. "How do you know what my rib cage looks like?"

Devon chuckled and opened the door. He whispered, "Another conversation for another time. I promise I was a perfect gentleman."

Anne blushed, but when she entered the room and saw the assassin, she understood what Devon had meant. At first glance, the woman could have been her sister. Tall and fair. Her hair, the color of light autumn leaves, hung down her shoulders in tangles. Her eyes may have been the same color of the moss that grows by the Irish Sea, but they were cold and fierce, without a touch of the gaiety Anne's father always told her shined in her green eyes. The face was most startling—pale skin and from a distance, she could have been mistaken for Anne herself.

Anne walked toward the other woman, careful to stay by Devon's side. The woman's watchful eyes followed Anne's slow movements. When Devon's light touch on her back tried to guide her to one of the chairs, Anne glanced up at him, silently telling him she preferred to stand. With a brief nod and a quick look to their prisoner, he stepped a few feet away. Derek stood behind the chair to which Anne's would-be killer was presently tied.

"You tried to kill me in my own home. The least you could do is tell me why."

DEVON NOTICED THE GLINT of anger in their captive's eyes when Anne had entered the room. Either Derek or Haverly had been by the woman's side for two days and nights. The woman did not even speak or protest when they refused to give her any privacy. Her glare told them without words that if she managed to get free, she would kill them all.

Anne's bravado made him proud, yet he wondered if it would work. The woman's angry stare darkened at Anne's statement but did not deter Anne from her task.

"You already know me, but I imagine these men surprised you. Did Lord Gaspar truly believe my cousin would not have someone close?" Anne smirked, her actions and words growing bolder. "Or did his lordship care nothing for you and sent you knowing it was a trap? Either way, the future does not bode well for you."

Anne and her near-double stared at one another, neither

relenting. Anne taunted the woman, and Devon couldn't help but appreciate her tactics.

Anne said, "I imagine someone like you is not used to bars and dark caverns. I've heard tales of the wretched conditions at Newgate. Brick walls with barely enough light to see your hands."

Anne managed to surprise him with her callous words and cold tone, though he did nothing to interfere. Devon noticed the other woman's eyes narrow at the mention of Newgate. Perhaps their captive killer was familiar with the prison.

Anne finally lowered herself into a chair, and Devon resisted the urge to help her. Anne asked, "If not your name, then what shall I call you?"

"Fianna."

Where had he heard that name before? Devon half-listened to Anne thank Fianna and continue her questions while he searched his memory. He looked up to his brother but saw no recognition of Fianna's name.

Anne leaned forward in her chair until she was less than a foot away from Fianna. "How much is my life worth?"

Fianna stared at Anne, and for the first time, her eyes softened. "My life."

"What do you mean?" Devon moved to stand beside Anne's chair, his curiosity as rampant as Anne's.

Fianna looked from Anne to Devon, but it was Anne to whom she gave her focus. "My life for yours."

Willing to bargain, Devon asked, "What is your freedom worth to you now?" He heard Anne gasp beside him, but he focused on Fianna. "I have heard of you, Miss Mac Branain." She was rigid in posture yet Devon saw a slight resistance in Fianna's body. "Yes, I know your name, though I daresay you've gone by many. Your mistake was in using your real name once, long ago. Your first kill, perhaps?"

"What do you want?" asked Fianna.

"Who sent you?"

Fianna turned away and remained silent. Devon reached forward and turned her head until she faced him, locking her chin in his strong hand. "You can make the crossing back to Newgate and keep your head, or you can be found beneath the ice in the river." He released her and leaned back until his arm rubbed against Anne's.

She shuddered, and Devon couldn't wait to take her away from the memories of this place.

"I call him Arawn," Fianna said.

"God of the underground kingdom of the dead." Devon stood up. "However appropriate for you, the name is no use to us."

Fianna strained against the ropes binding her to the chair. "He has a scar."

Devon turned back.

"Across his face on one side, from eye to mouth. I don't know his real name."

"Death is your trade and has been for many years, Fianna." Devon loomed over her. "How much did they pay you to kill her, and don't tell me it's for your life."

Fianna turned away and looked at Anne. "You're not safe anywhere."

Devon looked to Derek and nodded once before he held his hand out to Anne. She stared at it, not accepting his help. Instead, she spoke to Fianna. "You said my death would win your freedom, and yet you came here, free to kill, free to run."

"I'll say no more. Do what you will with me, but know this, Lady Anne, Arawn will see you dead, and if he doesn't succeed, you will wish he had."

Anne slipped her hand into Devon's and accepted his help in rising. "I don't want to see her again."

Devon helped her toward the door, but Fianna called out Anne's name. "Áit a gcasann na cnoic agus an t-uisce ar na fothraigh. Ná hinis do dhuine ar bith nó gheobhaidh siad uilig bás."

Anne turned away and walked from the room. She remained silent until they reached her bedroom. Devon stoked the fire and waited, but Anne did nothing more than stare out the window.

"Where the water and hills meet the ruins. Tell no one or they will all die." Anne turned around and looked at Devon from across the room. "I understand the threat, but the first part is a riddle. What could it mean?"

Devon approached her, careful to keep some distance between them. The lines between protector, friend, and lover blurred in his mind, and yet, her eyes shone bright, pleading with him for answers. "I would venture to say it's a location, but where, I don't know."

"Do you think they'll find my family?"

"I don't see how they could, but if they managed to find them, Tristan is there."

Anne gripped his arms. "I want to be with them. I need to see they are all right."

"They'll have someone watching Fianna in case she failed. You could end up leading them back to your family."

Her eyes shined with a mischievous sparkle. "Not if she didn't fail. You said yourself, Fianna could be my sister. Of course she's not for I have only one sister, but the opportunity—"

"No."

"But, Devon—"

"No." Devon raked long fingers through his hair in frustration. "Yes, you look similar, but up close, there's enough of a difference, and anyone who knows Fianna will realize you're not her."

"You have a better idea? This would gain us time and you

know it."

Devon lifted her chin with a gentle touch of his fingers. "Every time I believe you're going to be gentle, submissive, and cooperative, you surprise me by wanting to do exactly what you shouldn't."

Anne mimicked one of his ever-present grins. "You know I'm right."

"Right doesn't always mean right." Devon could ensure her safety, at least as much as they had thus far. He sensed her fear, but also her courage, and beneath that, a longing for adventure. She allowed fear to fuel her actions rather than debilitate them.

"We don't have much time." Devon ran his hand over her hair. "We'll need to make a few changes so there will be no mistaking you're her, at least not until we're ready for Gaspar to know."

"Thank you, Devon."

"Save your thanks for after Charles has finished with me."

Anne's soft smile warmed his heart in every way a smile like hers should warm a man. He would be speaking with Charles about many things when the case ended. "Rest tonight. Derek and I will have answers by tomorrow."

"I saw the fierce determination in her eyes, Devon. Fianna seems like a woman used to hiding, and she won't reveal her secrets so easily."

"You're right. She won't tell us everything tonight, but I promise in time, we will know all of her secrets. I don't believe she's here to save her own life, but I do believe she would set a trap. Whatever she told you, don't trust it."

He walked away from her, but she stopped him with a question before he reached the door. "How do you know Fianna?"

"Only by reputation. One of my first cases involved the brutal and methodical slaying of an agency informant. It was rumored that the man's mistress killed him, only later to be discovered she was an assassin, as rare then as they are now. She made the mistake of using her name, Fianna Mac Branain, but I never heard the name again until this day. She's better than most men I've encountered, and her only motive is money."

Anne leaned against the bedpost and lowered onto the oak trunk. "You don't believe she only killed for her freedom?"

Devon shook his head. "No. Someone may be blackmailing her, but a woman with her skills has choices. Whatever she claims they are holding over her, it has to mean more to her than any life, including her own. She's been doing this for at least half a decade. Do not try to rationalize her actions. Fianna Mac Banain is a murderer, and tomorrow, you will become her."

Fourteen

Uisce agus Fothraigh
(*Water and Ruins*)

So this is what it was like to be reborn, Anne thought. Lady Anne Doyle, wrapped in linen, lay in the ground. Miss Fianna Mac Banain had done her duty and killed the lady. Another success in a long career of death. Their plan had worked . . . so far.

The sweeping folds of the cape enveloped Anne as she stood on the deck of the small ship, her eyes fixed on the land ahead. She'd said goodbye to her home once again, without a promise or guarantee to when she'd return. Wales stretched out in front of her, from one end of the sea to the next.

Charles's ship sailed the seas somewhere behind them, while she traveled aboard the hired vessel, a transaction Devon managed with little difficulty. An assassin would not have trouble finding her way back to England, to her employer. To the world, Anne Doyle died in a tragic accident, and she had no way to tell her family. Devon assured her that Charles and Devon would know it was a farce.

"How?" she had asked.

Devon had smiled at her the way only he could and said,

"They just know."

Anne understood that to mean he had sent one of his cryptic messages, but it did little to reassure her.

Her only consolation was knowing her mother and sister had no contact with the world beyond Greyson Hall. Haverly and Nessa had sworn to keep her secret, so for now, Anne was the murderess Fianna. Devon had been right about someone watching Fianna, for before Anne boarded the ship, a man approached, handed her an envelope, and then disappeared into the mist.

"Are you ready?"

The deep familiar voice calmed Anne's nerves. Not another soul stood on the deck. The fierce ocean winds kept them inside. "Impersonation proved easier than I thought."

"You're not done yet." Devon stood a few feet away, braced against the railing. "They'll have someone else waiting at the docks. The man in Ireland would have sent a telegram telling them you're coming."

Waves crashed against the ship, pushing the vessel home. "What if this one knows Fianna?"

"You are Fianna. Remember that, and you'll do well."

Anne sneaked a glance from beneath her hood. "And who pray tell, are you?"

Devon chuckled and turned so his back leaned against the railing. "A gentleman gambler traveling from port to port."

"You don't look like you."

"That is the idea, my dear." Devon pushed away from the railing and splayed his arms around her, leaning into her back, his hands covering hers on the railing. "No one would think it odd for a gambler to seduce an assassin, certainly not her employer."

Anne closed her eyes and for a moment allowed her body to lean back into his. She knew it would not last, but even the few seconds proved unsettling. His warm breath caressed her cheek as he leaned farther into her, his lips close to her ear.

"When the ship docks, proceed to the carriages. You have money to spare, but do not flaunt it. Fianna would not wish to bring attention to herself. I will follow."

"They'll see you."

"No, they won't. Do you still have the dagger I gave you?"

Anne blushed from the memory of Devon securing the blade to her leg. She nodded.

Devon's hand brushed over the top of her arm. "Your shoulder?"

"The pain is manageable."

"Good."

Devon's warmth left her body, and when she turned around, the deck was empty.

Aberystwyth, West Wales
February 1892

DEVON SAT IN THE hotel dining room for an hour, watching every man and woman who came down or went up the main staircase. Another hour passed and Devon suspected the man he'd been waiting for had arrived. Middle-class, but not too low that the hotel wouldn't admit him. To Devon's surprise, the man walked past the front desk and directly to the stairs. Devon followed him to the third floor and saw the man stop in front of Anne's room. He slipped an envelope beneath the door and quickly left the way he came.

Ten minutes later, not another guest or hotel worker had stepped into the hallway. Devon reached Anne's room, and using the extra key she had procured for him, let himself into the room. She stood near the door reading a single sheet of paper. Her face appeared paler than usual.

"What is it?" Devon took the paper from her and scanned the few lines.

"They want Fianna to kill again . . . for her usual payment."

Devon walked into the room and tossed the paper and envelope into the fire. "You're not Fianna in this sense. Don't think about it because she won't kill again."

"Do you think they've arrived?"

Devon nodded and guided her to the single chaise in the room. "I've received word, and I've sent a telegram to Charles. Everything is going as planned, and you will soon be back with your family. This farce won't last long, but it has allowed us the time we need."

Anne brushed a hand across her face, but Devon stopped her hand from doing any further damage to his work. "That disguise has to work a little while longer. Once you leave this hotel, you can shed the façade."

"You've already done away with the gambler. Who is this new man?"

"You don't like it?"

Anne laughed and tugged on the long black hair flowing in loose waves over his shoulders. "You look like a pirate."

"Then I've succeeded."

"Will you be near tonight?"

Devon's relished in her closeness. "I'll be near."

Anne leaned back. "You look tired, Devon. Sleep tonight. We've made it this far without incident."

Luck had been on their side but that's what bothered Devon. He could attribute their luck to years of skill and careful planning, but it was all too tidy for him. Devon expected Gaspar, or at least one of his men, to bring Anne/Fianna in for questioning. Charles expected them at Greyson Hall in three days, and it would not be an easy journey for her. Devon preferred to travel by coach and avoid crowds, but the train would help them cross the same distance in half the time.

He studied her, worrying over the dark circles around her eyes. "Are you still in any pain?"

"Only when I move my shoulder too much, but otherwise I'm healing." Anne leaned back against him. "When this is all over, I want to sleep for a week."

Devon held her close and pressed his lips to the top of her head. "Sleep now. I'm not going anywhere." Anne didn't have to be told twice and lowered herself into the closest chair. Within seconds, her breathing slowed. Careful of her wound, Devon lifted her in his arms and carried her to the large bed. He removed her shoes and stockings and loosened the back of her dress, but he dared not do any more. Devon thought of the suite down the hall and the warm bed waiting for him. Anne was right, he needed to sleep, but he could not leave her. For Charles's sake or for his own.

He had chosen their route because the captain of the small ship on which they gained passage traveled often from the Wexford coast to Aberystwyth, and from there the train could take them safely into England, but someone had anticipated their route, leaving him to believe Fianna had planned to travel on the same passenger ship. It seemed Fianna's mind worked similar to Devon's, much to his annoyance.

Devon returned to the chaise and lay down on it the best he could, his legs hanging over the edge. He would sleep later, when she was safe.

ANNE WOKE FROM ONE of the most glorious dreams of her life. Dreaming of Devon came as no surprise since he'd been a constant in her thoughts. A single quilt covered her body, and it was moments before Anne remembered she wasn't at home. Gentle breathing from across the room drew her focus to Devon. She left the bed and walked on bare feet to stand beside the chaise. Even in sleep, he appeared intense. Anne suspected that hiding his emotions was easier while awake.

A faint light from the hallway seeped beneath the door, illuminating another envelope on the floor. Anne stood close to the door but heard nothing. The nondescript envelope was identical to the last, but the message within was quite different. She looked over her shoulder at Devon, reluctant to wake him. Anne read the note—threat—again.

She stood above Devon and lightly touched his shoulder, which is all it took for him to wake. His hand snaked out and grabbed her arm, but he immediately released her when recognition dawned.

"What's happened?" He moved off the chaise and swore. "How long have I been asleep?"

"You don't lack for quick reflexes asleep or awake." Anne passed him the letter. "This was slipped under the door like the last one."

Devon's quick study of her began at her feet and traced every inch of her body, before he put his attention to reading. "You're not going."

"This could be a chance for us to learn more or to find the evidence needed for you to legally take in Lord Gaspar."

Devon crumbled the paper and tossed it in the fire. "I said no."

"And I want to do this." Anne stood almost toe-to-toe with Devon, not in the least intimidated by his towering frame.

"You'll get yourself killed. You die, I'm at fault, and I have no intention of letting you die today, tomorrow, or any other damned day in my lifetime. You're not going."

Devon brushed passed her and walked to the adjoining suite door.

"Don't go." Anne closed the distance between them and pressed her hand to his back. "Please, don't be angry."

"I'm not angry with you." Devon leaned into the door, and after a few deep breaths, turned around and faced her. "You think too much like us, and it terrifies me." His hands gently gripped her arms, holding her steady in front of him. "Don't you understand, it doesn't matter how well a plan is executed, the deeper you get, the greater the risk. For God's sake, Anne, you all but begged me to get you back to your family. We're doing that, with the least amount of risk to you or to them. Three days and you can be back with them, safe until this is all over. None of us should ever have agreed to let you take part."

Anne wished he hadn't said the words, and yet, she could not fault him for wanting to protect her. Devon put high value on Charles's opinion. What he failed to realize was he already knew her better than Charles did and possibly better than her own mother and sister.

"I am a part of this, Devon, deeper than before. Yes, I want to get home, and I'm terrified every time I ask to be given a chance to help you. And then, I think of hiding away while you and the others fight my battles. Don't tell me I can't do this because I'm a woman or because Charles wouldn't like it. I love and respect Charles as family, but my cousin has learned by now that I'm my own person. You know me better now than he ever has. Do you truly believe I cannot do this?"

Devon's penetrating eyes darkened like the sea on a winter's day. Anne wondered at the turbulence behind them, praying he would not ask her to back down.

He said, "I know you can do this, but I also know this time I cannot promise you'll be safe. We don't know who you'll be meeting, and Fianna has given Derek no more information. They could know you're not her, which would make this a trap."

"You'll agree to let me go?"

"I can't." Devon pulled her close to him. "I'm sorry, Anne, but I cannot. We leave in a few hours."

"Forgive me."

Anne waited outside of the Queen's Hotel as instructed, careful not to draw notice to herself. The cold air stung her cheeks, and she resisted the temptation to burrow down into the mink-trimmed black cape. Her insides twisted in an uncomfortable knot of guilt and unease. The hood of her cloak covered her carefully braided hair and long black gown. The knife Devon strapped to her leg offered her some comfort.

Ten minutes and three carriages passed, but no one stopped for her. A man and woman walked out of the hotel, laughing and holding onto one another. Another man in a black frock coat and wide-brimmed top hat walked toward her. The smoke from his cigar billowed and disappeared into the night. The scent of the salty sea permeated the air, and Anne's conscience chose that moment to protest her actions.

A strong arm circled her waist and drew her into the shadows. "Don't say anything."

"I—"

"Not a bloody word."

He gathered her close and dragged her around the corner, away from the street lamps.

"I can explain."

"You damn well better."

Devon's hand swiped roughly through his thick hair, leaving it a disheveled mess. Upon closer inspection, she saw he was without coat, hat, or his gun, for there was no place to conceal it. He held up a crumbled sheet of paper.

"Did you honestly believe this would work? That I would allow you to walk into the snake's den unprotected."

"It's what I've been doing."

"No, it's not, Anne." Devon stepped back and closed his eyes.

His body shook, and it was the first time Anne saw him truly angry.

"I have been there every bloody step of the way. When you thought yourself alone, someone watched over you. You've never been unprotected."

For a man as furious as she believed him to be, Devon held remarkable control over himself. She wished she could say the same for herself. "You should have let me go. We had a chance to end this sooner, to find the evidence you need to—"

Devon slumped forward against her but somehow managed to right himself. Anne stared at the end of a gun barrel, the round opening close enough for her to smell the powder and steel. The second passed and the gun was gone. In the ensuing struggle, Anne was pushed face first against the brick side of the hotel. When she turned, one of Devon's arms was wrapped around the neck of their assailant. Devon stood half a head taller than the attacker and used a hand to pull his arm tight against the man's throat. Anne watched in surprise as the man's eyes fluttered close and his struggles ceased. He collapsed, falling at Devon's feet.

"Devon?"

Devon hoisted the man partway off the ground and dragged him farther into the shadows.

"Say nothing and stay close." Devon looped her arm through his and walked back into the hotel. He didn't stop until they were in her room and the door lock clicked into place.

"What happened out there? You killed that man as if—"

"I didn't kill him." Devon braced one arm against the door. "He'll awaken with enormous pain, but he's not dead. Anne, you can't go off on your own."

"You've likely ruined my cover as Fianna."

"I don't care." Devon leaned back against the door, staring at her. "We don't need the evidence. Charles telegrammed. Patrick has agreed to bring Gaspar in for questioning based upon what we already know. The problem is, no one can find him. Zachary watched him go into his townhouse and never come out, but he's not there."

Anne remained on the other side of the room. "Did you consider that Gaspar might have been at the other end of this meeting?"

Devon pushed away from the door, reaching her in a few slow steps. "Did you consider that he might have slit your throat or worse, given you to his men? Fooling his men, or even him from afar is one thing, but he would have known you're Anne Doyle."

"No."

"No, what?"

Anne straightened to full height, not that it made a difference when standing next to Devon, but she refused to cower. "Do not speak to me as a child. I hadn't considered that he might . . . give me to his men, but I did consider the other risks. I'm not entirely naïve to believe death was not a possibility, but I owe it to my family, Cillian, and my father to take the risk." Anne untied her cape and threw it onto the bed. "I shouldn't have left you the note."

Devon raised his arms and they fell heavy against his sides. "Then why did you? If you believed what you risked was worth your life, why bother to warn me?"

Anne crossed her arms and stared up at him. "I didn't think you would get to me before they did."

She watched Devon rub both hands across his face and hold them there. An odd sound escaped his lips and he dropped his hands. In one swift movement, Anne nestled in his arms. His lips, warm and urgent, pressed against hers. Her anger diffused and a spark ignited. The spellbinding moment lasted only seconds before he backed away. Anne stumbled forward into his arms. He leaned in close and brushed the fallen hair away from her face.

Anne sidestepped him and walked to the window for no other reason than to put some necessary distance between them.

"You shouldn't have done that."

"I know," Devon whispered. "I don't want to fight with you, Anne."

"I don't want to fight with you either." What Anne wanted in this moment, she couldn't have. Foolish dreams for a foolish woman who had spent her life sheltered from love. She wouldn't deny her desire for Devon, neither could she encourage it. Anne could not give herself to this man for only one night, for one night would not be enough. Unlike Charles and Tristan, Anne sensed Devon would not willingly give up his life as an agent. Anne had to consider Claire, if not her own heart.

"We have a task to complete, Devon, and I intend to see it through."

"You're angry. Fine, as am I, but anger isn't going to solve anything right now." Devon opened the wardrobe and the drawers in the bureau and small desk.

"What are you doing?"

"Checking for anything left behind." He closed the last drawer and walked to the bell pull. "Your alias is possibly in shatters, but in case it's not, we won't leave the hotel together. I'll still be able to see you, so do I have your word you'll not try anything else foolish?"

Anne picked up her cape and secured it over her shoulders. "I promise, but if an opportunity presents—"

"You're not serious." Devon shoved his arms into his great coat. "Of course you are. I'm going to leave before they arrive to gather your luggage. Go to the train station, Platform 3." Devon walked to the door, listening for anyone in the hall.

Anne asked, "How long will it take to get to Greyson Hall?"

"We're going to Blackwood Crossing," Devon said before he slipped from the room.

Devon strode across the platform to Derek. "I can't say it's good to see you, brother. You're early. Where's Fianna?"

Derek said, "Secured in the car behind you."

Devon turned and saw their prisoner through the small window. "What are you doing here today? I expected you to follow us in a few days."

"Plans changed. I was going to leave a letter with the train master until I saw you. I updated Charles and he sent another telegram. We're to meet him in Birmingham. Zachary heard a rumor which indicated Gaspar was en route to Wales."

"Damn." Devon looked around at the bustling platform. "Your train will leave soon."

Derek nodded. "And I'll be on it, but what's happened?"

"We'll discuss it when we meet Charles." Devon's eyes met Fianna's through the train window. "Has she said anything else?"

"Clues that mean nothing until she either gives us more or we piece them together."

Devon reeled at the possible discovery. "Anything about the ring or pendant?"

"Nothing."

Devon slowly nodded and said, "Give me five minutes alone with her."

"That's about all you'd have before the train departs."

"I know." Devon squeezed his brother's shoulder before boarding the private car. Fianna's eyes widened a fraction when he approached her, as though she finally registered the danger she could be in. Regardless of her bindings, Devon reminded himself that Fianna Mac Branain was as deadly of an assassin as they'd ever seen.

"Did you kill Lord Doyle?"

Fianna's eyes registered a spark of recognition. Devon advanced, his knife drawn, tapping against his thigh. Devon didn't enjoy violence, but he was no stranger to it. He didn't set out to kill people, but he wouldn't hesitate to take a life if necessary. "Did you kill him?"

"Does it matter now?"

"It does to me and to his family." Devon hunched low enough not to be seen through the window. The blade settled at the base of Fianna's chest. "Did you kill him?"

Fianna ground out her answer between tightened lips. "Yes."

The tip of the knife pressed into the skin beneath her ribs. "You've failed this time."

Fianna's brogue thickened when she spoke. "I did not fail. They want her dead, but they don't tell me why, and I don't care."

"You are the one playing games."

Fianna ignored him. Devon heard the train whistle and glanced out the window to see Derek about to board. "Tell me who hired you to kill Lord Doyle."

"The same man who sent me to kill his daughter."

"Your scar-faced Arawn."

Fianna nodded. "I was sent to kill him and find a ring. I cannot tell you anything more. They will find me, and kill me, even in Newgate, and none of you are worth that fate."

"Why not do the honorable thing with the last days of your life?"

Fianna turned her face away. "Thrust upward into my heart and make it a clean death if you will, but I won't tell you anymore."

Devon sheathed his knife and stepped away. "I believe you."

"If I were an honorable person, I would have told you not to allow Lady Anne to play my part. She will only be safe far away from this, or until he's dead. Until they're all dead."

"Then they'll die." Devon moved toward the door when the final whistle shrilled.

Derek stepped into the car and asked in a low voice, "Did you get what you needed?"

Devon shook his head and moved passed his brother. Fianna called out his name, halting him. She warned, "He won't stop looking for her, and he won't believe she's me. He knows me . . . well. He won't stop until she's dead."

Devon stood with one hand on the railing just outside the car door. The wheels began a slow turn. "If she had not witnessed the boy's death, would he have left her alone?"

"Perhaps." Fianna's deep green eyes stared up at him and her face softened, looking more like Anne than ever before.

Anne watched the passengers board the train when she sensed his presence. He joined her arm with his and led her down the platform to the last car. Without a word, he helped her inside and locked the door behind them.

"We'll have privacy until we reach England."

Anne set her purse on one of the chairs and removed her velvet coat and hat. "That's it?"

Devon lowered the shades on each window. "The greeting I'd prefer would not be appropriate considering you're still angry with me and I with you."

"I'm not angry."

Devon's raised brow and sardonic smile said he didn't believe her.

"Not too angry." Anne walked the length of the car, but there wasn't anywhere to go. "Why are we going to Charles's home instead of to see my family?"

"Because Charles asked us to meet him there."

"We could go to London."

The train pulled away from the station with enough of a lurch for Anne to reach out and grip the back of a seat. Devon clasped onto her arms and held her until she steadied. When she settled into the plush chair, he released her.

"It's not necessary. Gaspar, or his men, will come to you."

"How do you know? He didn't come when I was in Ireland."

Devon stood and filled two glasses with brandy, handed one to her, and then took his seat. "Your assassin has assured me they won't stop until you're dead."

Anne stared at him wide-eyed and swallowed the two fingers of brandy. "Are you trying to scare me?"

"I've already tried, unsuccessfully." Devon drank his brandy at a more leisurely pace. "I don't believe you can be properly scared, though I wish you could. Lord Gaspar could be anywhere, and I see only two solutions. You either disappear until all of this resolved, or we kill him before he gets to you."

Anne's study of Devon revealed nothing because he gave away so little. Despite his show of amusement and passion, and the occasional expression of anger or humor in his eyes, Devon proved to be one of the most contradictory people she'd ever known. If he wasn't, and if it was all for show, Anne could not begin to guess his thoughts, and yet, he seemed to be able to read her as if she was an open book on his lap and he read the pages one by one.

She didn't wish anyone else's death, even if the man deserved it, but she longed for justice, and she would not give up until the truth was uncovered. "Has all of this been for nothing?"

"Not nothing, Anne. Though it may not seem like we've made progress, we know more now. You don't have be the one in the midst of danger all the time in order to see justice done."

"I don't like the waiting or not knowing." She raised the shade on the train window to reveal a winter mist coating the landscape. Anne turned back to Devon and saw that he still watched her. "You said using me as bait was a good idea, but what would you have done differently?"

Devon finished his drink and set the glass on a tray. After a few seconds, he moved to the seat next to her. "What's done is done, Anne."

"Please, I want to know. Did you and Charles agree to my plan to humor me, or would you have done the same thing?"

Anne's heart skipped a little beat when Devon grinned. If he could do that, all was not broken between them. He said, "We agreed to the plan because it had merit. What it did reveal was that Gaspar is coming after you, but not on his own and not directly. Someone else is helping him. I believed that from the beginning."

Curious now, Anne laid her hands on the small table secured to the side of the car. She leaned forward, eager for more information. "Why did you not tell me this?"

Devon shrugged. "I can't prove it. I don't like Lord Gaspar, but even from what little I know of him, he's not the murdering kind—at least not without someone else encouraging him. He doesn't have the mind for it."

"Devon, I swear to you, I saw him slice a knife into Cillian."

"I haven't figured everything out yet, but as I told Charles and Tristan, there's more to this than any of us can see right now. Until we know what ghosts are haunting this case, I cannot go along with any more ideas that will deliberately put you in danger. Fianna managed to get too close."

Anne reached across the table and held onto Devon's strong bare hands. His heat penetrated her leather gloves, and she held fast, needing his strength to course through her. "Fianna wasn't your fault, and you said capturing her has helped. I don't know what happens next, but I do feel . . ." Anne leaned back and released Devon's hands. "Where the water and hills meet the ruins. Devon, I know where they're going!"

Fifteen

Géilleadh
(Surrender)

Thunder cracked and echoed through the night, giving noise to the hail pounding down upon the coach. The horses seemed to lose their footing on the slick roads covered in wet snow. They traveled on, only ten miles from Greyson Hall. Anne held onto whatever she could inside the conveyance, and Devon wondered at the sanity of their driver. Charles had sent one of his men, Hugh, to drive them back to Greyson Hall, but it seemed the man was incapable of handling the weather.

"Are you all right?" He shouted to be heard above the wind.

Anne nodded without releasing her grip on the seat, until Devon opened the door of the coach.

"You're crazy!" Anne yelled.

"We're going to be dead if the driver doesn't slow down."

The wind swung the door open, crashing it into the side of the coach. Devon glanced back to Anne, but she'd already moved to the opposite side. With his back to the gusts of cold air, Devon held onto the door frame and eased himself outside enough to shout to the driver again. He swore, and the words were carried away by the storm.

Blackness surrounded them, offering no hope that help may arrive and stop the rampaging horses. Devon pulled himself up and out, grasped the bar along the top of the moving vehicle, and hoisted his tall frame onto the roof. The driver was nowhere to be seen. The coach bounced, almost knocking him off. He inched his way to the driver's seat and thrust himself forward, the ferocious wind battling his efforts.

"Damn!" Devon fell forward, managing to right himself before he was flung over the side of the coach. The reins lay across the animals' backs. Two failed attempts nearly saw him on the road. He jumped from the seat onto the back of one of the black steeds, an act which only caused the horse to rear back before speeding up. Devon pulled back on the reins and harness, contending with an animal determined to escape the storm.

Rather than stop the team on the road, Devon forced them to veer off to a copse of trees, tugging on the reins until yard by yard, the horses slowed and finally stopped. The trees offered little protection against the fierce hail and wind, thunder causing the skittish team to rear back before settling down. Devon tied off the reins and rushed to the coach door.

Anne huddled against the far seat, her knuckles white and her breathing deep. Devon sat beside her, easing her fingers from around the leather strap hanging by the window. "We're safe."

Her eyes, presently the color of a storm-tossed sea as the waves crashed over the surface, rose to meet his. "Crazy is too mild a term for what you . . . Have you climbed out of a moving carriage before?"

Adrenaline pumped through Devon's blood, but he'd learned over the years to control the rising energy brought on by excitement and fear. Anne may be his match in many things, but he doubted she shared his enthusiasm now that the danger passed.

"Once, though not in the heart of winter." Hail continued to fall outside, and an inspection of the open door revealed one of the hinges had broken.

"What happened? Where's the driver?"

"Missing, but I can't see anything out there. We'll wait until the worst of the storm subsides to travel the last few miles."

Anne nodded and released a slow breath. Devon waited for anger, tears, or a combination of both, but she remained calm despite the turmoil in her eyes.

"You're bleeding." Shaky hands rummaged through her pockets and lifted a folded white handkerchief to his cheek. Devon's hand covered hers, and the linen came away soaked with blood.

"I'm sure it looks worse than it is. I barely feel it."

Surprising him, Anne poked his face, arms, and legs. "You need doctoring."

Devon glanced down to where she parted the torn sides of his trousers, revealing a long gash on his leg. Anne ripped a section of her petticoat, giving Devon a nice view of her trim legs.

"My supplies are in the trunk outside, but this should decrease the bleeding until I have more light and room." She pressed the fabric to the wound and moved his hand to replace hers in applying pressure. "How are you not in pain?"

"I've had worse." Devon raised the cloth to inspect the wound and realized it would need a few stitches. He left the coach and returned a few minutes later with her satchel. "Is this what you wanted?"

Anne nodded and pulled a bottle from the bag. She released a few drops from the bottle onto a torn cloth. "Give me your hand." Anne covered the wound and used a strip of cloth to secure the bandage. "It's not enough but will help clean the wound and slow the bleeding."

"Thank you." Devon made a fist around the bandage.

"I should check for other injuries."

Devon grinned. "As much as I'd enjoy that, the weather has eased enough for me to drive the team, but first I have to go back and look for the driver."

"I'll drive." Anne gathered her skirts together. Devon gently pushed her back into the seat.

"You'll stay here."

"I know how to drive, Devon."

"I don't doubt it." A soft chuckle escaped his lips. "But you're still staying inside. Do it for me." Devon climbed down from the coach, careful to keep his back to Anne. The cut on his leg pained him more than he'd admit to her, at least until they arrived at the house and she let go of any more foolish ideas.

Devon smoothed his hands over the wet coats of the horses. "You've been good chaps. There's a warm stable waiting for you both." The horses flicked their heads as if in agreement and remained still while Devon untied them and climbed onto the coachman's seat. He drove the team back to the point where he estimated the carriage's speed had increased and found the driver.

"Praise to the saints for you, sir." The driver huddled against a large oak, his left leg twisted.

Devon climbed down from the coachman's seat, his leg throbbing with each inch.

Anne poked her head outside of the coach. "Did you find—heavens!" Anne stepped out of the coach and walked around to the driver.

Devon didn't think he'd get back up if he knelt down. "You're going to have to help me, Hugh." The driver lowered his eyes to Devon's leg. "You're bleeding fierce, sir!"

"Not as badly as you are." Devon leaned against the tree, gripped Hugh under his arms, and lifted him up with care.

"Tarnation, sir!"

"I know it hurts, Hugh, but we have to get you inside."

Anne stepped up beside Hugh on the other side. "Lean on me a little, Hugh."

"I couldn't, my lady."

Devon would normally agree, but they had to get out of the rain. "Anne, can you do this?"

Anne nodded and braced herself against Hugh's side. When the driver didn't put his arm around her shoulder, she did it for him. Together, they half carried Hugh the short distance to the coach. Devon heard Anne's labored breathing and lifted the bulk of Hugh's weight away to help her.

"You can't drive in your condition, Devon."

Devon ignored her comment and hoisted her inside. "See what you can do for Hugh." He latched the door and returned to the driver's seat.

An hour later saw them at the gates of Greyson Hall. The front door swung open and Theo, the footman on loan, hurried down the steps carrying an umbrella.

Theo halted mid-stride when he saw the condition of the vehicle. "Are you all right, sir? Is her ladyship—"

"She's unharmed, Theo, but our driver is injured."

"We didn't expect you until tomorrow, sir."

Devon stepped down from the coachman's seat. "How did you know we were coming?" Devon helped Anne from the coach while Theo protected her from the rain.

"His Grace received a telegram from Lord Blackwood yesterday."

Tristan appeared at the doorway, carrying a second umbrella. "What the kind of bloody luck have you had?"

Devon grinned at his friend and stepped beside Tristan, out of the rain. "No luck at all. Our driver, or Charles's man, Hugh, was badly hurt."

"We'll take care of him and meet you inside." Tristan followed the footman, allowing Devon to escort Anne into the mansion.

Once inside, they were divested of their outer clothing. Rhona appeared at the top of the long staircase and hurried down. She pressed a kiss to Devon's cheek and embraced Anne. "Charles told us you'd be coming, but I didn't believe it."

"It's a long story, and one we'll gladly share." Devon run a hand through his sodden hair and accepted a towel from Rhona.

"My mother and sister?" asked Anne.

Rhona was quick to reassure her they were well. "Your mother is resting—as she does often—and Claire is in the kitchen with Rozalyn. She said she likes the smell of cooking, and Rozalyn lets her help. Shall we fetch her?"

"Not yet. Devon needs tending and we have things to discuss—matters I don't want my family hearing."

Tristan and Theo walked in, holding up the driver on either side, the wind howling behind them before Devon rushed to close the door. "The poor chap is unconscious." Tristan leaned down, braced Hugh, and hefted him over his shoulders like a sack of grain.

"Unfortunately, there's little I can do for Hugh's leg. Can we get a proper doctor?" Anne asked.

Theo said, "I can go for a doctor, my lady. There's sure to be one in a nearby village."

"Thank you, Theo." Anne looked pointedly at Devon. "We need to care for your wounds."

Everyone seemed to give Devon a cursory study, but it was Theo who exclaimed, "Good Lord, sir, your leg!"

Devon glanced down to his soaked trousers and saw blood had seeped through Anne's petticoat bandage and presently dripped down his limb.

Anne instructed Devon to follow her into the study where she placed a cloth on the sofa for Devon to sit and lay his leg upon. Amused with her, Devon complied, aware the others hovered nearby, seemingly ready to step in and help, if necessary. However, once a footman came in with tea, followed by a maid carrying a tray with hot water and clean cloths, Anne thanked them and appeared as though she wanted to dismiss them all.

Tristan smirked and shook his head. "You're not getting rid of me so easily, Lady Anne."

"Nor I," Rhona added.

Devon remained quiet while Anne ministered to his wounds. He was no longer amazed at her ability to take charge of a situation and do what must be done. He thought about how she looked when discussing the brutal murder she'd witnessed, but Devon had come to see it was the act itself and not the blood or death that sickened her.

"You need at least half a dozen stitches to close this laceration. Would you like to be put out?"

Tristan coughed on the brandy he'd poured himself and smiled. "Put out? Whiskey works wonders."

Anne shot Tristan a disapproving glance and looked back at Devon.

He thought his friend's suggestion held merit but thought better against saying so. "I've had—"

"Worse. Yes, you've said. Please keep still."

Anne cleaned her hands and set out a variety of small bottles, a scalpel, scissors, thread, and a small needle.

"Rhona, would you mind ordering tea, and please ask for a pitcher of fresh water with an extra drinking glass."

If Rhona thought the question odd, she remained silent, but Devon didn't miss the questioning look she gave Anne's back.

"Tristan, would you please come over to this side and hold his leg?" Tristan did as instructed while Anne cleaned the wound first with water, followed with a clear liquid that caused Devon's leg to jerk. "This is going to hurt."

Devon shared a glance with Tristan and thought about the

incident years ago in Scotland when they'd all been through worse and seen much worse. For all the pain inflicted on others during the execution of their duties, this suffering was the least Devon would endure. He steadied his breathing, nodded to Anne, and closed his eyes. The first few threads of the needle through his skin burned, but something about the way she massaged the skin along the wound lessened the stabbing pain, making her ministrations almost bearable.

Once she finished with the stitches, she wrapped a fresh bandage around the wound. "This should hold if you don't exert yourself."

Theo entered the room with a tea service. Rhona thanked the footman and poured Anne a cup. Instead of accepting it for herself, she handed it to Devon.

"You've lost too much blood, and this will help. Once you've finished, you'll drink water until your color has returned."

Devon accepted the cup, watching her over the rim.

"You should be resting," said Anne.

"I'll rest when you do. Besides, you're not going anywhere."

Devon shifted but decided against moving from the sofa with Anne in the room. "Now is as good a time as any to tell you what's happened. Will Alaina be joining us?"

"She's asleep. I'll fill her in later." Devon saw the worry etched around Tristan's eyes. "Why did you veer from the plan and come here? Charles's telegram gave us no details."

"Our lovely assassin said something to Anne before we left her company. A riddle of sorts that Anne has unraveled. The location is here in Northumberland."

"The location to what?" asked Rhona.

"Where I hope the men behind this will meet next." All eyes turned to Anne. "Coventina's Well. I didn't know what Fianna had meant by her words, but I remember something written in my father's papers."

Devon shifted, wincing at the sharp pain when his stitches pulled. "I've read your father's papers, every word of them, and I read no mention of Coventina's Well."

Rhona raised her hand as though a schoolgirl in a classroom. "For those of us unfamiliar with this Coventina, who is she, or what is it?"

Anne poured a glass of water and mixed in a white powder before passing it to Devon. "Coventina is a Roman-British goddess, but who she was isn't important. It's the place itself."

Tristan was the only one who remained standing, his arms crossed and expression grim. To Anne, he seemed like a man used to commanding, and she wondered if that was due to his former position within the agency or to his dukedom.

He said, "You're certain what Fianna said meant Coventina's Well?"

"As Devon says, I know, but I don't have the evidence to make it a fact. My father's journal talked about a place he once visited, and he described it much like Fianna had. He didn't say specifically that it was Coventina's Well, but he was in this region at the time and geographically, it's the only place that makes sense."

Devon shrugged and looked at Tristan. "It would be smart."

Tristan nodded in agreement. "The area is private enough. I'll go tomorrow." His suggestion was met with two vocal objections. "Devon, you can't ride yet, and Anne, you'll be safer here."

Anne stood and faced Tristan. "I'm going. Devon, there is no humor in this."

Devon's grin mingled with light laughter. "Tristan, you may as well give in because she doesn't give up. However, give me two days for this leg to heal. I'm going with you."

Anne turned on Devon. "Two days is not long enough."

"Then you don't go."

Anne shifted her focus to Rhona, hoping to find support from more understanding minds. Rhona's answer was a smile she didn't bother to hide.

"Anne, I agree with you. I've been in a similar predicament, but . . ." Rhona looked from one man to the other, her expression no longer showing amusement. "These men have saved my life, and I've lived through what happens when someone tries to resolve matters on their own. I didn't listen, and it nearly got me killed."

Frustrated, Anne paced. "What about Fianna and your brothers?"

"Derek will escort Fianna to London where the agency is mostly like to become involved in her questioning."

"If you couldn't force her to talk, how do you know they can?"

Devon managed to rise from the sofa and gritted his teeth against the ache. He stopped her pacing and held her arms close to her body. "You're making me dizzy. I believe Fianna has said all she's willing to tell us, for now. My brothers will draw the rest of the information from her, but it will take time."

Anne addressed Tristan and Rhona. "Would you please give us a few moments?"

Tristan nodded once, but Rhona hesitated briefly before finally agreeing. "I'll look in on Christian." They exited the room, leaving the door ajar.

"After all the time we've already spent together, she worries about what's proper?" Anne inched closer to Devon. "I've been my own mistress for many years now."

Devon's arms cradled her in the circle of his embrace. "Rhona isn't worried about propriety. She's doing what she believes best for you in Charles's absence."

"Your supervisor. Will he call you in?"

"I'm still here, aren't I?"

They stood in a house filled with people who would object to Devon's thoughts, and he didn't care. Devon drew her closer. Without encouragement, she laid her head against his chest and embraced him.

"Devon?"

His chin rested against her silky hair. He had no desire to ever let her go again. "Hmmm?"

"What will you do when all of this over?"

Devon's heart mimicked the increased pounding of Anne's against his chest. He had always believed himself incorruptible, honor-bound to serve his country until death, and yet, the temptation to defy his duty grew stronger every moment he was with her. He looked into the beautiful green eyes he'd come to love. He wasn't ready to answer her questions.

"Promise me something, Anne." Her eyes glistened, though he didn't know why. "When this is over—"

Her voice was barely above a whisper. "Yes?"

Devon lowered his lips to meet hers. Every ending in his body responded, and he knew hers had, too, when she flattened her body against his. Running his hand over her back, he deepened the kiss. The soft moan that escaped her lips told Devon he'd gone far enough. He broke their connection and set her away from him.

"Forgive me."

Anne sensed the willingness of her own body and realized her mind was not far behind. Consequences be damned, she wanted Devon—all of him. She lost herself in every stroke and touch of his fingers over her back and up into her hair, driving her need and his.

He set her away and released her arms, leaving her cold. She watched him limp from the room without a backward glance. Forgive him for what? For kindling her passion, for showing her kindness, and bringing laughter back into her life? She needed the cold winds off the coast to clear her thoughts. Anne longed for the cliffs near Ballinrock Castle where she would seek solace when her mother went through a difficult period or when the estate funds dropped so low she could no longer keep the servants. The salty sea air would caress and envelop her while the waves crashed against the rocks. She'd never felt more alive than those moments by the sea . . . never, until Devon.

Anne didn't want to know there was a better life out there, especially one she couldn't have. She rushed from the study and collided with Theo. He steadied her and immediately backed away.

"My sincerest apologies, my lady."

"It's not your fault, Theo. I didn't know you'd returned. Was the doctor available?"

The footman stood almost as tall as Devon and her cousin, and beneath his rigid exterior, she saw kindness in his shrewd eyes. "He was, my lady. Dr. Abbot was his name. They took Hugh with them in their ambulance."

"Took Hugh where?"

"To the village, my lady." Theo appeared hesitant as though he didn't wish to upset her. "His Grace spoke with Dr. Abbot. I'm sorry, my lady, was that wrong?"

"No, of course not." Anne would have liked the doctor to examine Devon's leg, but she understood the urgency to get Hugh proper care. As it was, the poor man may walk with a limp the rest of his life, if he didn't lose his leg.

Anne didn't want to think about Hugh or Devon or anyone else. "My cape please, Theo."

"It's snowing, my lady, and Mr. Clayton has asked Rozalyn to prepare a light dinner."

Anne softened her request with a smile but offered little explanation. "I'm in need of fresh air, and I promise not to be too long."

"Very good, my lady." Theo returned a minute later with her cape and gloves.

"Thank you." Anne stepped outside and welcomed the frigid air. Her boots left small indents in the wet grass, and the falling snow soon filled each footstep with a fresh layer of white. Halfway across the lawn, she turned back to study the mansion. The home stood as a sentinel on the hill watching over the vast, barren landscape dotted with trees, hills, and the wild creatures that called the northland their home.

A tug of worry formed in her heart over her mother and sister. She needed to see them, yet she had escaped instead of seeking them out. Knowing her family was here while she traveled with Devon had eased the burden she sometimes carried when they were near. She loved them both dearly and would never leave them alone, but these last days and weeks had ignited a passion for more than just the man who kept her safe. The experiences inflamed her desire to see what the world held for her. Healing had been her solace these many years, a way for her to go into the world and help others, and it had been enough—until Devon came into her life.

Anne wished the circumstances had been different, but she could not regret Devon's presence in her life, no matter how unpleasant the events. Whether fate or luck brought them together, with him, Anne believed she could face anything. Fearless and dependable, he didn't lie to her and he didn't try to appease her with false answers. Anne wished to stay with him for as long as she could, a truth she could hardly confess to him.

A light flickered in the distance, drawing Anne closer to the stables, but it quickly disappeared. The winds increased, tossing the hood of her cape off and almost knocking her to the ground. Snow quickly turned to rain. Anne stumbled over the grass, falling forward on the slick snow. She heard shouts, but a crack of thunder cut through the words. She pushed her body up and knelt in the rain, but she wasn't there long. Strong arms lifted her to her feet.

"Can you walk?"

Anne nodded and pulled the edges of her cape closer together. Tristan ran alongside her toward the house, her feet slipping once more. Before she could fall to the ground, he'd lifted her into his arms. Anne didn't know how long it took to reach the house, but when her sodden cape was removed from her shoulders, two pairs of eyes stared down at her—one held disappointment, the other anger.

Theo gave them both a small towel and moved away as silent as a grave.

"Thank you." Anne brushed her wet skirts, but they still clung to her legs. The towel soaked up the water dripping from her hair, and she used the distraction to avoid making eye contact with Devon. When he said nothing, she shook off her cowardice and looked up at him. Anne realized Tristan had come looking for her without his hat or even a coat but didn't shiver from the cold as she did.

"I'm sorry you had to come after me, Tristan. One of the servants was also out in this storm, so I don't believe . . . Devon?"

Devon's cheek twitched, an affectation Anne hadn't noticed before now. He turned and limped away, leaving Anne alone in the foyer with Tristan.

"He's angry."

Tristan sighed. "He's angry that you might have been in danger, and his injury prevented him from running after you. Devon does not do well injured. In fact, none of us do, but Devon is different."

"I wasn't gone long, and I could see the house." Anne realized how foolish the words sounded even as they tumbled from her lips. "I'll apologize. How did you find me out there?"

Tristan's grin reminded her of Devon's. "Theo came to us

immediately. You should know, Lady Anne, that everyone here is charged with your safety, even if it means protecting you from yourself."

"I didn't intend to worry anyone. I'll make this right."

Tristan offered her an encouraging smile. "Devon will come around, just give him a little time."

Anne watched Tristan walk up the stairs and disappear around a corner. She couldn't wait until morning to apologize to Devon. Anne and her family were guests in his home, and they'd all gone to considerable trouble to help her. Her erroneous actions may not have been intentional, but Devon obviously thought otherwise.

When she reached the upstairs hall, Tristan's suggestion seemed the better choice, so she passed Devon's room and entered hers. A single lamp burned near the bed and the fire blazed low in the hearth.

"I'm not angry with you, Anne." Devon emerged from the shadows, causing enough of a start to set Anne's heart racing.

"What are you doing in here?"

Devon stood only a few feet from her now. "I didn't want you to think I was upset. We're all overly cautious right now."

Anne held his smoldering gaze with her own. "You shouldn't be here."

"I know."

With a flash of movement, she was in his arms. Her breath quickened and her fingers caressed, gliding over his taut body. His lips moved lower, skimming her neck, and lower still until she arched her back and waited, anticipating. His warm breath excited every nerve, every point of pleasure. His hands took exquisite care with her body, allowing no curve or hidden place to go untouched. She arched again, unable to stop the natural response when his lips crept below her bodice line, moving aside the constricting fabric, freeing herself for his pleasure, her pleasure.

His strong arms brought her nearer, both in body and soul, until nothing stood between them except the clothes they both fought to remove. He wouldn't allow her to rush, though her body ached for it—demanded it.

She pulled him closer, begging with her hands, her body, for him to release the building pressure. He slowed his exploration, distressing her. She reached out, no longer willing to wait for whatever may come. Her lips found his, the friction making hers more sensitive. He worshiped her, drawing her in, deepening their kiss in a way she never imagined they could. She succumbed willingly, denying herself any control for just one more moment, one more of anything.

He released her. His eyes, dark with passion, met hers and moved inch by inch down her body. She stood, unmoving except for her thundering heart and rising chest. He turned her, his fingers deftly undoing each button down, drawing the edges away. His lips soon followed the same path, moving down the line of her back and up again, warming her neck as his hands circled her, pulling her back toward him. Without thought, she reached behind and gave herself up to his hands, his lips, his knowledge of her body. He turned her again until she faced him once more. With a gentleness she expected from this man, he lifted her into his arms.

"I won't be able to walk away. Tell me now."

"Your wound."

Devon chuckled and wrapped his hands in her long hair. "What wound?"

Anne smoothed her hand over his cheek and smiled. Taking her touch as the answer they both wanted, Devon carried her from the room.

Devon knew the servants would be in their own beds, thinking he had done the same. He could have remained in her room, no one ever knowing, but he wanted her in his bed. He carried her down the hall, nearly to his room, when a sense of foreboding hit him with a force he couldn't ignore. He stopped, closed his eyes, and listened.

Anne must have sensed something was terribly wrong, too, but he could not give her an answer he didn't have. His only longing was to continue with this night, to remove everything between them, to make her his. Not even knowing what Charles would do to him, what it might do to their friendship if it became known, would not have tempered the raging passion that had overpowered Devon since he met Anne. But for her safety, he would give up anything, do anything, and commit any inconceivable wrong. Giving her up this night was unimaginable, but he had no choice.

"Devon?"

He lowered her to the carpet and cupped her face, brushing his lips over hers.

"What's wrong?"

"I don't know, but something here in this house isn't right. I feel it, Anne." He guided her to his room, though not for the purpose he had planned. He searched the darkened corners and adjoining rooms before locking the inner doors and handing her the key. "When I leave this room, lock the door behind me. Do not answer any knock or open to anyone until you hear me."

"Don't search alone. You don't—"

Devon silenced her quiet plea with another kiss and caress. "Lock the door."

Sixteen

Brón agus Misneach
(Sorrow and Courage)

Sconces lit the wide corridor that ran from the family bedrooms to the guest quarters. Devon knew Tristan and Alaina shared a room next to Rhona. Kathryn and Claire occupied adjoining rooms next to Anne, leaving three rooms empty between his and the others. Silence filled the cavernous house, and yet when he didn't move, didn't breathe, Devon swore he heard something. His pistol sat on the bureau in his room, but his spare knife was secured in his boot. His hand reached down and raised the hem of his pants. A moan? A cry? Then footsteps, too light to be Tristan's, and a lantern illuminated the great stairway.

"Mr. Clayton?"

"Rozalyn." Devon dropped his leg and walked toward the maid, lifting the tray from her hands. "Whatever are you doing up at this hour? Is someone ill?"

"No, sir. Her ladyship, that is Lady Doyle, often wakes in the middle of the night. I fetched her some warm milk and hot tea."

Devon glanced first at the offerings on the tray and then down the hall to Kathryn's door. "Is her ladyship awake now?"

Rozalyn bobbed her head. "She awakened a short while ago. His Grace suggested I set up a bed in her ladyship's room so I didn't have to walk up and down the stairs all night. Was I wrong, sir?"

Devon smiled to ease the young maid's worry. "Not wrong at all, but this is hardly fair to you. I'll inform Lady Anne of the situation in the morning, but for now, let us see after Lady Doyle."

Rozalyn appeared torn between obeying the master of the house and speaking up about the master performing servants' tasks. Devon made the decision easy for her and started down the hall, eager to get the maid safely inside Kathryn's bedroom. The unease which prompted him to leave Anne remained. Rozalyn opened the door and turned to accept the tray. Devon peeked over the petite maid's head and paused.

"Did you say Lady Doyle was awake?"

"Yes, sir, but she claims the light sometimes bothers her and blows out the lantern when she's alone."

Devon brushed past the maid, tray still in hand, and set it on the edge of the bed. "Come over here with that lamp." The maid hovered close enough to light the area around the bed, but it was empty. "Where is she?"

"I don't know, sir. She was here just a short time ago. Perhaps she is wandering the halls. I'll go—"

"A party I don't know about?"

Devon glanced to the dark doorway where Tristan stepped into the lamp's light. Devon gave his friend a quick shake of his head and said, "It seems her ladyship has taken to sleepwalking. Rozalyn, please go and wake Theo and we'll start a search of the house." He needed to tell Anne, but he couldn't ask the maid to go to his room and fetch her. The maid left and Tristan came into the room.

"I do believe your house is haunted, old chap."

"Then we're both hearing ghosts, though it's possible what we both heard was Kathryn wandering."

"Where's Anne?"

Devon ignored the question and lit two more lamps in the room.

Tristan walked to the adjoining door leading into Claire's room. Movement drew his gaze to the bed, but it took a few seconds for his eyes to adjust to the darkness. A willowy figure cloaked in darkness stood beside the bed. Chanting? He couldn't tell what she said, but it wasn't English. "Lady Doyle?"

Devon headed toward the door so he could fetch Anne, but he shifted direction at Tristan's words. He reached the door soon enough to see a woman with her arm raised to her chest and a single blade pointing downward. Tristan lunged at her and Kathryn's knife plunged into his arm.

"Good God!" Devon surged toward them and wrapped his arms around Kathryn's waist, pinning her arms to her sides. She released a high-pitched shriek before bringing the steel down once more, but Devon managed to deflect her arm, tear the knife out of her hand, and throw it across the room. Kathryn kicked and pounded him with her fists, but Devon held fast. Claire's muffled moans turned to cries when her eyes opened.

Tristan ignored the blood oozing from his wound and grabbed Kathryn's legs.

"Theo will be . . ." Rozalyn stood in the doorway, eyes wide and transfixed on the grisly scene unfolding before her.

"Rozalyn, see to Claire!" Devon's shouted order went unanswered for a few seconds before the maid hurried past the trauma to the young girl crying for her mother. Together, Devon and Tristan carried Kathryn into the other room, but they now had company.

"Mother!"

Anne rushed forward, but Rhona pulled her back toward the

door. "Let me go!"

Rhona held tight and shook her head. "Not yet. Look."

Now subdued, Kathryn lay limp in their arms when they set her on the bed. Devon looked up and nodded once to Anne who quickly rushed to her mother's side. "So much blood." She poked and prodded, searching for the source.

"It's not hers, Anne." Devon pointed to Tristan.

Tristan leaned against the wall and closed his eyes, trying to control his breathing and heartbeat.

Anne's eyes glistened with tears begging for their release, but she held them back and exhaled a shaky breath. "I need my bag from my bedroom and clean towels. Hurry!" With one hand touching Tristan, Anne looked down at her mother who appeared to now sleep with the angels. The slow rise and fall of her chest belied the gruesomeness of the scene Anne had witnessed only moments ago.

Alaina stood at the door, a hand pressed to her chest. "The screams woke Christian. What's happened? No!" Alaina saw her husband across the room and hurried to his side.

Tristan ground out his words, causing Anne further worry when his skin whitened.

"I'll be all right, love."

Alaina hovered near the bed, and though Anne had heard tales of the woman's past adventures, she was in no condition to watch what Anne was about to do. "Alaina, I need you to wait in the other room."

"No."

Anne looked at Tristan, silently pleading him to help.

Tristan smiled at his wife. "Love, I'm in good hands. You saw how well she cared for Devon's leg."

"Tristan, I can't."

Tristan squeezed his wife's hand, though Anne saw the effort cost him dearly.

He said, "Rozalyn is in the other room with Claire, but neither of them is in a good state after what they saw."

Anne waited for Alaina to make her decision and with great reluctance, Alaina kissed her husband and stepped away. "You promise he'll be all right?"

"I promise." Anne knew the wound itself wasn't fatal, but any more blood loss could prove otherwise. She watched Alaina walk in halting steps toward the other room, as though her own body objected to her departure. Anne exhaled the breath she'd been holding, relieved she could work on Tristan's wound without his wife's emotions distracting her.

"I have them! I sent Theo downstairs for hot water." Rhona rushed into the room and set the bag on the bed, her gaze drawn to Kathryn. "Should this be done here with her there?"

"Tristan shouldn't be moved."

Devon lifted Kathryn into his arms. "I'll put her in your room, Anne."

Anne nodded and guided Tristan to the edge of the bed. "I may need your help here, Rhona. Perhaps Rozalyn can sit with my—"

"No." Devon stopped at the doorway, Kathryn's head against his shoulder. "Rozalyn saw too much. It wouldn't be fair to ask her."

A timid voice came from the doorway. "I can do it, sir." Rozalyn huddled halfway between the bedrooms.

Anne's heart ached for the young woman whose courage was to be admired. She had only seen her mother in a fit once before, but never with such devastating results. Anne didn't yet know how Tristan received the gouge in his arm but knew her mother seemed to be the cause.

"You don't have to, Rozalyn."

"It's all right, my lady."

She watched Devon carry her mother out of the room and

rummaged through her bag for a small bottle of liquid. "Take this, Rozalyn. If my mother wakes, mix three drops of this in a small glass of water and get her to drink it. It will keep her calm until I can see after her."

The maid clutched the bottle to her chest as though it might be her salvation and followed Devon from the room. Anne turned back to Tristan and asked him to lie back on the bed and spread his arm.

Theo carried in a bowl of water, steam rising from the surface. A heavy iron kettle rested on the same tray. Tristan's eyes remained closed. "Can you manage with me upright?"

"I'll try." Anne covered the bed with an extra quilt and laid a towel over it. She pulled out the instruments and ointments she would need and pointed to each one, telling Rhona the names. "When I ask for something, please pass it to me. Theo, please prepare a bath in His Grace's bedroom. It should only be half full."

Devon returned to the room and said, "Your mother is still asleep."

"Rozalyn?"

"She's shaken but resilient."

"Devon, would you please mix this powder with hot water to form a paste?" Anne handed him a small glass jar that held yellowish-brown nettle root powder. "Not too thick. The consistency of mud after a light rain."

Anne washed her hands and set to work on Tristan's arm, but the wound was far worse than she initially thought. "Would you like something strong to drink?"

Tristan surprised her by managing to grin, though it obviously pained him. "I thought strong spirits weren't allowed in your surgery."

Anne returned the grin. "We'll make an exception."

"I promise not to move."

Anne turned back to her task, taking special care to excise the edges of the cut before sewing them together. The depth of the cut worried her more, for she saw it had sliced through muscle, and she couldn't know what had been hit to cause such bleeding. "This may scar."

Tristan choked out a laugh. "Alaina won't mind."

Anne smiled in relief at his good spirits. She accepted the nettle paste from Devon. She dipped clean fingers into the paste and spread the substance over the wound, careful not to disturb the stitches. "It will aid with the healing."

Almost finished, Anne said, "Rhona, pour some of the iodine onto the bandages. It's labeled and in the large amber bottle. I'll be ready for them soon." Anne dabbed around the wound to remove the excess blood. She wrapped the treated bandages around Tristan's arm and covered those with a second strip of bandage. "A doctor should look at this arm, and your leg, Devon. Can we fetch one from the village?"

Tristan shook his head. "That won't be necessary. You've patched me up after worse, Devon, and Anne's a far better nurse than you." His grin, though strained, brought smiles all around.

"Very well, but if you feel any pain in a few days, or have trouble with your arm, we're sending for a doctor."

Tristan's slow nod was offered with some reluctance. "Agreed."

"Rhona, will you please help me move everything into Tristan and Alaina's room?" Anne motioned for Devon to come around the other side of the bed to help Tristan. Devon draped Tristan's arm around his shoulder and helped his friend stand.

Concern etched in lines around Anne's eyes when she noticed Devon's slight wince. "How is your leg?"

"I can manage."

Anne dropped a heaping spoonful of herbs and leaves into the kettle and left the tray for Rhona to carry. She put all her other supplies back into her satchel and stood on Tristan's other side. "We'll manage it together."

When they entered Tristan's bedchamber, Anne heard soft singing drift in from the other room. Devon assisted Tristan to the bed, leaving Anne free to walk into the small dressing room that currently served as a nursery to Christian. Alaina sat in a large wooden rocking chair, Claire snuggled in her lap. Her smooth voice, as pretty as the stars twinkling on a clear night sky, filled the room while tears drifted down her cheeks. When Alaina looked up and saw Anne, the singing stopped.

"He's going to be fine, Alaina."

"Thank you." Anne rushed over and helped move Claire from Alaina's lap to the large chaise and covered her with a quilt. "She doesn't understand what's happened."

Anne smoothed the blond hair back from her sister's forehead. "Neither do I. What say you we find out?" They returned to find Devon in discussion with Tristan and Rhona nowhere in sight.

Devon moved away from the bed to make room for Alaina and held out his hand to Anne. "Rhona has gone to check on your mother, but I imagine you'd like to see her."

Anne nodded. "Claire is sleeping, and I do need to see my mother, but I need to know what happened first." Anne caught the shared glance between Tristan and Devon. "If she's a danger, I need to know."

Devon's arm circled her waist, and Anne hoped he never stopped touching her. "She's not well, but there's more."

"What was my mother doing when this happened?"

Tristan shifted to make room for Alaina by his side and said, "I heard chanting, words I didn't understand. They sounded more like Rhona's old Scots language. When she turned, her eyes didn't look like hers."

Anne followed along, but they held something back.

Devon said, "She held a blade above Claire while she slept, the same knife that injured Tristan. Your mother was mad, but Tristan is right, there's more to it. I need to ask her some questions."

A deep and foreboding notion etched its way through Anne's thoughts and over her heart. She held Devon's hand when they walked into her mother's chamber. Rhona and Rozalyn sat on either side of the bed, and to Anne's surprise, her mother sat up, braced against the pillows and headboard.

Rhona handed a teacup to Rozalyn and met the pair by the door. When she spoke, it was a whisper. "Your mother refused the drink. She doesn't understand why she's in here, or what's going on. I don't believe she's aware of what's happened."

Anne studied her mother, who presently stared at her from across the room. The woman lying in her bed looked like her mother, down to the questions lurking in her eyes. "Charles is going to want to know what's happened, but I don't know what to tell him. Rhona, I haven't the right to ask for more help—"

"Of course you do."

Grateful, Anne reached out and squeezed Rhona's hand. "Would you stay with Claire for a short while? I'll bring her in here with me, but she's sleeping. I don't want her to go back into the bedroom where it happened."

Rhona leaned forward, embraced Anne, and pressed a gentle kiss on her cheek. "Leave her to me, and don't worry about Charles. You're family, Anne, and nothing else matters."

Devon called Rozalyn over when Anne replaced her at Kathryn's side. "Go and sleep now. There's nothing more to do here tonight, and you've been through an ordeal."

The maid glanced back at Anne and her mother. "It breaks my heart, sir, to see her ladyship and Lady Anne suffer so."

Devon contemplated the young woman, who in truth looked only a few years Anne's junior. She'd risen to the tasks as they came, no matter how difficult. He would have to speak with Tristan about releasing Rozalyn from his service so she could remain with Kathryn—if that was her desire. He knew they could trust Rozalyn, and a familiar face could be a comfort to her.

"Your compassion does you credit. Go now and rest."

Rozalyn bowed her head once and said, "I will, sir, thank you. I'll just see to the fires first." The maid quietly exited the room.

"Devon?"

Anne's questioning voice brought him to her side, but it was Kathryn's expression that drew his notice. Gone was the woman who held a knife above her daughter while she slept. No longer present was the woman who thrust her blade in Tristan's arms and thrashed as though hell's demons had risen from their graves.

"Where is Claire? Anne says I cannot see her."

Devon lowered himself until he leaned back on his heels and braced against the arm of Anne's chair. Kathryn followed his movements, her eyes blank and uncertain. Either she truly didn't realize what happened, or she was the best liar Devon had ever seen.

"Claire is resting now. Do you know why you're in here, Lady Doyle?"

Kathryn looked away while smoothing the quilt covering her legs. "I'd like to see my daughter now."

"Perhaps later, Mother, but you need to answer Mr. Clayton's questions."

Kathryn lifted her chin. "I have to do no such thing. Where is my daughter?"

"The one you tried to murder tonight?"

"Devon, please." Anne's hand squeezed his shoulder, but he couldn't relent.

"I did no such thing!" Kathryn's frenzied eyes darted from one to the other.

"What's the last thing you remember?"

Kathryn slinked her arms beneath the covers. "The maid, Rozalyn, gave me some tea and I went to sleep, just as I do every night. I like Rozalyn. I want to see Claire."

"Do you know where you are?"

The woman shifted her head right to left. "I'm not in my room."

Devon slowly rose and sat on the edge of the bed. He gently pressed a hand down on Anne's leg when she moved to stand. "No, you're not. Are you at Ballinrock Castle?"

Kathryn's gaze became blank once more and she shook her head. "I'm in England, young man. I'm not senile. This is my husband's country."

"No, mother, your husband was Irish, like you."

Devon shot Anne a quick look asking for her silence. "When did you last see your husband, Lady Doyle?"

The question seemed to bewilder her, but Devon didn't relent. "Do you remember when, Lady Doyle?"

"He'll come for me. He promised, and when he does, we will take our Claire with us to my castle in Ireland."

This time Devon didn't stop Anne from stepping away. Confusion and sadness marred her lovely features, but he couldn't comfort, at least not yet. Rather than leave the room, she walked to the fireplace and stood with her back to them.

Devon's patience dwindled with each vague answer, but Kathryn revealed more in those responses than she realized. Her eyes widened, and the blank stare disappeared. In its place, alertness. "Lady Doyle?"

"It should all be mine. Ballinrock Castle, all of it. My daughter belongs there with her mother and father."

"Claire and your husband."

Kathryn nodded and crossed her arms neatly against her chest. "My husband is a good man. I must ready myself for him."

"You're not going anywhere right now." Devon rose from the bed and crossed the room to Anne. He looked at her upturned face and in a lowered voice, he said, "Will you bring Claire in here?"

"You can't be serious."

Devon shifted so as not to turn his back on Kathryn. "Trust me. Nothing will happen to her."

Anne peered around Devon to look at her mother and nodded once before leaving the room.

Devon returned to the bedside, not mistaking the sudden and deliberate change in Kathryn. "How long did you think you could keep your secret?"

"I have no secrets, sir."

Devon's smile was only for the lady's benefit. "Of course not. When you leave here, will your husband take you back to Ireland, or would you like us to escort you?"

Kathryn smoothed back the flyaway strands of hair that managed to escape their loose knot. "My husband will come, just as he promised, but I must be ready for him."

"We will see you are." Devon heard whispers in the hallway. "But first, your daughter."

Anne walked into the room, her arms around her sister's shoulders, with Rhona standing behind them.

"Oh, my beloved. Come here to Mother." Kathryn held out her arms wide. Devon nodded for Anne to release Claire, and the young girl hesitantly walked toward her mother. "Hurry, child. I have missed you so."

With the innocence of a child who lacked understanding, Claire fell into her mother's arms. "There now, child. Don't cry. We'll be home soon, and we can get you a pony like you've always wanted. Papa will see to it."

Claire peered up at her doting mother. "Papa is dead."

Kathryn's body tightened, and her chin rested on her

daughter's head. "Yes, he is. I forget."

"Are you still mad at me, Mama?"

"Never, child." Kathryn rocked her daughter.

Devon stepped closer to Anne and Rhona. "Don't worry. She never meant any harm to Claire."

"How can you know that?" Rhona asked.

"I need you to trust me. If I'm right, we've been looking in the wrong place this whole time."

"You can't mean . . ." Anne lowered her voice to a whisper, ". . . my mother."

"We can discuss this further, in private. Rhona, would you take Claire back to your room? The doors lock."

Incredulous, Anne whispered, though Devon understood she was yelling at him. "You said my mother wasn't a danger."

"I said she never meant harm to Claire. Your mother can return to her room or stay here, but you're not remaining alone with her."

Devon watched the soft rose tint in Anne's cheeks deepen. Rhona intervened on Anne's behalf. "She can stay in my room. We'll alternate sleeping."

Devon shook his head. "No, you'll all sleep. Keeping watch will fall to me, and there are only a few hours left until daylight now."

Anne crossed her arms, her eyes traveling the length of him. "I need to check your leg first." Anne walked to the bed. "Claire, it's time to sleep."

Kathryn's arms tightened around the girl. "She can stay with me."

"You must rest. You used to tell me that when a woman does not rest, her beauty fades faster. Do you remember?"

Kathryn released her hold on Claire. "Of course I do. Yes, I must rest. I shall stay here."

"Yes, you'll stay here, Mother."

Claire left her mother's embrace and exited the room with Rhona. Anne and Devon waited until Kathryn sank below the covers before they turned down the lamp and closed the door.

"If she has another fit . . ."

Devon slipped a key into the lock. "I took care of the other door while you gathered Claire."

Anne appeared skeptical. "Let's see to your leg."

Anne led the way into Devon's room, where he promptly settled into one of the large plush chairs. She knelt on the carpet and cut away Devon's pant leg. She already knew his wound no longer bothered him, but Anne couldn't be certain if the pain had truly left or if other more amorous sensations had simply masked the discomfort. Her cheeks blushed from the memory of what might have happened only a few hours ago.

"I'd like to leave these stitches in another day, but your leg is healing well."

"I told you." Devon's grin caused the heat to course through her entire body. How the man could think of such things at a time like this she didn't understand. Then again, her own body betrayed her, wishing this night had ended differently. Anne spread more healing salve around the wound and changed the bandages. Her fingers worked nimbly at their task while she remained conscious of Devon's eyes following her movements.

"Be careful when you bathe." Anne blushed once more and avoided eye contact with Devon as she gathered her supplies.

"Anne."

"Yes?"

He leaned forward and cupped her face. "Will you look at me?"

Anne released a shaky breath and focused her eyes. Such a beautiful and powerful man who wore his scars with pride and kept his memories locked away, protected under a veil of grins and laughter.

"You're nervous." Beneath Devon's smiles and gentle chiding hid a compassionate and sympathetic heart.

"I'm not." Though once Anne spoke the words, she knew they were a lie. "What almost happened, Devon . . . we cannot risk it again."

"Because you're afraid, or because you don't feel what I know is between us?"

Anne's body trembled at his words. "When this case is over, there will be another and another. It's who you are, Devon. Your duty is to your country and mine is to my family."

Devon's fingers glided over her cheek even as his eyes ensnared her. "You didn't answer the question, Anne."

She refused to shed the tears which so desperately wanted to fall. Anne rose from the carpet and put a few steps between them. "I don't know if my mother will ever be herself again. I don't know if my father was a traitor. I worry about Claire, and how she'll move on after this is over. I fear for Alaina and her unborn child, and how close she could have come to losing her husband. Rhona and Charles barely began their lives together when I pulled him into my mess. I am afraid for many reasons, Devon, but loving you is not one of them." Without giving him a chance to say a word, Anne hurried from the room, her satchel tucked close to her body.

YOUR DUTY IS TO YOUR *country and mine is to my family.* Devon repeated Anne's words over and over in his mind. He wouldn't deny the truth of her words. His duty lay with his country, to the men and women who could no longer speak or fight for themselves, who lost their lives, homes, and rights because of men like Lord Gaspar. No man can serve two masters . . . duty and love.

"You're thinking too much."

Devon shook away his own misery and glanced up at his friend. "And you're not resting. Where's Alaina?"

"Sleeping." Tristan poured himself a glass of brandy with his good arm and settled in the other chair before the large hearth. "Lady Anne is a skilled healer."

Devon thought of his leg, and the dull ache which he now barely noticed. "She is, and she won't appreciate you ruining her hard work if you pull your stitches."

Tristan grinned and held up his glass. "This is worth the risk."

Devon watched the strong flames, which danced and flickered in the fireplace. His long fingers tapped the side of his own glass, still full after an hour of quiet contemplation.

"I'd wager our healer is the reason you're brooding."

Devon swallowed his brandy, emptying the glass. "I don't brood."

"It is unusual, which is why I mention it."

They sat in companionable silence for a few minutes while Devon continued to brood. "How did you walk away?" Devon didn't look at Tristan, though he sensed his friend's gaze on him.

"Well, I am still here, aren't I? We don't walk away, Devon, not completely." Tristan crossed his legs and nursed his drink. "How many times have I come back despite my better intentions to leave this life behind? I was luckier than Charles because I had you both to carry the extra work while I spent time with Alaina. Charles has you and your brothers. Zachary and Derek have learned quickly, and they're as skilled and eager as you've ever been, but for you, it's different. You're the last of us, and that's a burden."

Devon leaned forward, his arms resting on his thighs, while the heat from the fire warmed his skin. "I don't consider it a burden."

"You may not have, but that was before Anne." Tristan chuckled and said, "I remember when I first met Alaina.

Passionate, sharp-tongued, and determined to keep me away. She may have started out as a case, but I didn't expect her to captivate me. I fought my feelings until I lost, or should I say gave in to the inevitable."

Devon grinned. "You're a romantic, Tristan."

Tristan returned the smile and said, "When it comes to the love I have for Alaina, yes. We both saw Charles go through the same torment. Loving a woman is the most agonizing experience a man will ever endure, and the most incredible. You've managed to reach the tormenting stage, so the question is, do you continue to resist or tell her?"

"It's not that simple, Tristan."

"It never is, my friend. Charles and I didn't admit how we felt to ourselves, or the women we loved, until we almost lost them. Don't make the same mistake."

Seventeen

Muinín agus Gealltanais
(Trust and Promises)

Shadows lurked beyond the walls of Greyson Hall, hidden in a sea of snow and wind. An eerie howl sneaked through the window, but Anne welcomed the tormenting sound for it mirrored her heart. What had she done? Sleep had alluded her, despite every effort to find solace in slumber, but Devon's blank expression burned her thoughts. Anne spoke the words because the truth always found a way to be heard. She knew love was one of life's cruel and unstoppable events, and a person could either embrace it or lose everything. Anne had already lost enough and struggled to hold onto what was left.

Anne knew what it would mean for Devon to walk away from the agency, from his life of uncertain risks. She'd witnessed his excitement when danger lurked or a puzzle required solving. He lived the life of an agent as a man born into the frays of war, and he relished it. How could she ever want or expect him to give that up?

A soft knock at the outer door brought Anne around. Who else but Devon would think to look for her here? "Come in."

Alaina's head peeked around the door. "With your mother in

your room and Devon downstairs . . . are you all right, Anne?"

Anne wiped away the few tears which had fallen in her solitude. "How do you do it, Alaina?"

Alaina crossed the room and stood beside Anne at the window. "It's not always easy." Alaina smiled. "Actually, it's never easy. I have watched these men risk their lives and sacrifice their own desires and wants over and over again until they have nothing left to give, and still they give more. The question to ask, is not how we do it, but how do they?"

Unease shrouded in self-loathing snaked into Anne's heart. "You must think me terribly selfish."

"No." Alaina pulled Anne into her embrace, the way Claire sometimes did when she thought Anne needed comforting. "I believe you're a woman torn by love and duty, who feels honor bound to give up what she desires for the sake of others." Alaina leaned back, her hands sliding down to embrace Anne's. "I went through this agony and self-torment, as did Rhona, but it was different for us. We didn't have the responsibilities to family that you carry."

Anne's chest rose and fell with calming breaths, as her tears flowed freely. "It is different for me, but I've only just now seen it. I do have family, and I will do everything in my power to keep them safe, but I'm not in this alone, and I can accept that now, without guilt."

Alaina embraced her once more, kissed her cheek, and giggled. "My dear, Anne, we're not done here. Let me share with you the other advantages of loving a British Agent."

DEVON SLOWLY BACKED AWAY from the ajar door until he reached the balustrade. He leaned against the railings, his heart filled with more love than he thought himself capable of feeling. Anne dazzled him with her beautiful mind and unwavering strength. He'd always considered Charles and Tristan his brothers, and their wives his sisters, but Devon had failed to see they were much more—they were a single family unit bound by friendship, love, and enduring devotion.

Devon stepped into the shadows when he saw Alaina slip from the bedroom—his bedroom. Of all the places Anne could have sought comfort, she went to him. Alaina opened the door down the hall to the room set up as a nursery, and once he was alone again in the hall, Devon walked to his room, his hand on the knob and a smile on his face.

"Mr. Clayton, sir."

He whirled around, his hand inches from the handle of his knife. "Theo. Is no one in this house sleeping? You should know better than to sneak up on an armed man." The young footman seemed out of breath. "What's wrong?"

"His Grace sent me to find you. Two riders approach."

Only insanity or an emergency could compel someone to ride north in this weather under the shroud of darkness. "Theo, stay here, and don't tell anyone unless they ask."

"Very good, sir."

Devon hurried down the hall, bounded down the stairs, and reached the massive foyer in time to see two snow-covered figures walk into the mansion with Tristan. "Insanity it is."

Derek brushed snow from his coat and grinned. "You wouldn't be talking of us now, would you, brother?"

"Lost my bloody hat a few miles back." Charles removed his coat and gloves and shook the layer of snow from his head. "It's not insanity as much as it is timing that brought us here so urgently."

Devon slapped his brother on the shoulder. "Drinks and a fire are in the study, then we'll talk."

Derek led the way into the warm room and helped himself to a bottle of whiskey at the sideboard, fixing a second one for Charles. Devon knelt in front of the blazing fire and added another log while everyone else settled.

Tristan said, "We expected you, but not this soon. Devon and I had a little reconnaissance mission planned."

Surprised, Charles asked, "Where?"

"Coventina's Well." Devon leaned against the stone mantel and shrugged. "Anne figured out Fianna's riddle."

"So did Zachary." Derek moved into the chair Devon had occupied and swallowed half his drink. "Better than your usual brand, brother. Zachary managed to extract quite a bit more information from our lovely assassin. She's in the agency's custody now, and Zachary remained behind to continue the interrogation."

Devon swore, knowing what came next. "Patrick is going to offer her a deal, isn't he?"

Charles nodded. "We offer them all the time, Devon, and if this one helps us close this case . . ."

"Yes, to scum who pose no real threat, but Fianna is an assassin, and she nearly killed Anne. Since when did the agency align themselves with killers?"

"Devon, don't do this to yourself." Derek stood directly in front of his brother. "Fianna has asked for immunity, but her deal has not been finalized yet. Zachary promised he would do everything he could to get the information before that happens."

Devon tossed the remaining contents of his glass into the fire, igniting the flames into a temporary frenzy. "What else did you learn?"

"Patrick gave us official orders." Derek handed the packet to Devon, who accepted it with some reluctance. Devon read the top page outlining the official order and skimmed through the subsequent pages, which offered details on the evidence supporting the investigation. "This is good news, Devon."

Devon slapped the orders down on the desk. "I know, but I had hoped for a little more time. Before anything else is said,

Anne should be here."

Charles spoke up. "You might want to hear this first."

"I promised Anne no secrets." Devon set his glass on the mantel and walked to the door. "We'll be right back."

THE GENTLE PRODDING ROUSED Anne, but she wanted more than anything to remain in this blissful state of slumber. She slapped the offending hand away until unease invaded her dreams. Anne awakened fully, her hand reaching for the knife still strapped to her leg. A warm hand covered hers.

"You won't need that."

"Don't be so sure." Anne fumbled in the dark to light the lamp beside the bed, but Devon managed to light the wick first. "My mother, or is it Claire?"

"I checked on them first and they're both fine and asleep."

Anne glanced toward the window, but the only light beyond the glass radiated from the moon. "It's stopped snowing. What time is it?"

"Half past four. The snow stopped only a few minutes ago." Devon moved from the edge of the bed, leaving the air around Anne a few degrees cooler. "Charles and Derek have arrived, and they have news."

Anne lifted her skirts out of the way and scooted off the bed. In her exhaustion, she had only bothered to remove her shoes. "They rode all night?"

Devon nodded. "Apparently it couldn't wait."

Anne hurried to the dressing table where she poured cool water from a pitcher into a porcelain bowl. "I only need a minute."

"Anne, wait." Devon crossed the room, concern etched around his eyes. "Charles led me to believe some of the news might upset you."

"He didn't say anything else."

"Not yet, but they're waiting for us now."

Anne watched Devon walk from the room, and she went through a quick washing while Devon waited for her in the hall. Reluctant to risk waking her mother, Anne decided she and everyone else would have to make do with her rumpled appearance, though at this point, she doubted anyone would care about her wrinkled dress. She met Devon in the hall, and they immediately made their way downstairs, Devon remaining impassive the entire time. Three men stood when she entered the study, but her eyes went first to her patient.

"You should be resting, Tristan," Anne scolded, and walked to her cousin. "It is good to see you, Charles. Rhona will be pleased to know you're safe and back with her." She looked around at the men. "Shouldn't she and Alaina be here?"

Charles motioned her to one of the chairs. "We'll update them in the morning."

"Your tone says you don't bring good news."

Charles smiled and kissed each of Anne's cheeks. "Some good, some not. Perhaps you should sit for this."

"Please, just tell me, Charles. Nothing could be as dreadful as my worst imaginings."

Derek motioned her to the chair he'd once occupied, and when Charles remained silent, she relented and sat down, thanking Derek.

Charles leaned against the edge of the great desk and crossed his arms, a stance which didn't offer Anne any encouragement. The grim line of his lips and the darkening of his eyes only caused her further worry. "The good news is we believe we've linked Lord Gaspar with the money forgery which has taken place for more than three decades. I've met with the agents who are currently investigating the forgeries, and we spent three days examining every piece of evidence they have and checking to see where the evidence crossed over with Gaspar's known movements over the years. The proof isn't concrete, and we do believe there are others involved, but the link was enough for Patrick to open an official investigation. Once Gaspar is located, he'll be arrested and returned to London."

Anne looked up at Devon whose expression was equally somber. "Is it possible that Fianna gave us the clue to Coventina's Well to lure us there?"

Devon nodded. "It's possible, but still worth going. If it is a trap, we'll be prepared. If it's not, we have a chance to catch Gaspar or at least whoever else is involved."

Excitement and worry blended and coursed through Anne. Finally, a step forward. "Will I need to go to London to tell them about Cillian?"

Derek and Charles exchanged a brief glance, and though Anne didn't know what it signified, Devon must have, for when he spoke, anger reverberated through his words. "No, Anne. What they haven't said yet is that Cillian's murder is secondary."

Anne rose from the chair and faced her cousin. "Please tell me that's not true, Charles. I understand why the money is important to your government, but I came to you and began all of this because of a Cillian Ó Fionnáin. His death haunts my dreams, and I swore to myself if I did nothing else, I would find justice for him."

Devon stepped close to her, his hands cupping her face. "And it's justice you'll have. I swear to you."

"It's not that easy, Devon."

"Like hell it isn't, Derek."

Charles placed a hand on Devon's shoulder. Anne looked into her cousin's eyes and saw his concern, for although he and Tristan were free to help her, Devon still took orders from the agency.

"It's all right."

"No, Anne, it's not." Devon turned and faced Charles. "You

know we can't let this pass."

"And we won't, I promise," said Charles. "But if Gaspar is not at Coventina's Well, Patrick wants you and Derek to find him and return him to London. It was an order, Devon. Patrick said his telegrams to you have gone unanswered."

Devon's jaw clenched and he moved away. "I don't work for the agency any longer."

Anne gasped. "Since when?"

"Since now."

The room's occupants all stared at Devon in silence. Anne knew this was her doing. Her insistence on justice for Cillian could have compromised the investigation because she truly believed that without Devon, the chances of catching Gaspar lessened.

"Please think this through, Devon."

His blue eyes, dark as cobalt now, met hers. "I have, and I won't have my hands tied in this way." Devon turned to Charles. "Patrick has always imbued us with the authority to make our own decisions in the field. Why is this time different?"

Charles sighed and leaned back onto the desk. "This is the bad news, or what I believed would be the worst of the news." Charles reached out, took Anne's hands in his, and pulled her close. "There is a possible link between your father and the forgeries, dating back to the time of the Duke of Hambleton's death."

Anne stepped back, shaking her head. "No, I won't believe it. My father left behind enough debts to bankrupt us—to lose everything. If he had money, real or otherwise, where did it go?"

Charles said, "We don't believe it, either, but it is part of the theory the agency is working, and if they can't find proof of his innocence, they will name him when it comes time to charge Gaspar."

Worn down by disbelief and despair, Anne lowered herself

into the chair and closed her eyes against the tears fighting to be set free. She was tired of crying, tired of wondering who to trust, and what to believe. "This cannot be the end of it. I won't allow Cillain's death to go unnoticed . . . it could have been Claire. How can money mean more than murder?"

Devon experienced Anne's agony as if it was his own, and looking at Charles and the others, he knew they experienced a similar reaction. Devon looked first to Tristan, who nodded once, and then to Charles, who after a few seconds, did the same. Devon faced his brother. "Derek, you should go back to London."

"That's not going to happen."

Devon walked to his brother and set a hand on each of his brother's shoulders. "You need deniability, Derek. I haven't officially resigned, which means I'm disobeying a direct order."

"You've done so plenty of times."

Devon nodded. "I know, but this time is different. Patrick has never stepped in the way of justice when it's called for, which tells me someone else is calling the orders."

Charles said, "It was the same situation with Rhona's case."

"True," Devon said over his shoulder, "but Patrick didn't stand in your way, not when it mattered. We know Lord Gaspar has influential friends—almost as many friends as enemies. He's valuable to someone."

Anne interjected with a question of her own. "Why would he not call Charles away? I know Charles isn't an agent any longer, but could he not force him to stay away from the investigation? Charles is my cousin and has more reason to help me than anyone."

Devon laughed for it all made sense. He turned to Charles. "I shouldn't have doubted your motives. Patrick did order you to stay away from this case."

Charles smiled and shrugged. "Of course he did, but I'm no

longer under his purview, at least not officially."

Derek said, "I'm not going anywhere, Devon. With Tristan's arm the way it is, you'll need the extra man either here or out there, but I won't leave."

Devon slapped his brother on the back and grinned. "England love you, brother. Thank you." To Tristan he said, "I know how much you hate keeping out of the action."

"I know, this arm is useless for . . . how long exactly, Anne?"

"A few days at least. So, this means we're not giving up?"

Devon grinned. "We're not giving up."

"I'm going with you tomorrow."

"No, you're not." Devon laid the map of the region out on the desk and pointed to the area of the old well. "The old temple ruins will suffice to—"

"Excuse me, gentlemen." Anne tapped her cousin on the shoulder and scooted in between him and Devon. "I said, I'm going with you tomorrow."

"Devon heard you, Anne. We all did, but that doesn't mean you're going."

"Why not?"

Tristan and Derek both snickered, or at least to Anne it sounded like snickering. "I realize I haven't your physical prowess, or your skills with guns, but I can throw a dagger, and at least protect myself. I'm the only witness to the murder, and I can identify the other man who was there."

Devon set a book on the edge of the map and turned around to sit on the edge. "You can identify the man, if he's among those who show up, when we capture him."

Anne couldn't argue with the logic, so she took another approach. "I'm not asking permission. Before you say anything else, hear me out. Devon, you've been with me long enough to know I won't back down." Anne watched in surprise as Charles left the room without a word, though none of the men seemed surprised.

"Where is he going?"

Devon ignored the question and said softly, "We don't question your passion, Anne, or even your ability to take care of yourself if necessary, but the risk is too great. If we're focused on keeping you safe, we risk the lives of everyone."

"I don't accept that."

Devon grinned. "I didn't think so."

Anne couldn't reconcile the seriousness of the situation with Devon's newfound amusement. "So, I'm to wait here for news, doing nothing?"

"Not nothing."

Anne spun around to see Charles and Rhona standing in the doorway.

"Giving them peace of mind is not doing nothing, Anne." Rhona crossed the room with Charles by her side, and once again, Anne envied their solidarity. Only a short time together, and they already moved as one.

"What did you do, Rhona?" Anne asked. "You have been in this situation, have you not?"

Rhona had the graciousness to blush and the honesty to say, "I did what I wanted to, what I thought I needed to do, and it nearly got me killed."

"This is different." Anne felt her argument had no foundation, but to give up entirely, to watch others fight her battles, was not something she could bear.

"How?" Charles asked. "We have a job to do—"

"Not just 'we.' Tristan, when you met Alaina, were you not on assignment? And Charles, you and Rhona were brought together again because of another case. This time it's my doing. If I had any inkling that all of you would become so embroiled with my problems, I would have found another way. I did this, and it's only right for me to see it through."

Devon opened his mouth as though to speak, but Anne cut him off. "Please, don't ask me to stand by and watch, not any longer. My conscience won't allow me to let others risk their lives while I wait."

Anne did wait . . . for the silence to pass. Charles, Tristan, and Devon all exchanged glances which she could not interpret. They had their own language, these three men who had worked and bled together.

"I know what I ask of you is not fair, but I don't want to do this without you or in secret. All I ask is you give me a chance to be there when justice is found for Cillian."

Devon said to Charles, "I need you to indulge me while I speak privately with Anne." Devon knew his request meant that he was removing the others from the decision, but he counted on Charles's trust. Relations only bonded people to a certain point, and right now, Devon knew Anne better than anyone else there.

Charles stared long and hard at Devon and Anne for almost a minute and nodded once. Devon grasped Anne's hand and led her from the room, down the expansive halls, through the spacious ballroom Devon doubted had ever been used, and into the conservatory. He'd walked through it briefly during his initial inspection of the property, and it immediately became his favorite room in the house. The glass-enclosed room was in need of greenery and small trees to take advantage of the full sun, but right now it boasted only a few chaises while rain cascaded down the windows.

Devon led Anne to one of the chaises and waited until she was comfortable. He sat down beside her and gathered her hands into his. "My life has been lived on secrets. From the time I was a young boy, I learned not to ask my father questions about his work as a solicitor because I knew he couldn't tell me, and if I pressed, he would have to lie about where he went and with whom."

Anne continued to watch him in silence, and Devon pressed forward. "My father, Marcus, knew how to keep a secret or tell a lie better than anyone I've ever known. Perhaps that is where I learned, and those skills have been used to great advantage over the years, especially with the work we do. It wasn't until I'd met Charles and Tristan that I knew what it meant to trust someone other than my brothers, and yet over time, I didn't allow anyone else into my circle of trust. I learned to trust Alaina, and more recently, Rhona, but it's not been easy."

Devon wanted to look away as Anne stared at him with understanding and compassion in her eyes, but her calm and soft smile encouraged him to finish. "I told you there would be no secrets between us during this investigation, and I meant it. It's a promise I've never made to anyone."

Anne broke her silence and said, "Surely with Charles and Tristan, and of course your brothers."

Devon shook his head and exhaled a deep breath. "No. We often leave information out until it becomes necessary for everyone to know. That's a part of the job. For instance, all the time Charles and Derek spent in London, we didn't know the details until tonight. We won't know everything Zachary is doing until it's imperative we be told. It's not about trust but about keeping everyone involved safe, and allowing us each to do what we do best."

"Then why did you make me that promise, Devon?"

"I don't know," he said with absolute honesty. "But I have never intentionally broken a promise, and neither have the others. They are not in the same position as me, for I know Charles would have preferred you remain unaware, but only because he wishes to keep you safe. He's your family, Anne, and he feels responsible for you."

"I do understand, Devon, and I'm sorry if I've been difficult.

I tell you I'll cooperate, and then I insist on playing my part. I have been using your promise to my advantage, and I realize that's unfair to all of you. Charles is my family, and I can't convey in words what it means to know he's there for me, my mother, and sister, but I've stood on my own for so long."

"Everyone under this roof is here to help you, possibly risk their lives for you, to offer you friendship, love, and hope everything will be all right. That is not someone who is alone."

"My heart aches with worry that if I'm not there with all of you, somehow you won't be safe, that someone may die and it will be because of me—because of my family."

"You want justice."

A few tears fell silently down Anne's pale skin and dropped onto their joined hands. "I do want justice."

"Trust us—trust me—once and for all, to find the justice you seek."

"You ask for complete trust, Devon. You aren't the only one who finds that difficult."

Devon brushed away her tears. "I know, but I've given you mine."

Anne removed her hands from his grasp and walked to one of the expansive windows. After a minute of waiting, Devon walked up behind her.

Anne's soft voice gave him the promise he sought. "I do believe in you, in all of you." Anne turned around, leaned her head back, and raised her eyes until they met his. She surprised him by holding out her hand in the narrow space between their bodies. "Unconditional trust."

With a wide grin, Devon shook her hand. "Unconditional trust."

Eighteen

Tagann Craiceann ar Chneácha
(Wounds Heal)

Devon returned to the study alone, after escorting Anne to the base of the stairs. He wanted so much to depart with a kiss because when he kissed her, the jumbled mass of confused thoughts about his future seemed to unravel until everything made sense. Instead, he brushed his lips over her hand and watched her ascend the staircase and disappear into the shadowy hall.

Charles and the others stood around the desk, studying the map he'd laid out earlier. Charles's eyes posed questions of their own, and Devon appreciated the position in which he'd placed his friend. He hoped his own silent gaze assured Charles they would speak, and soon.

"Anne will remain here."

"She agreed to this?" Charles asked.

Devon nodded. "Willingly." He felt the weight of responsibility in a way he'd never understood before. Each assignment came with its own set of difficulties, and some with exhaustion, heartache, and defeat. No matter who was involved, Devon had managed to hold back a piece of himself, enabling him to do the job with a clear mind and little emotion. This time, defeat would mean heartache for Anne, and that possibility tore through his last resolve. "What have you decided?"

Tristan pointed to the area of Coventina's Well on the map. "The wall isn't far from the well, and there's another set of ruins nearby, small, but they should provide enough cover, allowing you to wait on one side and Charles on the other."

"And where will you be, Tristan?"

"Derek and I will remain here with the women. Enough time has passed, and we can't be certain Gaspar hasn't discovered the connection to this estate. Besides, Derek has proven that my arm is of little use to you out there."

"It was only a tap, Tristan."

Devon laughed and grinned at his brother. "A tap? Zachary did the same thing when I injured my shoulder last year. It hurt like a son of a bitch."

Devon grinned back at his brother, and Tristan rubbed his arm in mock pain.

"I hate for you to all have the fun without me," said Tristan.

"Once we arrest Gaspar, or whoever makes an appearance, there will be more fun to be had." Devon thought of what Anne had told him about feeling responsible if one of them were to be injured. She bore the unnecessary burden of guilt over Tristan's current injury, and his own. If further harm came to Tristan, Anne may not overcome the guilt. "Alaina is strong, Tristan, but she is carrying your second child, and you should be with her. I know Anne is grateful you've already done what you have, but your place is with Alaina."

Charles and Derek seconded the sentiment. Devon saw Tristan was torn between watching his longtime friends and partners go into the fray without him, and remaining with his wife, which is where he wished to stay.

"I know," Tristan said, "but I'd still like to be there with you."

The choice between love and the work was a decision Tristan had to make many times since he married Alaina. What Devon hadn't appreciated until now was that Tristan never had to actually choose between one or the other. He did what was necessary and right, but his ultimate loyalty was always to Alaina. With a bond such as theirs, Alaina didn't have to be reassured of her husband's love because it was everlasting.

For the first time in his life, Devon ached for that same infinite bond. "You are here, friend." Devon grinned. "And someone is going to have to help keep Anne's mind occupied. She thinks as we do and would rather be out there."

"Anne won't try anything, will she?" Derek asked.

"No, she'll keep her promise," Devon assured them, and to Charles he said, "I'll wait at the ruins, and you at the wall. As much as I'd like to kill these bastards, we'll do this the agency's way one last time."

Three pairs of questioning eyes settled on Devon, but he shook his head, refusing to offer an explanation. He still searched for answers within his own mind in an attempt to reconcile what he swore he'd never do, with the choice he'd already made. Devon glanced up at the clock on the mantel. "We have only a few hours until daylight, and we may not be back for a few days. If the information is accurate, they'll be arriving at the well soon."

"And if it's not?" Derek asked.

Devon rolled up the edges of the map and his eyes lit up. "Then we take the fight to them."

KATHRYN WRESTLED WITH DEMONS in her sleep, or so it appeared to Anne. Her mother turned over and over during a restless slumber while Anne watched and waited. Sleep had escaped her already this night, and she didn't bother to try and lay her head down again with the hope she'd awaken and the nightmare would be over.

"Anne?" Claire tiptoed into the room dragging a blanket behind her, the corner clutched to her chest. Anne motioned her over to the large chair by the bed and lifted Claire onto her lap.

"You should be sleeping." Anne smoothed back her sister's mussed hair and hugged her close.

"I saw the sun come up." Claire rubbed the blanket across the tip of her nose. "Will Mama open her eyes?"

"Of course she will. You know when you're asleep, your eyes are closed, but every morning you wake up and your eyes open again."

"Can I ride a horse?"

"May I ride, and yes." Anne rocked her sister from side to side and thought of how one event and what seemed like a lifetime of days had changed their lives. Normalcy and hope were what Claire needed now. "If the weather allows, I will take you riding today."

"Will cousin Charles come with us?"

Anne's thoughts drifted to her cousin and Devon who by now must almost be at the well. "Not today, sweetheart, but if you ask Derek or Rhona, one of them might come along."

"Anne?" Rhona stepped inside the room partly brightened by the rising sun. "Claire got away from me while I checked on Christian."

"She's an independent one," Anne said. "How is Alaina?"

"I'm afraid a bout of nausea has plagued her. Tristan is in with her now, but he said it's the worst Alaina's experienced."

Anne lifted Claire off her lap. "Will you sit with them until I return? I'm going to look in on Alaina and fix her something to keep her comfortable."

"You can do that?"

"Not always with success, but a ginger tea should help. I keep a bag of the herb in my satchel for the pregnant women in the village. Alaina should be home resting."

Rhona pulled Anne aside. "You're not going to start in again, are you? Alaina would rather be with Tristan."

"No, I'm sorry. I'm cooperating, but the guilt hasn't gone away."

"It might not, at least until this is over."

"You're reassuring me, Rhona."

Rhona smiled. "It's not meant to be. I carried so much responsibility and regret when Charles and the others helped me. Whenever one of them was injured, I blamed myself. When Blackwood Crossing suffered the fire and we nearly lost the servants, I held myself accountable. It took time, but I eventually allowed for the possibility that I wasn't responsible for the actions of others."

Anne considered and saw the truth in what Rhona said. "You're right, of course. I'll look after Alaina, and afterward Claire and I plan to go riding. Would you like to join us?"

"I could do with a bit of fresh air, but I should stay and look after Christian while Alaina rests." Kathryn murmured and her eyes fluttered open. Rhona lowered her voice and said, "Will your mother be all right?"

Anne shook her head. "I'll ask Rozalyn to stay with her, and when this is all over, she deserves a king's ransom for all of her help." Anne thanked Rhona and went into Devon's room for her satchel of medicines. She made her way downstairs in search of the kitchen but managed to get lost. Theo stopped her in the hallway, his arms filled with wood.

"May I be of assistance, Lady Anne?"

"I'm in need of some hot water for a tea."

"I'd be pleased to get that for you."

"Not at all. If you could direct me to the kitchen, I can manage well enough."

The young footman stared at her, mouth agape and eyes wide.

"I couldn't possibly, my lady. Rozalyn will be down straight away."

"I assure you, Theo, I can manage this, and Rozalyn has been awake much of the night."

Theo wavered and then instructed her how to find the kitchen.

"Thank you," Anne said. "For everything. I know it hasn't been easy here with no one else to help. I'm grateful to both you and Rozalyn for all you've done."

Theo wore shock and humility well. Anne left the stunned servant in the hallway and followed Theo's directions to the kitchen. She stopped at the entrance of the immense room, overwhelmed by admiration for every cook that had ever worked in such a place. "Good grief." The kitchen was three times the size of the one at Ballinrock, with more cupboards, shelves, and cooking implements than anyone should ever require. The fire in the cook stove needed only a little stoking, much to Anne's relief. The kettle was easily filled, and while she waited for the water to boil, Anne went in search of a teapot for the herbs.

"Lady Anne?" The soft voice startled Anne, and a quick thump against the open cupboard door landed her on the floor. "Ooh." Anne rubbed the top of her head as she stood and leaned against the counter.

Rozalyn rushed forward. "I'm so sorry, my lady. What can I do?"

"It's quite all right, Rozalyn." Anne closed her eyes and rubbed the assaulted area of her head until the throbbing subsided. "I should have asked for help, but it was only water." Anne smiled at the maid in an effort to reassure the young woman that all was well. "How do you find your way around here?"

Rozalyn's eyes twinkled. "It's a challenge, my lady, but I do love it." The maid brought out a teapot and cups from a cupboard on the opposite end of the kitchen and took over where Anne left off. "This kitchen is a dream for someone like me."

Curious, Anne sat on one of the low stools and watched Rozalyn move efficiently about the room. "What do you mean?"

As though confessing a great secret, Rozalyn lowered her voice. "I've always wanted to run a kitchen of my own, to prepare grand feasts, and experiment with new ideas and recipes."

Anne dropped the herbs she'd sorted into the teapot. "When you went into service, why did you not work in a kitchen?"

Rozalyn shrugged, deftly lifted the kettle of boiling water off the stove, and filled half of the teapot. "My uncle Henry, the butler at Claiborne Manor, always wanted more for me. His dream was for me to become a lady's maid in a grand house like this, but I prefer working with food."

Anne admired those who dreamed of a better life for themselves, but she admired even more, those who strived to do what they loved. Anne thought of Nessa Ó Fionnáin, Cillian's sister, who despite her brother's death, had become the cook at Ballinrock Castle. What would happen to her when they returned home? Would they be able to save Ballinrock, or would the few tenants and staff still there be forced out? Anne longed to save her beloved family home, but asking Charles for the funds necessary to do so was not an option.

"If a kitchen is where you long to work, then you should."

Rozalyn raised her shoulders and shook her head. "It is not so simple for us, my lady. In service, we must do the best we can ourselves."

Anne wondered how many servants believed their lots in life were so much worse than those of the upper classes. Anne's family, and many more like theirs, bore the burden of title while inhabiting homes they couldn't afford and staff they could not pay. Ballinrock's coffers would not last six more months.

"I believe all anyone can do is their best, whether in service or in a grand home like this." Anne lifted the tray before Rozalyn could. "I'll see to this."

The maid bobbed her head, but Anne could see that Rozalyn did not like to see a lady do a servant's work. "These past days could not have been easy for you here, especially with what you've been tasked to do."

"I don't mind, my lady. We all have our demons, and I don't believe . . ."

"Don't believe what, Rozalyn?" Anne prodded.

"I was frightened, my lady, when I saw her ladyship in a fit, but I don't believe it's her own doing. She's misses his lordship fiercely."

Anne set the heavy tray back on the counter. "Why do you say that?" When Rozalyn hesitated, Anne encouraged her. "Please, speak at will."

"Lady Doyle speaks of him often, saying his name, 'Asher,' over and over again in her restless sleep."

Anne remained still. "When did she say this?"

Obviously concerned that she overstepped her position, Rozalyn was quick to apologize. "I'm sorry, my lady, I didn't realize it would disturb you so much."

"I'm not upset with you, but I need to know when Lady Doyle said this."

"Why, all the time, my lady."

Anne composed herself the best she could and offered a reassuring smile to the maid, though she felt anything but heartened. "Thank you, Rozalyn."

"Of course, my lady. I will have breakfast in the dining room shortly and a tray ready for your mother."

With a silent nod, Anne left the kitchen. When she reached the upstairs landing, she couldn't recall how she had managed. Could her mother's delirium be worsening, or did Kathryn truly believe she was wed to Lord Gaspar? Anne hurried to the end of the hall and knocked on Tristan and Alaina's room, though no one answered. Anne balanced the tray and opened the door. Alaina and Tristan walked in from the adjoining room, Alaina leaning on her husband. "Tristan, please bring her over to the bed. Alaina, I want you to remain in bed and try to sleep. No matter how much you think it will help to move around, your body needs to rest."

Alaina groaned and leaned back against the mass of pillows Tristan placed behind her. He said, "If you can get her to rest, I'll be indebted."

Alaina scoffed and pushed the top quilt off her body. "As will I, but I can't very well get sick in here."

Anne handed her the tea and instructed, "There's a full pot of this. I want you to drink it all, and then I'll prepare another pot. When you're not drinking the tea, drink water."

"I can't possibly, Anne."

"You're dehydrated and the water will replenish your liquids and the tea should soothe the nausea. I'd feel better if the doctor could look in." Anne looked at Tristan.

Tristan nodded. "I sent Theo for Dr. Abbot."

Considerable relief coursed through Anne, for where her remedies have proven to help, and even cure many ailments, she did not wish to risk Alaina or her unborn child. "When the doctor arrives, I'd like to speak with him."

Alaina reached out and grasped Anne's hand. "I'd like you in here with the doctor. I trust you, Anne, especially after what you've done for Tristan. I do not believe a doctor could have done better."

Anne passed over the compliment, ever uncomfortable with praise in any form, and merely nodded. "Speaking of Tristan, why don't I check your stitches?"

Assured that his wife was as comfortable as she could be, Tristan sat at the small table, allowing Anne to unwrap and inspect the wound. "There's no infection. I'd like to leave the bandage off and allow the wound to breathe. Is there any stiffness?"

Tristan moved his arm up and down. "A little soreness, but I can move it."

"I can remove the stitches tomorrow if you'd like."

Tristan nodded. "Thank—"

A cacophonous wail echoed through the halls, a wail too familiar for Anne's comfort. She rushed from the room, followed closely by Tristan. Derek bounded up the stairs and met them outside of Kathryn's bedroom.

"Wait, Anne," Derek said, and cautiously opened the door.

Claire, her eyes wide and dry, sat huddled in the corner watching her mother writhe over the bed. Kathryn's arms and legs flailed about, blood staining the sleeves of her nightgown. Her moans sounded more like the howl of wild animal caught in a trap. Anne hurried to her sister's side while Derek and Tristan approached the bed from each side, careful to avoid the knife in the lady's hand."

"Anne, get over here and check on Rhona," Tristan said, his eyes never leaving Kathryn. Anne rushed to the other side of the bed where Rhona lay unconscious. Anne checked for a pulse, grateful to find it strong. Rhona stirred, but Anne leaned over her until Kathryn could be subdued.

Kathryn's thrashing soon subsided, but her moans did not.

Derek wretched the blade from Kathryn's hand. "How did she get this?"

Tristan shook his head and cut through the bedsheets with his own knife to create makeshift bandages. He tossed a few to Devon who wrapped Kathryn's arm while Tristan wrapped the other. Tristan said, "Is Rhona harmed?"

Anne shook her head. "It appears she hit her head but otherwise unharmed."

"I'll take care of Rhona. Your mother needs tending, Anne."

Rozalyn rushed into the room with a tray, but it slipped from her hands, crashing to the floor in a clatter that startled Kathryn out of her subconscious. "I'm so sorry."

Anne whispered to her sister, hugged her close, and guided her to the maid. "Don't fret, Rozalyn. Claire's all right. I should have come directly here, she's my responsibility. Please take Claire downstairs to the kitchen with you."

"I'm terribly sorry, my lady. Is Lady Blackwood all right?"

"Calm yourself, Rozalyn. This isn't your doing. Lady Blackwood is fine. Will you be all right watching over Claire for a while?"

Rozalyn gave her a brisk nod and ushered the young girl from the room. Anne inhaled deeply and hurried down the hall where she'd left her satchel and returned to her mother's side. Derek held the bloody knife wrapped in one of the bandages. "This is a different blade."

Anne glanced at the dagger. "Claire confessed that she gave it to her when my mother asked. She didn't know any better, but I did. I gave my mother enough sedative to keep her asleep for hours."

Tristan lifted Rhona and set her down in one of the stuffed chairs. Her eyes fluttered open, and her hand immediately went to the back of her head. "Is Claire hurt?"

"No, she's safe. What happened?" Anne asked from her place beside the bed.

"I stepped into the bathing room to fetch your mother a wet cloth. When I came back in, she had that knife. I couldn't get it away from her."

"You shouldn't have tried." Tristan moved his fingers over Rhona's injury. "You're certain you're well?"

Rhona nodded and then paused as though noticing the scene for the first time. "Oh, my. I'm sorry."

"It's I who am sorry." Anne looked into the blank eyes of her mother.

Tristan said, "I'll check the room for anything else she could use."

Anne removed the white strips of cloth from one of her mother's arms. "Why have you done this, Mother?" She cleaned each cut, applied a salve, and rewrapped Kathryn's arms. All the while her mother stared blankly at the ceiling. Anne beckoned both men into the hall.

"She's becoming so much worse. I can't keep her here and continue to risk everyone's lives, my sister's life."

Tristan said, "We can't send her away. Not right now."

Anne wished she could turn back the clocks to a time in her life when the world didn't pitch and tumble, when life made sense. "I can heal visible wounds, but I don't know how to treat her mind."

"I'll stay with her," Derek offered.

"I can't ask that of anyone else, not after what happened with Rhona. I'll remain with her."

"What of Claire? You can't stay with them both," Tristan reasoned. "Derek and I will take shifts, and no argument, Anne. It's not safe for anyone else to watch her. Rhona can stay with Alaina and Christian, and I'll take the first shift with your mother. I believe Rhona mentioned that Claire wished to go riding."

"I can't just leave to go riding."

"Yes, you can," said Derek. "I'll go with you, and Claire will have an activity to keep her mind off of what's happened."

Anne peered back into the room where her mother lay motionless. She acquiesced to their plan, not because it's what she wanted, but because she had no other choice. Alone, she would fail, but with their help, she and her family had a chance. It wasn't only Devon whom she must trust unconditionally, but all of them, if she wanted her family to survive. Anne prayed Devon and Charles were successful in their hunt.

A short while later, Anne went in search of her sister. Alaina slept comfortably, and Rhona watched over Christian, though Anne worried she needed more sleep. Tristan assured Anne that he would have no trouble with her mother. Anne had given her mother a stronger sleeping draught. Claire stood alongside Rozalyn in the kitchen, a smile of sheer delight on her face.

When Anne entered, Claire held up both her flour-covered hands. "I made a pie!"

Anne laughed and clapped her hands. "Well done, Claire. What kind of pie?"

"Apple!"

Rozalyn praised Claire's efforts. "She's a natural, my lady."

"It appears she's had a good teacher."

"My lady . . ." Rozalyn glanced at Claire. "Is her ladyship all right?"

"Claire, please wash up now. Derek is taking us riding."

"Horses!" Claire jumped off the stool and hurried to the sink. Anne moved closer to the maid. "She's sleeping."

"I know I haven't the right to ask, my lady."

"Nonsense. You have every right. This household has been anything but normal since you've arrived, and we're all in this together. I must apologize to you for what you've had to endure."

"It's quite all right, my lady. I'm sorry for her ladyship's troubles."

"Thank you." Anne pointed to the mess of flour and dough. "And thank you for your patience with Claire."

"She's a true delight, my lady." Rozalyn wiped her hands on her apron and said, "I'll clean up here and then see to the breakfast."

"There is no hurry. His Grace and Mr. Clayton have both had their breakfast and we brought trays up to the rooms for the others."

"But, my lady. Surely you—"

Anne held up her hand and said, "You are only one person. Theo should return soon from the village, but no one expects miracles with all of us and only two of you."

Claire hurried over to her sister and held up her hands, now clean and dry. "Can we go to the horses now?"

"May we go, and yes." Anne smiled at Rozalyn, thanked her again, and followed her enthusiastic sister from the kitchen.

Derek waited at the base of the front steps for them with two horses, his own impressive steed, a brown Thoroughbred, and one of the Friesians they'd used to pull the coach. "Can you ride?"

"Yes, but Claire has not before."

"We don't have any ponies for Claire, but I'll ride the Friesian and Claire can ride with you on my horse. He's sound."

Claire, in her excitement, almost tripped down the steps. Anne managed to catch her before she tumbled headfirst into the stone. "You must be careful, Claire. Horses can become scared, just like people." Anne led her sister to the Thoroughbred, and showed her how to slowly approach the animal. Anne stopped her sister a foot away from the steed and instructed Claire to hold out her hand. After a few seconds, the horse stepped forward and nudged Claire's small hand, delighting the girl.

Tristan and Derek had been right to urge her outdoors with Claire. Worry accomplished nothing, and if Anne remained inside, she'd be plagued only by her troubled thoughts, wondering what else she could do to help. Anne hoisted herself up onto the back of Derek's horse, and Claire was lifted so she sat in front of Anne. Derek mounted the great black horse and together they made their way across the moorland. Claire was captivated by a pair of fox scurrying through the snow and tall grasses. She was charmed by a trio of red deer standing majestically on the hilltop. Anne closed her arms around her sister and enjoyed the moment.

More than one hour later, the snow began to fall, a few flakes, and then at a steadier pace. Derek led them back toward the mansion and into the safety of the stables. He lifted Claire off of the horse and held the reins while Anne slid out of the saddle. "Thank you, Derek."

"My pleasure. Did you enjoy the ride, Claire?"

Claire bobbed her head up and down and jumped from one foot to the other, too excited to keep still. "Can we go again?"

"May we." Anne laughed. "And yes, but when the weather is good again."

Claire pulled her kerchief from her pocket and rubbed at her nose. "When will Aunt Alaina have the baby?"

Anne and Derek exchanged an amused glance. Anne said, "Not for a while yet. We'll be back in Ireland by then." Once she'd spoken the words, Anne realized she didn't want to return to Ireland, at least not to the life they'd been living.

"Will Mama come home with us?"

"Of course she will." Anne tweaked her sister's nose. "I'm going to help with the horses and then we'll go back inside and see how Mother is doing."

Claire nodded and skipped off down the long center of the stables. Something fell to the ground, and Anne's gloved fingers retrieved a piece of paper which appeared to have been folded and crumbled many times over. The ink was faded, but Anne could make out most of the words. "Claire!"

Anne rushed after her sister who waited as told inside the stable doors. "Where did you get this?" She showed Claire the folded page.

Claire shrugged her small shoulders. "I found it."

Derek reached the pair, his hand hovering above the pistol at his belt. "What's wrong, Anne?"

"I don't know yet. Claire, when did you find this?"

"I don't remember. The man with the scar gave it to Mama."

"Anne, what is it?"

Anne passed Derek the letter and pressed Claire for more information. "What man with the scar, Claire?"

"Lord Gaspar. Don't you remember, Anne? He's our friend."

Derek clutched the letter in his hand and tucked it away in his coat. "Back to the house, now." He lifted Claire into his arms and together they crossed the strip of land separating the stables from the mansion. Derek set Claire down inside the foyer. "Look after her. I need to speak with Tristan."

"Wait, Derek. Do you know what it means?"

"Not with certainty, but I do know Lord Gaspar does not have any noticeable scars. But this letter, Anne, changes everything."

"WHERE'S CLAIRE?" DEREK ASKED, when he and Tristan walked into the study ten minutes later.

"With Rozalyn. How is Alaina? Theo told me the doctor wasn't in town."

Tristan smiled. "She's much better, thank you. I don't believe the doctor could have done any better."

"I showed Tristan the letter," Derek said.

"And what do you think?"

Tristan returned the worn letter to her. "Is there a possibility this is true?"

"I pray not, but I'm no longer certain of anything." Anne lowered herself into one of the chairs by the desk. "My mother isn't well enough to be asked such a question, especially if it's not true."

Derek knelt beside the chair. He looked so much like his brother, and for a moment, Anne could almost imagine it was Devon by her side. "But if it is true, Anne, we need to know."

"If it's true, Derek, my family is not mine." Anne swiped at the falling tears. "Could this not change the outcome of the investigation? Devon and Charles should be told before they make an arrest, if they haven't already."

Tristan sat on the edge of the desk, his arms crossed now that the sling was gone. "This doesn't change what needs to be done, but it does mean we've taken a man's child away from him, a lord of the realm. Gaspar may not be deserving of his title or status, but the law still recognizes the father."

Anne rocked her head from side to side. "No, I cannot believe it." She stood abruptly. "We need to get word to them, now."

Derek rose. "I'll go."

"Thank you, Derek." Anne walked from the room, leaving the men alone. She found her way upstairs to the room where her mother rested, only now she sat in a chair by the window.

"Mother?"

When her mother turned her head, Anne saw the face of a woman who appeared a decade older. Her eyes no longer looked hollow, but the woman Anne always believed to have been her mother had vanished.

"Where is my daughter?"

Anne choked back the tears and disappointment. "She's downstairs and happy right now. We went riding today."

"Lady Blackwood informed me. She's kind and proper. I like her."

Anne leaned against the wall by the window. "She's wonderful." Anne reached into her pocket and removed the letter. "I need to ask you a question."

Her mother turned her curious eyes upward. "Well, what is it?"

Anne handed her the letter. "Do you recognize this?"

"Where did you get this?"

"That doesn't matter."

"It does!" Her mother rose from the chair on weak legs, the letter fisted in her hand. "Where did you get this? Did you read it?"

"Yes, I read it."

Her mother tossed the paper to the ground and wobbled back into the chair. It would be a few days before she regained her full strength. "It wasn't your right to read my letter."

"Is it true?"

Her mother remained tight-lipped and turned her face away to stare out the window. The sun peeked through the heavy curtain of clouds, but inside, darkness still held her mind.

"He loves me."

Anne stopped the cry of anguish from escaping her lips. "Why did you or Father never tell me?"

"Tell you what? That your father loved another before me?" She waved her hand in the air as though dismissing Anne.

"Are you my mother?"

Kathryn glanced up at Anne, but said nothing.

"Why won't you tell me?" Anne looked closer at her mother's blank expression and realized she'd slipped away again.

"Where's Claire? I'd like to see her now."

"Claire will be up later. Leave her to her happiness for now." Without another word, Anne left the room, closing the door behind her. She left the house through the front door and raced across the snow-covered grass to the stables, where alone she could release the torrent of sorrow building up inside.

Once she'd released the last tears, Anne lowered herself to the straw-covered ground. One of the great black Friesians nickered in the stall beside her. "I imagine you long for freedom, as I do now. We both serve as we believe we're meant to, but duty can be exhausting, can it not, my friend?" Anne pulled herself up, leveraged against the stall door. The black beauty lowered his head over the door and nudged her shoulder. "I envy you right now." Anne stroked the horse's muzzle, her hand moving over his ears and down his mane. "You truly are a magnificent creature. What would your life have been like if you had been born free?"

Anne had not considered duty a burden until now, for caring for one's mother and sister was not duty, but love. All lies. She wanted to not care, to hate the circumstances and the people who put her in this moment of anguish, but she couldn't. Blood or not, Claire was her sister, and that would never change.

The horses joined the nickering and snorting. "Calm yourselves now. It's not all bad." Anne looked around the stable. "You've a finer home here than most humans. Perhaps you just want a little exercise, and—"

Agony dragged her into the void, devouring her thoughts until only blackness remained.

Nineteen

Níltear i measc na laochra ar lár
(Not Among the Fallen)

D evon crouched low behind the ruins. The crumbling stone offered little cover as he and Charles waited on the boggy ground. Two days had passed and still no sign of Gaspar or anyone else. If the information they'd managed to withdraw from Fianna proved to be accurate, a meeting should have taken place by now. Devon doubted they had been spotted, but they couldn't be certain.

Devon prayed they would soon find an end to the emotional torture he knew plagued Anne. He longed to be with her, to offer her another promise, one that would give them both a future unlike either had ever dreamed. Instead, he waited on the moors where so many had died before. Battles had been waged on this land, and it would bear witness to another.

Devon hoped death wasn't in the cards for him or anyone else today. As much as he despised Gaspar, Anne deserved to be a part of his downfall. Would it cure her misery? He didn't know, but he could hope. It seemed as though an ocean separated them, and every time he believed they were coming closer together, the waves would crash and roll, carrying them away on opposite currents.

A snow bunting's call carried from the north—Charles's call. Devon waited for the second call, and when it did, scouted the area behind him. Low on the horizon, a figure bent low to the ground and rolled down the hill to where Devon waited.

"What are you doing here?"

"You need to bring Gaspar in alive, no matter what."

"If he gives us no choice—"

"He may be Claire's real father."

"Bloody hell." Devon slammed his hand against his leg. "How?"

"There was a letter. Listen, Devon, we haven't confirmed anything yet, but if Claire is his daughter . . ."

"Who told you?"

"Anne found a letter that somehow Claire had." Derek set a hand on his brother's shoulder. "We need to end this. Anne is strong, or trying to be, but I don't know how much more she can endure."

Devon pressed hard against the wall, and Derek followed suit.

"An approaching coach," Derek whispered.

Devon nodded. "I hear it." He peeked his head over the top of the ruins. The vehicle rambled over the uneven ground until it could go no further. One man stepped down from the coach and struggled across the bog to within shooting distance from where Derek and Devon hid. They waited another thirty minutes before a horse rider made their way over the sodden earth. When the rider dismounted, another passenger alighted from the coach.

"Bloody hell." Devon's harsh whisper drifted no farther than the cold stone wall. Lord Gaspar raked his eyes over the landscape in every direction before walking toward the man who had arrived with him. The rider followed close behind. Devon placed the looking glass through a gap in the stone to watch the first exchange.

The unknown rider passed a leather pouch to Gaspar, who in turn examined the contents. From what Devon could see, it was no money, but what appeared to be official documents, bearing the seal of the agency at the top of the first page. Charles knelt on the ground beside him, looking through his own glass. Devon raised his looking glass higher to scrutinize each man, memorizing the faces of the two he didn't know. His vision passed over Gaspar once and quickly returned. A long thick scar traced from eye to chin in a half circle. The skin puckered around the edges to form a permanent white line across the hardened face.

Gaspar called out to his driver, after which the man climbed down from his seat and opened the vehicle door. The rider hurried over to help carry a bundle—a person wrapped in a blanket—from the coach to the horse. Devon's body tensed and he started to move, but Derek stopped him. "Wait."

An arm slipped from beneath the blanket and hair the color of burnt autumn leaves, flowed down in a tangled mass. "Son of a bitch." Devon gauged the distance he'd have to run to reach them.

"Devon," Derek whispered.

"That's Anne. How in the hell did they get to her?"

"You can't run on your leg."

"Like hell I can't." A rashly impetuous desire to race after her consumed Devon.

"You're faster on the horse. Charles is on the other side, and he'll have seen what we did. He and I will take care of Gaspar. You go after Anne."

Devon focused on slowing his heartbeat, but his rage would not be harnessed. He knew he had to keep a level head if he was to help instead of hinder. The rider swung up behind Anne and positioned her on his lap before heading north toward Scotland.

"Don't let the bastard get away," Devon said, and careful to stay below the line of sight, he dashed across the soggy land and rolled down the hill where the horses waited. He mounted in one swift movement and began the chase, keeping behind the hill until he heard gunfire in the near distance behind him. Devon kept riding, his sights on the back of the man. His stallion was faster and stronger. Keeping low to the steed's head, they raced against the wind, closing the distance one furlong at a time.

The rider finally saw he wasn't alone and fired a shot behind him, missing Devon by a yard. Devon continued to gain ground. His opponent pulled his horse to a stop and reared back before he turned around. The jarring movement must have roused Anne because Devon saw slight movement beneath the blanket. She wasn't given the chance to remove the blanket from her head before the man yanked her hair back and set the barrel of his pistol to her head.

Devon pulled back on the reins, forcing his horse to stop suddenly. "Let her go."

"Ye don't want your pretty lady to lose her head, do ye guvna?"

"I'd rather take yours." Devon raised his own Webley Revolver and took aim. The single bullet met its mark. The rider slid sideways off his horse, and Anne managed to hold on to the saddle. Devon dismounted and hurried to her side. He lifted her off the animal and held her in his arms. "You're all right?"

She nodded against his chest. "I'm not hurt, Devon, except for a dull ache in my head."

He inched back and pressed his lips to her. "You're certain?"

Anne cupped his face. "Yes, but I don't know what's happened."

Engulfed with relief, Devon held her close once more. He wanted nothing more than for this to be the end, but the danger wasn't over. He brushed his lips over hers once more and asked,

"Can you ride?"

"I think so." Anne nodded, this time with conviction. "Yes, I can ride."

Devon helped her back onto the horse and mounted his own stallion. They reached the well in twice the time Devon and the kidnapper had crossed the same distance, but he wasn't willing to risk injury to Anne.

Charles knelt over one man on the ground, but Derek was nowhere to be seen. Devon pulled up a few yards away from Charles, dismounted, and asked Anne to remain on the horse. His boots slushed through the bog as he walked to where Gaspar lay unconscious in the muck. The long scar was more prominent now than before. "Did you have to shoot?"

Charles nodded. "He took a bullet in the leg, and I've bandaged it, but he'll need a doctor. I don't want Anne near enough to fix him."

"Does his scar look older than it should?"

Charles looked closer to study Gaspar's face. "He could have come by it shortly after our encounter at Ballinrock."

"He already had the scar." To Devon's annoyance, Anne trudged up behind him.

"What are you doing?"

"Not waiting." Anne placed her hand against Devon's arm. "Lord Gaspar had the scar when he killed Cillian."

Devon exchanged a worried glance with Charles. "No, Anne, he didn't. He bore no scar when Charles and I saw him in Ireland."

"That's not possible." Anne looked from one man to the other. "I swear to you, he had the scar."

Derek turned away from the topic and asked about Derek.

"He ran after the other bloke," Charles said. "Ah, here he is."

"Derek?"

"He didn't make it. Bloody big fellow, too. We'll have to

bring the coach around to pick him up," Derek told his brother, and helped Charles heft their prisoner and carry him back to the coach.

"The other one is a few kilometers northeast."

Charles nodded and said, "We'll get him. Take her back and check on the others. I want to know that Gaspar's men didn't get to the house."

"They didn't," Anne interjected. "I went out to the stables, and I didn't tell Tristan or anyone else."

"Did you see anyone?" Devon asked.

"No. The horses fussed, but I was too upset to think." Anne sighed. "Derek told you about the letter?"

Devon nodded. Charles asked, "What letter?"

"I'll explain everything to Charles on our trip back to Greyson Hall," Derek promised.

Devon ushered Anne back to the horse and helped her mount. With a brisk nod to Charles and his brother, Devon led Anne away. Halfway home, another rider approached. They pulled up and waited.

"Thank God." Tristan looked mad. "Don't ever scare us like that again, Anne."

"Tristan, you've pulled your stitches."

He looked down at the small bloodstain on his arm. "I'll live. When I saw Theo in the stables, and you nowhere to be—"

"Theo wasn't in the stables with me."

"Anne," Tristan began, "I found Theo dead in the stables after he went searching for you. We all have been, but when I saw him lying there, and your shawl on the stable—"

"I'm so sorry, Tristan. I had no idea."

Devon reached out and covered her hand. "This isn't your fault, Anne."

"Then whose?" Anne skirted her horse around the men and set off at a gallop for Greyson Hall.

They buried Theo beneath an ancient oak on a hillside behind Greyson Hall, where Theo could watch the sun rise and set. When the small crowd dispersed, Anne remained at the foot of the mound, staring at the cross. Devon promised a proper headstone, one worthy of the young man who had done nothing but his duty. He shouldn't have been there.

Anne let the tears flow with abandon, her heart aching for the young servant who reminded her so much of Cillian. The loss of an innocent life started all of this, and now another went to join him.

His strong arm circled her waist, and without thought, Anne leaned into him. "This isn't over, Devon."

"I know," he whispered against her hair and brushed a kiss on her head.

"Theo deserves to have someone mourn for him, and we will, but I want to end this." Anne looked upward into his beautiful blue eyes—eyes which held such compassion. "Where is he?"

"Now is not the time, Anne."

"There is no better time."

"He's in the attics."

Anne slipped from Devon's embrace, and with firm resolve, she said a silent goodbye to Theo and returned to the house.

Derek stood when she reached the top of the stairs, Devon close behind her.

"Has anyone spoken to him yet?" she asked.

"At length," Devon answered, "but he hasn't said much."

"I want to see him."

Derek hesitated, but after his brother nodded, he unlocked and opened the door. Devon moved past Anne to walk in first. On a rough cot, their captive sat, his head bowed low.

"How could you?" Anne approached him cautiously, but Devon held her back before she could get too close.

Their prisoner raised his head, and inch by inch, Devon saw the truth they already suspected.

"You're him, but not . . ." She clutched her chest and stepped backward. The eyes, cold and void of humanity. "How . . ."

"You filthy bogtrotter," he spat out. "You and your stupid whore of a mother—"

Devon's open hand connected with the other man's face. "Watch what you say, Gaspar."

"Who?"

Devon leaned close in an effort to calm Anne and whispered, "This is Lord Bartley Gaspar, Asher's twin brother."

Anne wanted to ask more, but the cautious glint in Devon's eyes told her to wait. "I've seen enough for now." Anne backed out of the room, ignoring the expletive shouts from behind her.

CHARLES DANGLED THE GLASS of whiskey in front of her. "You'll want this."

Anne accepted the glass, closed her eyes, and drank half of the liquid. It didn't matter how much she drank, the truth crashing down around her would not be easily forgotten. Devon hadn't followed her from the attics immediately, and Anne wasn't sure she wanted to know what delayed him. When he finally walked into the study, the one room in the monstrous house where they were guaranteed absolute privacy, it was with a grim expression.

"Will someone please explain to me what's happening?"

Devon eased into the space on the sofa beside her and opposite Charles.

"Lord Asher Gaspar, the man you've known all these years, is not the man who murdered young Cillian."

"He told you this?"

Devon nodded. "Not willingly. He's crazed, but not stupid."

"I don't understand."

Charles leaned forward. "Anne, we have the man responsible

for Cillian's death. Justice will be done."

Tristan walked into the room, still clothed in the clothes he wore to the funeral. He poured himself a drink and walked to the hearth where he stared into the glowing flames. "Do you remember what happened that day, Anne?"

Anne grieved Theo's loss, but not as much as Tristan, for he had brought the boy here. She knew nothing she could say would release Tristan of his guilt. "After Derek left for the well, I spoke to my mother. Afterward, I needed to be as far away from her as I could, so I ran to the stables. I remember talking to the horses, and then everything went dark. I woke face down over a saddle. If I had known . . . You can't know how sorry I am, Tristan."

"Perhaps you should separate yourself from the rest of this investigation," Charles suggested, and Anne recognized the tone as one of utmost seriousness.

"No." Anne set her glass on a silver tray in the center of a small table. "I need to know why this happened. If these events were all about money, why kill an innocent young farm boy? Why kill Theo instead of tying him up?"

Devon drew her attention when he spoke next. "Your father left you the full estate, for whatever it's worth, in his will."

Confused by the sudden change of topic, Anne slowly nodded. "I believed it was because he expected me to look after the family. I had already taken over the small household accounts, paying local vendors and such."

"Yet, he must have known at the time of his death that debts weighed down the land and castle because he obviously went to lengths to hide his financial situation. You'd have no way to support your family for long, unless he knew something about the castle." Devon gripped Anne's arm and led her to the desk. "Can you draw the interior of Ballinrock? Just the layout, the rooms as you know them?"

Anne thought the request odd, but she sat down behind the

desk while Devon rummaged through the draws. He produced a single sheet of paper and a pencil. As though she stood in the hallways of Ballinrock, Anne drew line by line, room by room. Her mind walked through the foyer where the floor was in need of repair, down the hall that needed new paper and paint. She continued through each room, on the lower floor before ascending the stairs. Rooms that had long been closed off, now came to her memory.

When she finished the upper levels, Devon asked about the downstairs, rooms Anne had rarely thought of before. She sketched the kitchen, servants' hall, and storerooms to the best of her knowledge, and as an afterthought, drew the attic bedrooms which had been empty since she'd let most of the staff go. Once complete, she pushed the drawing toward Devon and Charles.

Devon pointed to her mother's room. "You forgot the room where Claire and your mother were kept."

"I didn't know about that hall or chamber."

Charles scrolled his finger over the downstairs. "There's extra space here below the castle next to the kitchen."

Anne shrugged, frustrated with herself for not knowing. "I believe they are servants' rooms of some kind. I haven't spent much time down there."

"And this space here . . ." Devon indicated a narrow stretch of emptiness between the entrance to the servants' staircase and the second-level landing.

"An empty room. I remember hiding in there as a child, but it's now used for storage, linens, and such."

Devon tapped the paper and straightened. "We need to return to Ballinrock."

"I cannot put Claire and . . . my mother through another long journey unless I know they won't have to come back." The thought of remaining in Ireland bothered Anne more than she wished to admit. Ireland—Ballinrock—was her home, so why should she feel more at home here than she ever did there?

"They don't need to go back, and neither do you," Charles promised.

"Charles is right." Devon smiled. "You never have to go back. We'll return to Ireland and search the castle."

"And what of my sister? You know Gaspar is . . ." She didn't want to say the words aloud for fear speaking them would solidify their truth. "Claire is Lord Gaspar's—Asher's—daughter."

"There's no proof until we speak with Gaspar," Charles said.

"Yes, but he has rights, does he not?"

Devon and Charles exchanged another one of the secretive glances to which Anne had grown accustomed. "I have no authority over Claire, do I?"

Charles knelt beside the desk chair. "Not if he's her father, but we can fight him if he attempts to take her away. He's made no claim to her all of these years, and a letter in his own hand is not proof enough for the courts, at least not with our solicitors on the case."

Devon grinned. "Derek and I would be honored to represent you in court, and we won't stop fighting until Claire is free." Anne realized how much she'd come to appreciate Devon's ability to find the humor, the hope, and the adventure during the most trying of times. His smiles somehow gave her the strength to press forward.

"Thank you." Anne stood and found herself close enough to Devon to feel his body's heat. Strengthened by his nearness, she asked her cousin, "Where will you go now?"

"Now that the immediate danger is over, we'll take Bartley back to London for questioning and trial, which is where Zachary comes in."

"What of Lord Asher Gaspar?"

Tristan tossed back the remaining liquid in his glass. "He'll be easier to find now that we have his brother. Devon, I'd like Alaina to remain here while we're in London."

Devon nodded, but qualified the nod by asking, "Shouldn't you stay with her?"

Tristan's grin was more sinister than Anne expected. "I'm going to pull rank, and every last favor I have, to ensure neither Bartley nor Asher escape with less than the maximum punishment. Within the confines of the agency, titles don't mean much, but outside, I'll use mine to our advantage."

Anne didn't wish to presume, but she took the risk. "Should we not all remain at Greyson Hall until you return?"

Charles's voice conveyed surprised when he asked, "You're not going to argue or ask to join us?"

Anne shared a brief smile with Devon, as her way of telling him she intended to keep her promise. To Charles, she said, "No argument. I ask only that when you find Lord Asher, I be allowed to speak with him."

Charles nodded. "Agreed. Do you want me with you when you tell your mother?"

"Thank you, but I don't believe that is wise. You're family, no matter how distant, and I believe your authority reminds her too much of my father."

"I'll go up with you."

Anne thanked Devon with another smile, which conveyed her gratitude. "When will you leave?"

"Tomorrow. We'll take the coach west and board the train in Inverness." Devon was quick to assure her they wouldn't be left alone. "Derek will remain here with you."

Anne nodded, though she wished Devon was the one to stay. She thought of the task ahead and inhaled a fortifying breath. "My mother won't take this well."

"You don't have to do this now, Anne."

"Yes, I do."

Anne and Devon made their upstairs to Kathryn's room, where she'd refused to leave until her husband came for her. "Mother?"

She didn't bother to look away from the window. "Where's my daughter?"

"Claire is playing right now." Anne walked toward their mother, motioning Devon not to get too close. If she wanted to have this conversation without bringing harm to her mother or anyone else, she had to play into the fantasies. "Will you tell me about Asher?"

Her mother turned and looked at Anne. "He's my heart, my true husband."

The worn letter had proven otherwise. Although Anne believed her mother loved Asher, Lord Gaspar had played on her loneliness and desperation. "You said he's coming for you. Do you know when?"

Her mother's lips formed a tight smile. "I will go to him when the time is right. That's what he said. When the time is right. You can't come with us, Anne."

Anne wasn't going to shed another tear for what she never had. "I know. Would you like to go to Asher now? You can leave whenever you wish."

Her mother's eyes widened. "I cannot go alone."

"Cousin Charles will escort you."

Her mother waved her hand, as though dismissing the idea but said, "I like Lady Blackwood. Charles may escort me. I wish to leave tomorrow."

"Of course. Where will you go?"

"To London, where I belong with my Asher. Claire should be readied."

Panic set in, and Anne did her best to temper it before speaking again. "Claire would be in the way for you when you meet Asher again. Perhaps she can come later when you've settled into Asher's home."

"Yes, that will be best." Her mother removed the blanket covering her lap and prepared to stand, but Anne wasn't finished. She swore to herself she wouldn't ask the question. "Did you ever love my father?"

"Of course. Asher is a wonderful man."

"No, Mother. Kevan Doyle. Did you love him?"

"I don't want to talk about this anymore, Anne. You talk too much, just like your father. He was weak, like your mother."

"What are you talking about?" Anne shook her mother's shoulders. "You're not weak, just sick. You're . . ." Anne saw the truth in her mother's eyes. "You're not my mother."

"Of course I am, you silly girl. Now, help me—"

Anne stepped away and stared down at the woman who had raised her, at the only woman who had sung her lullabies and said "I love you" when she tucked her in to sleep.

Twenty

An Fhírinne agus na Torthaí
(Truth and Consequences)

Ballinrock Castle, County Wexford, Ireland

Devon moved silently through the upstairs halls while Charles checked the lower rooms, but not a soul breathed within the castle walls. A whisper of suspicion clouded Devon's thoughts. No bodies, no stench of death, and no sign that a family had lived in these rooms. The absence of sound became more deafening as he walked from room to vacant room. Convinced the upper levels were empty, Devon made his way to the long narrow room from Anne's sketch.

The door adjacent to the small room opened, and Charles emerged from the servants' staircase.

"This place is a tomb."

Devon nodded. "Nothing up here, either."

"Too many things feel wrong about this."

"I agree, but we're almost done." Devon joggled the door knob to the room. "I don't suppose you have a key." Devon grinned before he stepped back and rammed the full force of his body against the door, cracking the wood around the lock.

Charles brought a lamp around, lighting up the first few feet of the storage room. As Anne told them, linens, pillows, and quilts covered every shelf on both walls. Trunks lined the base of the room toward the back, and what appeared to be old livery hung on a rack against the back wall.

Devon moved past Charles toward the back while Charles moved aside piles of linens. Devon lifted the lid on each trunk to find more of the same bedding. One trunk held yellowed children's clothing and a girl's doll, broken in pieces. Devon thought of Anne, much as he had been since they left her at Greyson Hall. Was the doll hers or Claire's? From the condition of the clothes, he'd surmise they belonged to Anne, but why hold onto a broken doll or old clothes?

"Anything?"

Devon shook his head and dropped the lid. "The walls."

Charles nodded, and together they ran their hands over the walls, Charles at one end, Devon at the other. Devon shoved aside the livery and continued his search along the seams. "Found something back here."

Charles set the lamp on a trunk and helped maneuver the clothing rack out of the way. Devon pulled the dagger from his boot and used it to pry away the old paint and paper until he had enough to pull. Inch by inch, wooden planks were revealed, and with a final tug, a narrow portal was exposed.

Barely the width of Devon's shoulders, the narrow hatchway was sealed by rust and age. Devon wedged his dagger between the wall and the door, moving up and down the length of the portal. "There's a solid statue in the last trunk there. It should do the trick on this lock."

Devon pounded at the rusty lock with the heavy statue, breaking it away after three hits. The lock fell to the floor with a clang. The small door gave easily, and on the other side, a musty stench permeated the air. Devon pulled back and coughed into his arm. He pulled back to make room for Charles and the lamp.

"Bags, five of them," Charles said. He, too, had a difficult time breathing the air and stepped back into the storage room. Devon covered his mouth with a handkerchief, grabbed the lamp, and squeezed through the door into the small compartment room. He set the lamp down and with one hand used his dagger to slice through the top of the first bag. He'd seen enough. Devon moved back into the storage room and lowered the cloth from his face. "That air is toxic," he said between coughs. "But the money is in there. From the look of the bills, they're at least two decades old."

They returned to the hallway where both men could breathe easier and speak freely.

"If all of those bags contain as much money as the first . . ."

"Hundreds of thousands of pounds," Devon finished. "I know. To amass that quantity in forgeries would have required access to the proper equipment. If they've continued, we need to find where they're producing the money and destroy it all."

Charles nodded. "We'll transport the bags to the coach, but I need to find out what happened to the servants. At the very least, Haverly, the butler, should be here, as should Nessa since her family lives on the land."

"You know this means Anne's father was somehow involved."

"I know," Charles said, "and we'll tell Anne, but it must be the right time."

"Agreed. We'll carry the bags out first, and then I'll go to the Ó Fionnáin's cottage and look for—"

"I heard it," Charles whispered. Revolver in hands, they stood on either side of the servants' stairway entrance. The door was pressed open a few inches, revealing a hand. Devon held up one finger and raised his gun when the figure stepped through.

"No, please!"

"Nessa?"

The young woman removed her hands from around her head

and gazed up at Charles. "Saints be praised, Lord Blackwood, Mr. Clayton. I prayed it was Lady Anne or her family who came back."

Charles looked around her into the dark room. "What happened here?"

Frantic, the young cook's words tumbled from her mouth in rapid succession. "Lord Gaspar told us that Lady Anne and her family were killed and he was master of Ballinrock now. He showed Mr. Haverly the documents and said he was married to Lady Doyle. He forced us all out without reference. Mr. Haverly, he refused to go, and Lord Gaspar struck him over the head and tossed him into the snow. My ma fixed him, and he went back to his family. Lord Gaspar was here for days. We watched him leave three days ago."

Nessa's accounting of Gaspar's timeline made sense considering three days ago they'd captured his brother in England. How Gaspar had learned of it, Devon didn't venture to guess, unless Gaspar didn't know where the money was located, only that it was inside the castle.

"Was anyone else hurt, Nessa?" Devon asked.

"No, sir. It was only me and Mr. Haverly here." Nessa tugged at her threadbare scarf. "Lady Anne?"

"Is alive and well," Charles promised. "Listen to me carefully. Lord Gaspar is an imposter and a thief. I assure you that your position here is secure."

A stream of tears fell down Nessa's pale face. "Thank you, my lord."

Charles reached into his pocketbook and produced a stack of bills. "Take this back to your family."

"I couldn't possibly, my lord."

"Yes, you can. For Cillian, you can do this."

Nessa timidly took the pound notes and tucked them into her pocket. "Thank you, my lord. Your generosity, and Lady Anne's, has been a blessing." She raised teary eyes up to Charles. "Will Lady Anne return soon?"

Devon caught the glance Charles sent his way before he answered Nessa. "I don't know, but Ballinrock Castle is her home and yours. Do you know how to contact Haverly?"

Nessa gave him a brisk nod. "Yes, my lord. He's with his family in the North. Mr. Haverly, he didn't believe anything Lord Gaspar told him."

"Have you seen anyone else lurking about?" Devon asked.

"No, sir. Not until tonight."

"Hurry home now, Nessa. I promise you'll hear from us soon."

"Thank you, my lord. Thank you ever so much." Nessa turned and hurried back down the stairs, the pitter-patter of her slippers echoing through the stairway.

Devon hauled the bulky canvas bags from the small hideaway, and with Charles's help, they managed to get all five bags down to the coach quickly. Devon, fully aware that Charles kept glancing his way, piled the last bag into the coach. "I've not dishonored Anne, Charles."

"I know." Charles closed and secured the door. "You wouldn't be standing if you had." He turned to face Devon. "You're my brother and my friend, but she's my responsibility, even if she believes otherwise. I've failed her once, and I won't let it happen again." Charles turned and leaned against the vehicle. "I've seen the way she looks at you and you at her. If you intend to walk away, I only ask you do so with care, and soon." He slapped Devon on the shoulder in a brotherly fashion and said, "We should take the money back to the ship tonight. I'll secure the doors as best I can, but I'd like to stop and check on the other tenants. Anne tells me there's one more farmer at the north edge of the estate."

Devon watched his friend disappear into the shadows around

the side of the stone wall of the castle. Walk away from Anne? The mere suggestion set him in a panic. His life had been complete before he met her. His work, his friends, his brothers— what more did he ever need? Devon hadn't before questioned his choices in life, and he had no regrets, but to walk away from the one woman who tested his willingness to change, would be a regret with which he could not live.

Honor and courage he had aplenty. Finely honed skills, extensive education, and coveted wealth were nothing more than tools he used to his advantage. The thrill of danger and promise of adventure had been enough for him these many years. Devon had been pleased for Tristan when he found Alaina, and elated for Charles and Rhona when they finally had a chance at love, but it wasn't a life he craved . . . until Anne.

Charles rounded the castle from the other side, locked the front entrance, and returned to Devon's side. With a casual air, Charles climbed up to the box seat, and Devon followed suit. Devon reached for the reins first and held them in his grasp.

"We need to talk about Anne."

Charles leaned back, but said nothing.

"I'm not walking away. I haven't spoken with her yet, but if she'll have me . . . *if* . . ."

Charles didn't hide his surprise. "I saw something between you from the first time in Ireland, but you've never been one to commit to a woman. Your work is your life, Devon."

"As it was for Tristan and for you, yet neither of you hesitated."

A soft chuckle escaped Charles's lips. "I hesitated far too long. You know I almost lost Rhona because of the work. Had we not been brought back together on that last case, she and I might never have had another chance. Men like us rarely get a second chance, Devon."

"Which is why I don't want to jeopardize this first chance."

"And you're willing to walk away, officially?"

Charles asked the question Devon had yet to answer. In his heart, he knew he could sacrifice anything, and everything, for Anne, but his mind raced to catch up with his heart. "If that's what it takes."

"Be certain, my friend. I'd leave behind a life of intrigue and murder over and over again if it meant living a life with Rhona. We can't always control what happens, as recent events have proven, but these women we love deserve to be first in our lives." Charles grinned. "And you'll soon learn they're worth it."

Devon grinned back. "I don't doubt it, but let me ask you this. How did you convince Rhona to marry you?"

Charles laughter filled the night air. "Turns out she loves me. It's a bloody wonder why, but she does."

Greyson Hall, Northumberland, England

"THAT'S WONDERFUL, CLAIRE!" ANNE lifted the drawing her young sister had spent the past hour sketching. "You've captured their true beauty."

Claire beamed. "Horses are my favorite animal in the whole world."

"Well, there are many magnificent creatures out there, and someday perhaps you'll see some of them." Anne set the drawing back down. "You're quite talented."

Claire's eyes sparkled, and she giggled with delight. In the week since Devon and Charles had left for Ireland and Zachary arrived to help Derek transport Lord Gaspar back to London, they'd existed in quiet at Greyson Hall. Except for Kathryn's daily reminder of what was still to come, they all managed to find peace and a sense of hope. Alaina recovered from her nausea after a few days of rest and Anne's herbal treatments.

Anne removed Tristan's stitches two days before, and he'd

spent most of the days since inspecting both the interior and outside of the mansion. She caught sight of him twice at the grave of young Theo, and the third time, she approached the snow-covered mound and stood beside him. They said nothing, but in the quiet she sensed an inner turmoil and a fighting spirt within him. In her heart, she knew that together, Tristan, Charles, and Devon would go to the ends of time and space for one another. Whether that meant avenging one of them or protecting the people they loved, it would not matter.

They'd left Theo's grave in silence and did not speak of those moments, but when Alaina pulled her aside the next morning to thank Anne, she believed Tristan had understood why she'd been there. Anne, too, would risk her life for any of them, for any reason.

Anne shook the past from her thoughts and focused on her sister in the present. Rhona had spent the morning with Kathryn, and a glance at the clock told Anne it was time for her daily conversation with her mother. It did not matter if Kathryn was not her mother by birth, for Anne knew no other. "Not important at all" were the words Kathryn uttered about Anne's real mother, but Anne refused to believe such a thing. A woman of no importance? No! She wouldn't believe her mother meant nothing to her father, for they bore a child together. Anne held onto that truth as she made her way to her mother's room.

Rhona sat by the hearth reading from a volume of Tennyson's poems.

The stream will cease to flow;
The wind will cease to blow;
The clouds will cease to fleet;
The heart will cease to beat;
For all things must die.
All things must die.

Tennyson had brought many hours of solace to Anne with his words of life as it was and not always as people hoped it to be. She loved the truth of his verses as if they spoke to her. "All things will die" had meant something different to Anne, a passage which to her meant every day was precious and to live it as though you may not have another, but listening to words with her mother staring blankly at the wall, the poem brought only sorrow.

Rhona glanced up and closed the book. "We'll read more tomorrow."

Kathryn bowed her head once and stared into the fire. Rhona stepped into the hall with Anne.

"She's dressed again."

Rhona nodded. "Every day the same thing. She believes today is the day she'll go to see him."

"Just as she did yesterday and the day before." Anne sighed and hugged her arms over her body. "Charles and Devon should return soon, shouldn't they?"

"Yes. Charles told me they would stay in Ireland only one night and travel by train. They'll be here soon, I'm certain of it."

Anne looked through the doorway to see her mother had not moved. She didn't have the strength to face Kathryn today because the story didn't change. Anne's mother was an unimportant whore, and she never loved Kevan Doyle. Nine years ago, Kathryn had given herself to another man and to this day believed that man loved her.

Rhona rubbed the side of Anne's arm. "You don't need to talk to her today."

"Am I a dreadful person for wishing her gone? I pray for Charles and Devon's speedy return because I wish them safe, but also because I want Kathryn away from here, away from Claire. With each day that passes, she drifts deeper into her delusions. Her mind is so fixated on Lord Gaspar."

"It may not feel like we're near the end of a long and dark tunnel, but the light isn't far away, Anne. Be patient a while longer, and you'll not only have justice, but perhaps something of greater value."

Anne's gaze met Rhona's gray eyes. "What do you mean?"

Rhona smiled and her eyes brightened. "As Tennyson said, 'Heart, are you great enough for a love that never tires?'"

Anne scoffed, though in truth it was one of her favorite poems. "Tennyson spoke of marriage."

Rhona cast another secret smile and returned to the room where she opened the volume of Tennyson and read.

WEARY AND FRUSTRATED WITH the delays, the constriction around Devon's chest eased when Greyson Hall finally came into view, but it was not the mansion which drew him. Three days longer than anticipated because of a storm on the channel, but they'd managed to transport their cargo into trunks on the ship, and then onto the train. Devon sent a telegram to Patrick the moment they reached England, another cryptic message providing him with an intersecting location. Devon and Charles planned to turn the trunks of forged banknotes over to Patrick with the promise they would return to England to see the investigation through.

Only Devon didn't believe Gaspar would be in London. Too many eyes watched and even more people searched the streets of the great city. Gaspar hadn't located the money inside Ballinrock, and by now he would have heard of his brother's capture. Crazy, not stupid, is how they had described Bartley Gaspar, but Asher lacked his brother's fervor for the macabre. Devon stood by his initial assessment that Asher Gaspar was indeed an abhorrent human being who deserved to live his life in the hallowed cages of Newgate, but he was not a murderer.

Devon reined in his stallion half a mile from Greyson Hall

and turned to look at Charles. "I'd like to be there when you tell Anne about her father."

"I assumed you would," Charles said, "but we don't know how involved Kevan Doyle was with Asher and Bartley."

"True, but it's safe to speculate that he was entangled from the beginning. He had Hambleton's ring and Lady Whitley's pendant. Either he played a part in Hambleton's death—which I don't believe—or the duke trusted him to keep the items. Unfortunately, we can't know the truth now for it was buried with her father."

Charles nodded. "Anything Gaspar says in his own defense taints the truth, but it's all we have."

Devon tapped his heels once against the stallion's flank and set the horse back in motion. They'd had cases go unsolved before, but at least some form of satisfaction had been meted to the guilty. Yes, Lord Asher Gaspar and his brother would be brought to justice, but without a confession, they could not prove a crime more than twenty years old, nor could they prove Kevan Doyle was murdered. Devon didn't believe his death an accident, but how did he tell Anne she may never know what really happened to her father?

The river flowed alongside the narrow road to the gates of the estate. A winter haze surrounded the mansion, and the barren branches of a tall sycamore rustled with the gentle breeze. The cold didn't keep Anne indoors. Devon's heart teetered on the edge, but when he saw Anne, her glorious hair flowing in the wind and a smile of welcome on her face, his heart took the final leap. His feelings toward her should have made the difficult truths pale in importance, but he didn't believe she would see things as he did.

Devon wanted to believe the darker days of Anne's life expired with the capture of Cillian's murderer, and he hoped what he could offer her and Claire would be enough. Devon kept his eyes focused on Anne and watched her smile fade. His eyes shifted to Charles, whose grim expression mirrored his own. Anne stepped halfway down when they dismounted. "What's happened?"

Charles reached her first. "It's freezing out here, Anne."

"I didn't want Claire to overhear any bad news." She glanced behind her.

Devon remained with the horses, holding the reins of both animals. "I'm going to stable the horses, and I'll join you soon."

"Wait." Anne whispered something to her cousin and bounded down the steps to Devon. "I'll help you."

Devon's gaze shifted from Anne up to Charles, waiting for his reaction. After long seconds, Charles gave Devon a brisk nod and walked into the house. Devon handed Anne the reins to Charles's horse and set a slow pace toward the stables. The wind whipped the edges of Anne's shawl as they crossed the frozen ground, but she didn't seem to mind. She remained silent until they reached the stables, and Devon secured each animal in a stall.

"Have I upset Charles?"

Devon rubbed the muzzle of his stallion and fed him a small handful of oats. "What made you ask that?"

"His reaction just now."

"He's not upset." Devon put away the saddles and returned to Anne. "Charles is torn between his position as head of your family and accepting your independence. He's used to taking charge, but he's also familiar with independent and headstrong women."

"I like Rhona."

Devon chuckled and leaned back against the stall door. "She's good for him, but you're changing the subject."

Anne pulled at the edges of her shawl, her eyes avoiding him. "I respect Charles's place in the family, but somehow bad news doesn't sound quite so distressing when you deliver it. I don't want Charles to see my weaknesses."

"I wasn't aware you had any." Devon grinned and held out his hand, waiting for her to accept his gentle invitation. She faltered for a second, but laid her hand in his. "We found the forged money at Ballinrock."

Anne instinctively tugged her hand away, but Devon held fast.

"My father was involved. Is that what you and Charles don't want to tell me?"

"There was a small compartment at the back of the room. I can see from your expression you didn't know about the space."

"No." Anne closed the narrow distance between them, her hand now relaxed in his. "I suppose I should be grateful my father won't be going to prison, though I'd rather wish him alive than dead. Why kill him?"

"I don't know, Anne. If he was involved, there are only two reasons to have killed him—greed and discovery."

"Which do you believe?"

Devon saw the hope in her eyes, though he believed she had no expectation that her father would be proven a good man. "The money was in your home for years, but I don't believe your father knew about it. As you said, we can't know what he would have done had he lived, but I believe his actions speak of a man who sought redemption and possibly forgiveness."

"I pray you are right, for that is what Claire will know someday. My father did not do right by us, but I don't believe he was an evil man. So long as I am alive, Claire will know Kevan Doyle was her father, and he loved us."

"Speaking of evil men," Devon began, "we have one more left to find."

"Lord Asher Gaspar. To think all this time, we didn't know he had a brother. What else could we have missed?"

"Gaspar's ruse went deep, Anne, with the imposters at Ballinrock when Charles arrived and then sending Fianna to kill you. Bartley will be interrogated by Derek and Zachary who both excel at extracting information out of subjects. Once they know something, we will."

Devon saw something more disturbed Anne, and she hedged around the question he believed she wanted to ask.

"You're worried about your mother."

Anne nodded. "Will you go with Charles when he escorts her to London?"

"Charles and I discussed this on the train." Devon removed his coat, draped it over her shoulders, and walked with her to the stable door. "Let's return and he can explain his idea."

The wind had mellowed, replaced by a gentle breeze and light snow. Anne didn't appear to be in a hurry to reach the front door. "What's wrong, Anne?"

"When I stand outside, the expanse of open land all around, and not another soul for miles, I feel as though anything is possible here. There hasn't been a day in my adult life when I haven't worried if I've done right for my family or if I've made the best choices. Despite everything that has happened, I've never felt so free."

Devon exhaled slowly and gazed out over his estate, trying to see the land as she did. When he first viewed Greyson Hall, Devon gave little thought to the role it might play in his future. To him, it was a monstrous building which required a good deal of upkeep and a large staff. Employing those in need of jobs was his singular pleasure in owing land, but Devon detested waste. Viewing Greyson Hall now, from Anne's perspective, he could see the beauty and the freedom such a place allowed.

"Anything is possible anywhere, Anne." Devon pressed his hand over his heart. "But the freedom you seek has to be found here first."

Anne's moss-colored eyes glistened. "How?"

"I've led my life with a singular purpose, to defend crown and country. Duty has always been the forefront of my existence, but it doesn't own me, at least not anymore. Watching the changes in Tristan and Charles's lives has helped me see there is more to living than duty. Only when you realize that, will you find the freedom you seek."

Devon's words flooded Anne's mind until all of her old beliefs overflowed into a river of confusion. Who would she be without duty? What purpose would she serve if not to give her life to her family? Anne walked beside Devon up the final stairs and into the mansion. The gentle press of his hand on her back bolstered her courage, and it was with an open mind that she entered the study with Devon.

Charles's grim expression only reinforced her desire to remain calm. Whatever they had planned, it couldn't be worse than what they'd already been through.

"Devon tells me you have a new plan regarding my mother."

Charles stared at her a long moment before answering. "One that should keep her calm, or at least we can hope." He indicated one of the chairs and said, "We'll have to forgo tea. Rozalyn is with your mother right now and quite out of sorts after what happened to Theo."

Guilt bore down on Anne's conscience. The young maid had been through more than anyone should, especially when the battle wasn't hers to fight. "My mother likes Rozalyn, though I don't believe she'd admit it. I will be glad for Rozalyn when she can be free of us."

"Rozalyn won't be alone any longer. We're going to London, and with us a full entourage."

Anne rose from her chair, her gaze fixed on Charles. "You plan to use my mother as bait."

"I remember you were quite adamant about us using you—"

"That was me, Charles, not my family." Anne drew in a deep breath and exhaled, giving herself time to calm. "I apologize.

You'll have a plan, of course, to keep them safe." She returned to her seat, crossing her hands in her lap. "What are we to do in London?"

"Attend a ball," Devon said with a grin. "A lavish affair hosted once a year by the Duke of Sutherland. Tristan and Charles both receive invites, though neither has yet to attend, until this year."

Charles continued. "As the Duke of Wadebrooke, Tristan's an honored guest who rarely makes an appearance in London since his official retirement. I abhor social gatherings, and so our presence will be noted."

"Lord Gaspar will assume it's a trap, for it was your plan, was it not?"

Devon cast her a devilish grin, the kind she'd come to associate with high risks. "It is indeed a trap, but Gaspar won't be able to resist the bait. We'll need your help."

She had a choice to say no, but excitement simmered within, the same frenzy she experienced when disguised as Fianna. Any reasonable woman would say no. "What do you need?"

Twenty-One

Baoite agus Gaiste
(Bait and Trap)

Stafford House, London, England

Anne entered the sumptuous ballroom feeling like a foreigner. No matter how near the Irish coast was to England's shores, home appeared farther away than ever before. The silk brocade of burnished gold and cream, accented with elaborate beadwork, was as unfamiliar to her as the upswept coiffure Alaina's lady's maid painstakingly arranged an hour before their arrival. No additional embellishment had been required, for the dress was a work of art, but Alaina had encouraged Anne to accept the amber drop earrings to finish off her ensemble.

Next to Alaina, who had recovered well from her sickness, and Rhona, who seemed to enjoy the conspiracy as much as the men, Anne's confidence was much like a wilted flower unfamiliar with her surroundings. Had it not been for the look of wonder and admiration in Devon's eyes when she emerged transformed, she might not have had the confidence to enter the ballroom.

Opulence abounded from the heavy chandeliers and crystal encrusted sconces to the women in stunning gowns. Anne had often wondered what it would be like to attend a grand ball and to mingle with the upper crust of London society. She'd prefer to have remained at Greyson Hall or even to return to Ballinrock, for there she knew the rules.

Couples cast curious glances in their direction while others whispered behind hands and fluttering fans. Devon bent his head close to hers. "Breathe. It will be over soon."

"Have you done this often?"

Devon's easy grin and gentle grip on her elbow calmed Anne's racing heart. "No, and I say that with great pleasure."

"Will this work?"

"We have no intention of failing tonight." Devon leaned in again and whispered, "Have I told you how stunning you look this evening?"

Anne gave in to a moment of girlhood giddiness and her cheeks reddened. She didn't respond, but she offered him a smile of appreciation. The heat in Devon's eyes startled her enough that she didn't hear Rhona the first time her name was said.

"You've dazzled them all tonight, Anne." Rhona linked her arm with Anne's. "My dear, you're shaking. Devon told us you composed yourself remarkably well as an imposter assassin. Draw on that same indomitable spirit now, and you'll do just fine."

Anne squeezed Rhona's hand and watched as Charles led her onto the dance floor. Tristan and Alaina followed suit.

"Lord Gaspar knows I'm to be here, does he not?"

Anne focused sympathetic eyes on Kathryn. Mother or not, she had been the woman who raised her, and Anne could not help but feel a measure of sorrow for the state of Kathryn's mind. "Yes, he'll be here soon, I'm sure."

"I should like to dance."

The music ended and with it, Charles and Rhona returned to the small group. Charles bowed and offered Kathryn his hand. The older woman beamed and joined Charles on the dance floor.

Rhona gave them a half smile and went off to find their hosts.

"May I?" Devon held out his hand. "We don't want to disappoint the gawkers."

The stiffness left Anne's body as Devon swept her into the throng of dancers. His eyes didn't leave hers once during their waltz. Anne now knew what it must have been like for the women in fairy tale stories. She'd long ago stopped believing in happy endings, but in this moment, Anne believed anything was possible. The freedom she sought within seemed in reach.

Kathryn appeared to be in her element, though Anne didn't recall her ever speaking of society life. Anne's childhood memories consisted of running in green meadows, walking along Ireland's shores, and riding her pony over the hills. What a glorious life it had been. She would trade every bit of glitz and glamour for a lifetime of simple country existence.

Devon caught her up in a second dance, but this time his gaze skimmed the crowded room. If he saw something unusual, he didn't give any indication. Anne watched Charles entice Kathryn to another dance, and hoped her mother had forgotten, at least for the moment, about Lord Gaspar. Devon gave Tristan a furtive nod before Tristan stepped into Devon's place and Devon danced away with Alaina. They'd seen what they needed to, but how had she missed it?

Anne looked over her shoulder with each rotation around the room. Tristan whispered, "You'll give yourself away."

"Has it happened?"

Instead of answering, Tristan asked, "Would you care for punch? I find dancing encourages one's intake of drink."

Anne gave him an absent nod and searched the room for Devon. She saw Alaina alongside Rhona as they spoke with the Duke and Duchess of Sutherland. Charles had stepped aside and allowed another gentleman to dance with Kathryn, and he soon joined her and Tristan at the refreshment table. Charles, in turn, swept her up in a dance, until they moved round and round, and each turn brought them closer to the open patio. Despite the cold winter air, a few dancers escaped the heat from the ballroom.

One moment Anne was in Charles's arms, and the next she found herself behind a holly bush, a hand clamped over her mouth. Gleaming eyes of indigo stared at her over the strong hand. Her heart thumped within her chest at a rapid rate, and she smiled when he released her. "That wasn't part of the plan."

"It's best if your departure goes unnoticed by the masses."

Devon clasped her hand and pulled her alongside as they dashed around the mansion. The St. James's district lacked an abundance of activity but offered the pair enough to cover their departure. Once safely inside Tristan's ducal coach, Anne turned to Devon. "I thought Charles and Rhona were going to leave the ball."

Devon grinned and laid a wool blanket over her lap. "And here I thought you didn't care for that part of the plan."

Anne tucked the blanket beneath the edges of her gown. "Well, I didn't. What else has changed?"

"We're the bait. Don't worry, you'll be safe so long as you follow the plan." Devon pulled back the curtain to look out at the streets. "Gaspar's life's work unraveled with the capture of his brother, and it's my estimation he'll try to leave the country. America is his best option now."

"Then why do you believe he'll bother with me at all? He abandoned my mother and Claire, so why would he return now? You've confiscated his money, which would have done him no good."

"Actually, he could have used the banknotes with some success in parts of America. They're bloody good forgeries."

The noise from the city drifted farther into background. Anne peeked out the window to see they had entered the countryside. "Where exactly are we going?"

"North."

The coach rolled to a stop at a quaint roadside inn. "You are Mrs. Clayton for tonight. Don't worry, it's only for show." Devon helped her down and instructed the driver to bring in their baggage. Anne peered over her shoulder to see a trunk secured to the back of the coach. Anne waited while Devon obtained their lodging, and they followed the innkeeper, an old man with graying hair and healthy girth, up the wood staircase to the second level.

"Dinner is served at half past six downstairs. If you'd like a meal in your room, just tell the missus."

Devon thanked the man and ushered Anne into the room, then left to help the driver bring up their trunk. He handed the driver a banknote and envelope, gave him a brisk nod, and without a word, the man left.

"Charles approved this part of your plan?"

"He voiced his concerns, but it was either him or me, and I can be quite convincing." Devon slipped out of his overcoat.

"There's only one room, Devon."

"And you'll be the only one in it." Disappointment sneaked up on Anne at the thought of Devon leaving her in the room alone, no matter how improper. She flicked through her memory to the night not long ago at Greyson Hall in Devon's bedroom.

"Anne?"

She removed her hat and turned her back to him. "Yes?"

His hands caressed her shoulders and drew her back against his chest. "There is an unspoken promise between me and Charles. When this is over . . ."

Anne shifted until she faced him. "When this is over, I return to Ballinrock with Claire."

"There's another choice. You can—" Devon pushed her behind him, her back to the wall while he faced the door. She heard it—heavy footsteps in the narrow hallway.

Devon gave her a slight shake of his head to ward off any further conversation and backed her toward the bed. He indicated for her to lower herself on the other side of the bed, hidden from the doorway. Without sound, Devon doused the lamp, crossed the room, and stood beside the door. The lock gave easily and the door inched open. Anne couldn't see the man in the shadows, only she didn't doubt it was Lord Gaspar.

He stepped into the room, and the door slammed closed behind him. Devon's arm wrapped around Gaspar's chest, raising a knife to Asher's throat.

"Don't even twitch."

Gaspar dropped his pistol. "I wasn't going to kill her."

Devon tightened his grip and dug the edge of the long blade into Gaspar's skin. "The gun says otherwise."

"I swear."

"Make me believe it." Devon eased his grip and shoved Gaspar against the wall. "You found us too quickly."

Anne listened intently to the heated conversation. How did Asher know? They'd been secluded at Greyson Hall for weeks. She peeked over the edge of the bed. Gaspar choked against the pressure Devon applied against his throat.

"You knew?"

Devon stepped back, allowing Gaspar to inhale, each breath exhaled came out with a cough. "Suspected, but couldn't prove. Kathryn never knew what part she played in your schemes."

Gaspar rubbed his neck and cautiously eyed Devon.

"You could have had her killed and ended it. Except, then you'd have to have Anne and Claire killed. Too many bodies for even you to cover up."

"I never would have killed Claire."

Anne turned on him. "Why spare her?"

Gaspar's eyes narrowed.

"It's true then. You're Claire's father."

Devon didn't look back at Anne. He could not risk taking his eyes off Gaspar for even a second. The truth was within reach, and Anne deserved to know the whole of it. "You're going to prison, Gaspar, but you may save your neck from the gallows if you cooperate."

Gaspar balked. "They wouldn't dare hang me."

"Is that a risk you're willing to take?"

Gaspar turned his head away, though Devon sensed the man would tell them what they wanted, albeit reluctantly.

Anne walked toward them until she stood only two feet behind Devon. "What did you hope to gain by any of this, or was it always about the money?"

Devon stepped in between Anne and Gaspar when she looked ready to advance. "Anne, don't."

"Don't what?" Anne shot him a glare that told him to back down. He complied for the moment but remained in her path. Anne turned on Gaspar. "How long did my mother believe you actually cared about her?"

"She's not your mother."

Anne reached into her boot where the blade Devon gave her had been sheathed. Devon reached for her hand, but she shot him another glare. It wasn't carelessness he saw in her eyes but determination. Before Devon could stop her, Anne threw the knife. It cut through the air and sliced into the wall a breath away from Gaspar's head.

"Answer the question, or the next one goes through your eye."

Contempt filled Gaspar's eyes, but Devon saw when the man decided he'd rather keep both intact. "From the beginning."

To Anne's credit, she kept her composure, though Devon would rather have put a bullet through Gaspar's head and whisked Anne away. He held back, reminding himself she deserved the truth, whatever it may be. "Why kill that young boy? He was innocent."

"He saw my brother. The boy shouldn't have been there."

"It was my home, not yours!" Anne turned away and faced the window.

Gaspar focused on Devon. "Can you guarantee I will live?"

Disgusted because he knew that Gaspar would likely live no matter what Devon said, he nodded. "But you have to tell us everything, and I want it written and signed in your hand."

After almost a minute, Gaspar nodded.

Anne spun back around and advanced on Gaspar. "You could have taken the money at any time. My father's death, Cillian, all for greed? Why?"

"You may not believe me, but I would never have harmed Claire or her mother. Kathryn and I could have accomplished great things together if she hadn't lost her mind."

"You're right, I don't believe you. You took away my father."

"Fianna did that."

Anne stepped forward once and then back. "You're a weak man without a conscience." Anne shuddered. "Get rid of him." Anne finally met his gaze, and she looked ready to stumble into a dark abyss of pain. "I don't want to see him again."

Devon guided Anne away from Gaspar and against her ear he whispered, "I need a few minutes alone with him."

Anne nodded once, said nothing, and walked from the room.

Gaspar held up his hands when Devon approached. "You can't kill me. It would be murder."

"That never stopped you, but I'm not going to kill you." Devon ground out the words, wishing it were otherwise. He'd rather be at Anne's side, but he had to finish this now. Devon tied Gaspar's hands behind his back and forced him into a chair. "You're going to tell me everything in your own hand. Your life for the truth."

"What do you want to know?"

"This has all been about the money. Did you and your brother conceive of the idea together?"

"Bartley drove my family into debt, and one day our creditors were paid and our wealth restored."

"With forged money. How did you do it?"

"We didn't. A man in Ireland knows the trade and was paid handsomely with what was left of our family's jewels. I had no choice."

"There's always a choice. What did Hambleton have to do with any of this?"

Gaspar shrugged. "He learned of our operation, though I don't know how. Bartley said he must go."

Devon fisted his hands but tempered the urge to run it into Gaspar's face. "And you are at the mercy of your brother. Why hide the money at Ballinrock?" Devon's eyes narrowed as he studied Gaspar. "We didn't believe Kathryn was involved, but nothing else makes sense."

"She began to lose her mind and with it her memory and my money!" Gaspar strained against the ties.

"It was never your money." Devon helped Gaspar to stand. "At the mercy of your brother and a crazy woman. You're a weaker man than I thought." Devon checked the ties on Gaspar's hands and then pushed him from the room.

Tristan waited at the end of the dark hall and emerged from the shadows when they exited the room. "Did you get a confession?"

Devon nodded. "Yes, but we're not done yet." Devon handed Gaspar off to Tristan. "Who came with you?"

"Derek's outside. With the help of Patrick, Zachary finally managed to get Bartley to talk."

"Tell Patrick that Bartley will have some company."

Tristan pushed Gaspar against the wall and lowered his voice, leaning close to Devon. "I saw Anne when she left the room. Will she be all right?"

"She will."

Tristan smiled and said, "We'll see you both soon." He forced a reluctant Gaspar down the stairs, and when Devon could no longer see them, he returned to the room. Anne sat on the edge of a wooden bench, her body hunched over, shaking from the tears. Devon lifted her into his arms and settled down on the bench with her in his lap. She turned her face into his chest, slipped her arms around his waist, and cried.

ANNE AND DEVON ONCE more stood in Lady Alexander's parlor at Brickstead. This time the butler had welcomed them inside before announcing them. Lady Alexander walked into the room, expectation in her eyes.

"You were successful?"

Anne closed the distance between them and removed the pendant from around her neck. The last gift her father had given her was never meant to be hers. Anne folded the jewel, along with the duke's ring, into the other lady's hand.

Tears welled in Lady Alexander's eyes. "You don't have to do this."

"Yes, I do. It was always yours, given in love. I'm only sorry you had to be parted from it for so long. And I believe he would have wanted you to have his ring."

Lady Alexander held the jewels close to her heart. "Thank you." She invited them to be seated. "Will you stay for tea?"

Devon grinned at Anne and said, "We can do better than that. We can tell you what happened and promise that justice for your duke has been found."

Anne and Devon spent the next hour sharing everything they knew about the Duke of Hambleton's death and the greedy motives behind those responsible. Anne watched the emotions play across the other lady's face alternating between sadness and disbelief. When the telling was complete, Lady Alexander sat in silence as the clock chimed the new hour. "All of these years, and I thought I'd feel better knowing what happened."

"I'm sorry if we've brought you more pain."

"You haven't. I would rather know, though I wish you could have been spared. How can I repay you for what you've done?"

"I do have a question for you, Lady Alexander."

"Of course, child."

"You said you knew my father before I was born, and my mother."

"Yes, both kind people."

Anne reached for Devon's hand and held tight. "My mother . . . who was she?"

Lady Alexander held the teapot in front of her, staring at Anne. "You don't know?" She set the teapot down on the tray. "I had heard that your father remarried, but for you not to know . . . oh dear. Your mother was Miss Elizabeth Cantrell before she married your father. She passed away shortly after your birth. I heard what happened when I was last with Harlan in Ireland."

Anne's gripped tightened in Devon's. "Did my mother have any family?"

Sympathy clouded Lady Alexander's eyes. "I don't know, child. I wish I could tell you more."

"You've given me more than I had before, and I'm grateful." Anne held back her tears.

Once back in the coach, Devon pulled Anne close to his side and covered her with a small blanket. "I didn't know you planned to ask her about your mother."

"I didn't either, but no one else knew my father back then. Even Haverly wasn't around before my birth." Anne huddled close to Devon's warmth. "Now I have even more questions. My father took too many truths to his grave, and I may know any of them."

"All questions have answers, Anne. We have your mother's name."

Anne leaned back and looked into Devon's eyes. "I don't know if I should look. What if she had no family? What if she did and they never knew about me?"

"Do you want those answers?"

"I don't know."

"When you're ready, tell me. We'll find the answers together."

Twenty-Two

I rith an ama, go deo na ndeor
(Ever and Always)

Rhona and Alaina rushed forward when they entered Tristan's London residence. Anne welcomed their embrace and had to force tears back. She looked over Alaina's shoulder to see Charles watching her. Anne left the women's embrace and approached her cousin. "Where is Claire?"

Charles smiled. "She's upstairs with Rozalyn. I do believe they've each found a kindred spirit in the other."

"And Kathryn?"

"How much do you want to know?"

"I want the truth."

Devon came up behind her and guided her into Tristan's library where a fire roared in the hearth. A footman walked in with silent steps and set a tea service down on the sideboard. He bowed once to Tristan and exited the room. Anne thought of Theo and how he would never work in such a lovely home again. She thought of her father, who regardless of his faults, had deserved a better wife than Kathryn.

Everyone waited while Alaina and Rhona served the tea. Anne accepted the cup without any thought of drinking the hot liquid.

"Please, Charles."

Once Rhona sat down, Charles joined her on the sofa. Tristan stood behind the plush chair Alaina occupied, and Devon remained by her side where she could see him.

Charles said, "It was always about the money. I had your estate books examined and contacted your father's old banker. At one time, he possessed great wealth. A few poor investments diminished his accounts until there was nothing left. The other account in London, at the bank you didn't know about, held a small sum. It's not enough to clear your family's debts, but the account is in Claire's name."

"He wanted her looked after," Anne said. "The debtors couldn't touch that money."

Devon pulled a chair over directly beside Anne's. "Your father was never a part of anything corrupt. Not the Duke of Hambleton's death, the forged money, none of it. He and Hambleton found out what Gaspar was doing, and Bartley had your father killed for it."

Anne closed her eyes, but the tears had a will of their own. She swiped the errant moisture from her cheeks. "I should not have doubted him. How involved was Kathryn?"

"She obviously had an affair with Gaspar while still married to your father, and considering that he cut her from his will, he may have known. We believe she was a pawn, but there's no way to know," Charles said, "Kathryn's mind . . . she's ill, Anne. It wasn't an act. The agency wants to release her into an asylum for her own safety."

"No, the stories one hears of those places are horrifying."

Charles took hold of her hands. "I've made other arrangements. A small manor in the country where she can be looked after."

Anne stared at her cousin. "At one time, Kathryn was involved. Will she be punished for it?"

Charles shook his head. "There would be no point to it. Her mind is gone."

Anne set her tea on the table and rose. "I'd like to see Claire now." She moved away from the group but turned back. "I will spend the rest of my life finding a way to thank all of you for what you've done." Anne left the room and hurried into the hall, only to realize she didn't know where she was going. She stopped a passing maid who directed her to the nursery room upstairs.

A child's giggles mingled with a woman's laughter, and the musical sounds brought a smile to Anne's lips and melted the layer of pain that had formed around her heart. When she opened the door, Claire bounced up and rushed into her embrace.

"You left and didn't come back, but Rozalyn said you would come back and you did." Claire bent her head back and grinned at the maid. "She came back, Rozalyn, just like you said." Claire looked back at her sister. "Cousin Charles said you would, too."

"Of course I did." Anne hunched down until she was eye level with Claire. "For you, I will always return." Anne rose and tweaked her sister's nose.

"When is Mama coming home?"

Anne brushed back her sister's soft curls. "She had to go away for a while."

"But when will she come back?"

"Think of it as a long holiday and that Mother is resting so that she can be well for you again. Do you want her to get better?"

Claire's head bobbed up and down, but Anne knew the child didn't understand.

"Can we go to the house with the horses again?"

Anne realized that Claire spoke of Greyson Hall. It wouldn't be right to return, knowing they'd have to leave again, but Claire's bright eyes, filled with hope and longing, could not be denied. "I'll ask Devon. Return to your drawing. I need to speak with Rozalyn for a moment."

Claire didn't look like she believed her. Anne laughed. "I promise to return."

Rozalyn followed Anne from the room. "Have I done something wrong, my lady?"

"Quite the opposite, Rozalyn. I need to speak with Tristan, and I can't pay much, but if you're willing, I'd very much like for you to come and be Claire's companion. You wouldn't be running your own kitchen or preparing grand feasts, but Claire is fond of you."

Rozalyn's eyes brightened. "Do you mean it, my lady?"

"Ballinrock Castle is nothing like what you're used to, Rozalyn."

"That's quite all right, my lady. I adore the young miss, and I'd be honored to be her companion. It's a grander position than housemaid. I know His Grace won't mind."

"Thank you. Now we'd best go back in before Claire comes searching for us."

Anne searched for Devon, finding him as he left Tristan's study. "Devon, may I speak with you?"

"Of course."

Devon motioned her to follow him into a small parlor. "Is everything all right?"

"Yes, though I do have a favor to ask of you."

"Anything I can give, it's yours."

Anne wished those words didn't fill her with false hope. "Claire has asked to return to Greyson Hall. It won't be a long visit, but I seem unable to say no to her right now."

Devon's immediate smile brought Anne enormous relief.

"I couldn't say no to her either, when she asked."

"You spoke with her?"

Devon nodded. "We can leave in the morning."

Devon didn't care where he lived, or how he lived, so long as Anne was there.

No matter how many times he pictured her in his future, surprise quickly followed. He didn't know if he'd ever become used to the idea of settling down with one woman for the rest of his life, but he couldn't imagine an existence without her.

He realized a perfect moment didn't exist for what he needed to tell Anne, but he could create the moment by asking her. Devon found her in the nursery, asleep on Claire's bed. Claire and Rozalyn looked up from their place at a short table, Claire offering him a beaming grin. In a whisper that sounded almost like a shout, Claire said, "Anne was tired. She's been sleeping and sleeping. Rozalyn said not to wake her."

Devon knelt down on one knee next to Claire. "Rozalyn's right." He sent the maid a brief look over Claire's head.

"Claire, dear," Rozalyn said. "It's time for a stroll. How about we ask the cook for a treat?"

Claire seemed quite agreeable to the idea. "Maybe she'll have pie?"

Rozalyn chuckled and nodded. "Maybe pie."

Devon waited for them to leave the room before he walked to the bed. Anne's hair, the burnished color of autumn, fell in loose tendrils over the pillows, a gentle contrast to the cream-colored bed linens. Her soft lips parted slightly with each quiet breath. Devon reached out and brushed back a lock of hair that had fallen over her eyes. The tender caress was enough to wake his sleeping beauty. Anne's eyes fluttered open and her lips curved.

"Claire?"

"The promise of pie tempted her away." Devon rested his chin on his hands, his face only inches from hers. "Will you walk with me?"

Anne shook the sleep from her mind and leaned up. "What

time is it?"

"Dinner isn't for a few hours."

"All right. I just need a few minutes."

Devon leaned down and brushed his lips across her temple. "I'll wait downstairs."

ANNE HURRIED THROUGH A quick washing and pinched some color into her cheeks. Exhaustion had been temporarily sated by her impromptu nap, but she knew it would take much longer to overcome the emotional turmoil. Claire proved stronger than Anne once again and went about her life as though little had changed. Someday Anne would tell her sister the full truth, but until then, Claire would be able to enjoy her childhood as a young girl should. Would she ever understand the truth? Anne couldn't be sure, but she would be there to answer Claire's questions and soothe the fears.

After a failed attempt to fix her hair, she plaited the long strands and grabbed her heavy cloak before leaving the room. As promised, Devon waited at the base of the stairs. Anne's step faltered when her eyes met his, and her heart seemed to ricochet within her chest. Devon's warm smile brightened his entire countenance. Despite his numerous grins and occasions of levity, Devon appeared more at ease than he had in any moment since she'd met him.

Anne reached the bottom step and immediately he offered her his arm. Together they walked from the house and into the cold afternoon air. She waited for him to say something, but he remained silent as the breeze blew in circles around them. Devon led her toward the tall oak under which Theo's body lay beneath the earth. The setting sun touched upon the snow-covered grave, and Anne could almost see Theo's smile as he held his face up to the sun's muted rays. Beside Theo, she saw young Cillian, his Irish green eyes bright and filled with life once again. Tears of both sorrow and peace fell unbidden down Anne's cheeks.

Devon removed a silver and gold dirk from his waist. He held the richly etched and gilded blade between them. "This dagger belonged to an Irishman named Eoghan Ruadh Ó Néill. Ó Néill gave it to a man who saved his life at the Battle of Benburb. That man was my ancestor, and this was passed down through the men in my family. My father didn't bestow upon me much beyond his wealth, but he did leave me with a legacy of strength and honor I haven't fully appreciated until now."

Devon knelt beside the grave and buried the dagger in the earth. "There are many great warriors in our country's histories, but I believe there are those men of honor worth remembering, whose considerable sacrifices too often go unnoticed."

Devon rose and reached out for Anne's hand. She embraced his warmth and strength as her heart overflowed with love. "I'm sorry we couldn't save them, Anne. This wasn't their fight, nor was it yours, but I promise you, they will be remembered."

Anne stepped in front of him and wiped her tears away with her free hand. "I have lived these last years of my life for the love of my sister. I can despise Kathryn for her treachery, but she gave me Claire. I think of Cillian's family and what they've lost, and I know how blessed Claire and I are for the family we have found in Charles and Rhona."

"In all of us, Anne." Devon cupped the side of her face. "We've been on a tumultuous journey these past weeks, and many times you and I have reached the edge of something remarkable. I didn't know if I could give you what you deserved or needed, but I've never been more willing to try." He leaned down until his lips caressed hers. "You and Claire have a home here if want it—if you'll have me. I love you, Anne Doyle."

An overpowering joy erupted within Anne's heart. "I love you, Devon Clayton. My heart is yours, and there's nowhere else I'd rather be than with you."

Devon's ecstatic laughter mingled with her own. So strong was his embrace that Anne had to pull back in order to catch her breath, but she never wanted him to let her go.

"I need to go to London for a few days."

Anne didn't want to be parted from him for a single day, but she understood. "I imagine there are matters in this case to finalize."

Devon grinned, his most endearing one yet. "To resign, Anne. I'm going to leave the agency, but I owe it to Patrick to tell him in person. When I return with my brothers, we can marry."

Anne immediately objected to the unexpected and casual announcement. "You love your work, Devon."

"Not as much I love you, and whatever family may join us in the future."

"What does one have to do with the other?" Anne held fast to him. "Whether it's one more case or a dozen, you're not done yet. We'll both know when it's time for a new chapter in our lives, but I'm not ready to say goodbye to this side of you."

"You are the most remarkable woman."

When they embraced, his gentle lips lovingly touched hers. Unrushed, both knowing the preciousness of each moment, they gave each other their pledge of everlasting devotion. Anne welcomed the passion she'd once tasted with this man and the promise of more to come. They parted, comfortable with the silence of the whispering breeze and the setting sun. With their arms around each other, Devon and Anne walked down the hill to Greyson Hall where a lifetime of adventure, surprises, and family waited.

Thank you for reading *Clayton's Honor!*

If you'd like to share your thoughts or comments with MK, feel free to email her at her website.

If you'd like to share your thoughts with others, consider leaving an online review.

Don't miss out on future books.
www.mkmcclintock.com/newsletter.

CLAYTON'S HONOR
BOOK CLUB DISCUSSION QUESTIONS

1. What do you feel was a turning point for Devon?

2. What were the dynamics of "power" between the characters? How did that play a factor in their interactions?

3. Who was your favorite character in the book and why?

4. How important is the setting and time period to the story?

5. Were there any moments where you disagreed with the choices of any of the characters? What would you have done instead?

6. What surprised you the most about the story?

7. How have the characters changed by the end of the book? What do you think will happen next to the British Agents?

8. If you could ask the author any question about the story, what would you ask?

A HOME FOR CHRISTMAS
Short Story Collection

A collection of three historical western short stories to inspire love and warm the heart, no matter the season.
Set in Montana, Colorado, and Wyoming.

PRAISE FOR *A HOME FOR CHRISTMAS*

"Ms. McClintock has a true genius when writing beauty to touch the heart. This holiday treat is a gift any time one needs to remember the true meaning of love!"
—*InD'Tale Magazine, 5 stars and a Crowned Heart for Excellence*

"The cold nips at your face and delicious Christmas cake leaves you wanting more."
—*M. Ann Roher, Author of "Mattie"*

"If you like the 1800s, like I do, you will love these stories!"
—*Diane Holm, The Reader's Cove, Amazon Vine Reviewer*

THE AUTHOR

Award-winning author MK McClintock writes historical romantic fiction about courageous and honorable men and strong women who appreciate chivalry, like those in her Montana Gallagher, British Agent, and Crooked Creek series. Her stories of adventure, romance, and mystery sweep across the American West to the Victorian British Isles, with places and times between and beyond. With her heart deeply rooted in the past, she enjoys a quiet life in the northern Rocky Mountains.

Learn more about the author, her books, and find reader extras at www.mkmcclintock.com.